Road Kills
short tales of dark horror

Road Kills
short tales of dark horror

Isaac Thorne

Lost Hollow Books
Franklin, Tennessee

For P.

There are only two mistakes
one can make
along the road to truth;
not going all the way,
and not starting.

—Buddha

Contents

Acknowledgments

Not even the most independent of independent authors goes through the entire publishing process alone. This collection of short tales of dark comic horror would not have made it into your hands without the assistance of some family, some friends, some professional services, and a whole lot of social media contacts. I am going to attempt to list as many of them as I can here. If I miss anyone, please do not take it as a sign of anything but a failure of my own memory. Here goes:

Billy Crash and Jonny Numb — who have repeatedly screamed out to me from their podcast, *The Last Knock*, and engage me regularly on social media. Their insights never fail to provide me with a new perspective on some old tales. You can find them on Twitter: @crashpalace and @jonnynumb

Bleeding Critic — the clown prince of horror himself, who has allowed me to share a horror memory and some horror therapy over at his place on the web: bleedingcritic.com. Moreover, his passion for providing an antidote to what he terms modern "fast food horror" is contagious. You can find him on Twitter: @BleedingCritic

Cleo — Her podcast, *Talk2Cleo*, was the first on which I appeared as a guest. After I appeared on her show, I suddenly began receiving invitations to appear on other programs. She's a brilliant interviewer, and her show is a great launchpad for thought-provoking conversation. You can find her on Twitter: @Talk2Cleo

The Fear Merchant — I was fortunate enough to be one of the first handfuls of guests on *The Bazaar Cast*, a horror-themed podcast by a man named Richard, otherwise known as The Fear Merchant. Richard has a passion for horror and a knowledge of the genre that bring a unique challenge and delight to being a guest on his program. You can find him on Twitter: @TheFearMerchant

Paula Hanback — for her limitless talent and tireless efforts at representing my twisted tales in a graphically appealing way. You can find more of her on Twitter: @ellezorart

Liane Moonraven — for bringing back the magic of radio theater in a new and entertaining way. I have been privileged to have Liane portray Tiffany in an audio version of *Because Reasons*, which is the first story in this collection. She also writes, directs, and produces her own online audio horror series, *The Burbs* and her own independent horror films. You can find her on Twitter: @LianeMoonRaven

My Little Rascal Film Productions — for being willing to read through most of the contents of this collection, searching for gems that they want to bring to the screen. Joey and Lisa have such a passion for the horror genre. I'm excited to be working with them. You can find them on Twitter: @MyLittleRascal1

One Sick Puppy – host of the Dead As Hell podcast, who offered me an opportunity to join a panel discussion about the classic horror comedy *Rocky Horror Picture Show*. Dead As Hell was the first podcast I'd been included in that wasn't specifically about me or my work, and I loved every second of it. I write horror, but at my core I am primarily a horror fan. You can find Dead As Hell on Twitter: @DeadAsHellHP.

The Rob and Slim Show — these guys are hilarious. Although not a specifically horror related show, Rob and Slim often features guests who work in the genre. Their show is in the style of morning shock radio and definitely worth a listen. Rob, Slim, Pete (Slamborghini), and Amanda provide an awesome way to pass the mid-week blues. You can find them on Twitter: @robandslimshow

Ron Shaw — his *Ron Shaw Show* podcast was one of my last appearances in 2016. Like me, Ron is a Southern gentleman with a penchant for topic-jumping, which makes for one hell of a conversation. You can find him on Twitter: @rongizmo

Tra Cee – singer, author, and podcaster all rolled into one, Tra Cee has been a huge supporter of my work for a while now. She's on Twitter: @tra-cee_tr. You can also catch up with her and a whole passel of other horror hosts at SCRM radio: @SCRMRadio.

And, of course, there are all the people I've encountered on social media who have taken time out of their day to retweet me, like my posts, share my books, and interact with me on a daily basis. There's also the readers who have taken the time to purchase, download, read, and review many of these stories in their single ebook forms. Without them, the words on these pages would simply be me standing in an echo chamber.

My thanks to you all.

Until our roads intersect again…

Introduction

Anyone who has ever fallen off a bike and skinned a knee can tell you that a road is a dangerous place. You can break a bone or crack your skull open just trotting along at whatever your leisure, never mind barreling down some stretch of interstate at 70 miles-per-hour in a cage of steel, fiberglass, plastic, and rubber. We all venture out on them. We have people to see, places to be, and things to do. All roads lead to nouns.

So it's no surprise to me that the paved pathways connecting the dots of civilization all over the United States have long been a fascination for authors and filmmakers. Road movies were an action and comedy staple of the 1970s and 1980s. From *Easy Rider* to *National Lampoon's Vacation* to *Thelma & Louise*, long and winding paths throughout the nation have served as the backdrop for story upon story. So too have novelists and journalists taken these fantastic trips, from Jack Kerouac's *On the Road* to Tom Wolfe's *The Electric Kool-Aid Acid Test*. Not to mention horror masterworks like Richard Matheson's *Duel* and Stephen King's *The Stand*. All of this serves only to illustrate our collective fascination with the act of long travel over potentially dangerous terrain to parts (and perhaps circumstances) undiscovered.

The stories you are about to read all involve a journey of some stripe. "But of course!" you say. "All stories do." And you're right. However, the journey in the majority of these stories takes place—at least partially—over the highways and byways of the United States. The ones that don't (*Dislike* and *Diggum*) are more-or-less journeys of self-discovery that *could have* taken place over the course of a road trip. If you require a defense of these: *Dislike* takes place over social media, which is a byway along the internet, which used to be called the information superhighway. *Diggum*, on the other hand, is pretty much the road to Hell.

The difference between the stories herein and any other highway-set literary journey is that every stop along your way through these pages includes an element of horror. These are not day trips to the beach or slow beats to a pleasant weekend retreat. These stories are intended to be visceral blind-spot stalking, tailgate riding, unwelcome passenger-discovering, road-rash burning, motion-sickness projectile vomit-inducing tales. They want to make you feel like they've disabled your airbag, slashed your seatbelt, and cemented your throttle to the floor while you scream at your body to *do something* to put a stop to the certain doom of the crashing halt toward which you rush headlong. Because the road is a scary, deadly place. We see the evidence every day on the news or hear about it in traffic reports while we impatiently tap our fingers on our steering wheels in miles and miles of bumper-to-bumper crawls through rush-hour commutes.

Right now you are safe, of course. You can comfort yourself with the fact that you're reading all these tales in a warmly lit room, perhaps curled up on your bed or in your favorite chair. It's possible you're even cozied up beside a loved one, or a pet, or a steaming cup of herbal tea.

Just don't forget about what's waiting for you just beyond the edge of your driveway. It's lurking there, quiet and dark, just waiting for you to come out for a walk or a jog. Or perhaps biking is your thing. Maybe you even have a job you need to drive to tomorrow morning. However you next confront it, the road is already there, plotting.

And waiting.

For you.

Enjoy the ride.

Because Reasons

Well. Hello there, sleepy head. I didn't expect you to wake up so soon. You must not have been as wasted as I thought you were.

Don't try to talk. I've tied that strap tight. Ever had a ball in your mouth before? I bet not. You look more like an alpha type. At least you think of yourself as one. Usually, the kinks who like the straps will tie them behind your head. I stretched this one way out so I could tie it behind you. You know, around the headrest. I'll bet you can't even move your head right now. Go ahead. Try to look at me.

Yeah, that's what I thought. Can't move much more than your eyes right now, can you?

Good.

The way I cuffed your hands to the frame of that seat should keep you from making any unwanted advances should we meet any other drivers out here. Did I say "advances"? Ha! I meant signals. I don't want you to be able to signal anybody. *If* we meet anybody. Not that I think we will. This stretch of desert is pretty well empty in the wee hours of the morning, I think. My daddy used to drive out here sometimes because it's so far away from everything. To get his head on straight, he said. I think he might've just been hooking up. Horny bastard.

So, I don't know much you remember. My name is Tiffany. Your name doesn't matter. We met in a bar just about six hours ago. You were pounding the drinks pretty hard and—I'm sure—undressing me with your eyes in the mirror. Do you remember that? Nod if you can. Yeah. Hey, remember when I said "unwanted advances"? Freudian slip. Ha!

I don't know how well you can see me from your angle, but I was the little hottie sitting at the table right behind you. Remember? You thought you were so cool, sitting on that barstool and eyeballing me in the mirror. You guys. You don't get it. Girls like me know when you're getting all predatory. It's like a pheromone you emit, like armpit stink. And we know how to use that against you if we really want to.

Oh, don't look so shocked. Let's be honest. You know I'm a hottie. I know I'm a hottie. And there's almost nothing you wouldn't do for me if you thought for one second it would get you that piece of my sweet, sweet ass. You want it *so* much.

Ha! I told you so. Look at your dick. Well, I guess you don't have to look at it, huh? I take it you can feel it getting all stiff and gross. So funny. You don't have the slightest idea who I am. I have you completely tied up and gagged in a car driving through the desert in the middle of the night. You have no idea what I plan to do to you. But there's some part of you that still thinks it's hot. There's some part of you that wants me to take control of you and ravage you and spank your naked ass.

Got news for you, buddy-boo. It ain't happening. Ha!

Oh please. You think because I stripped you down that I want to have sex with you? Nah. I don't want your sex, sweetie pie. I only took off your clothes because I thought it would be funny to see your reaction when you woke up tied up, gagged, and naked in a speeding car. Well, that and I figured you'd be less likely to run off on me if you're bare-assed. Face it, you'd be arrested for indecent exposure before the cops ever listened to one word about what happened to you. By the time they were done booking you, I'd be long gone. And nobody would believe you anyway. You were drunk, buddy-boo. Nothing spells wandering around naked and stupid like a drunk little blue collar boy who spends most of his weekly check on beer and titties. Hell, I bet you already have a mile-long rap sheet, don't you? How many DUIs you have, mister?

Oh. Right. You can't answer me, can you? Ha! My bad.

So anyway, it's not as much fun having you naked as I thought. It's a big disappointment, really. Ick. I sort of wish I'd left your clothes on. Unfortunately for both of us, they're all in a trash can outside the last titty bar I saw along this stretch, about a hundred miles ago. But, hey, sometimes I make mistakes, you know? Ever made a mistake? Ha! I guess you made a big one tonight, didn't you, buddy-boo?

Now you must be thinking "If she doesn't want my hot hard-workin' man body (and I don't and it ain't), what the hell does she want?"

That's easy. I want your blood. I want to watch you watching your life drain from your body. I want to see the look in your eyes as you watch your whole existence slip away and you finally get it that you're not going to live to see another full sunrise. I want to feel the hot thrill of taking your life from you running through my fingers and dripping off the tips.

Sound like fun?

Ha! Nice soft-off. Looks like I just let all the air out of your little flesh balloon there. No tears now. That wouldn't be very manly. My advice would be to just accept your position as a soon-to-be non-entity. Oh but don't feel all special or picked-on. See, you're not the first person I've killed tonight, man or woman. Let's see now if I count the accident in mom's bathroom at home, you'll be number four tonight. Yeppers peppers, that's right. Number four in my teeny tiny little life experiment. Maybe that's what I'll call you from now on if I bother to call you anything at all. Number four. I like the sound of it. Or maybe I'll call you Yeppers Peppers. I like that sound of that, too.

Over the past twelve hours, I've come to learn that I'm actually magnificent at this. Killing people, I mean. Honestly, I think the government should fucking hire me to take people out. I know how to do it all quick and terrifying. And I positively *love* it. My favorite part is when the eyes bug out at the very end, just as they realize this is not a dream and I'm never going to call for help. They open the lids up real wide, you see, right before their soul or life force or electro-chemical impulses, or whatever they are cry out for the last time. Then the lids relax, but the eyes don't close like they do on television. No sir. They stay open and stare straight ahead, except there's nothing behind them anymore. The lights go out. I like seeing the lights go out.

Did you ever hear that old story about how French executioners used to hold up the disembodied heads of the condemned and command them to blink until they finally died? They say some heads were able to keep blinking up to thirty times before they finally died. Can you imagine that? Being aware that you're dying? That your body is already lying lifeless on the ground while your head is performing its last actions on command like a trained monkey? What must it feel like to watch the world fade to black right in front of you? Does it fade, I wonder? Or are you just suddenly not there? Can you imagine watching it happen to someone else right before your eyes?

I knew what I was going to do for the rest of tonight when I saw my mom's eyes bug out. The last drops of her life circled the drain, and she looked up at me with her mouth all gasping like a fish out of water. Ha! You'll get why that's funny in a minute.

I got a real zing of electricity through me seeing that look on her face. That moment when she finally understood that it was me, not her, who held the power. Every drop of her life was in my hands, legit depending on me. Then, when it hit her that I was never going to help her? When she finally figured out that I was just going to sit there and look her in the eyes as death pulled her under? *That* was the best. Just. The. Best.

I guess I'm not *technically* responsible for mom's death, though, even if I was kind of responsible for just allowing it to happen. Mom slipped in the shower and cracked her skull open on that old chrome faucet. Get that fish out of water gag now? Ha!

Ever notice that old house shit is harder and heavier than the stuff they make houses out of these days? My mom's house was built ages ago, like maybe in the 70s, so it's ancient and everything's as solid as a rock. My mom's poor brain bucket was just too fragile to handle a blow like that. She went down *hard*.

I really do hate that house, though. Mom's a lawyer making six figures, for fuck's sake. My daddy's the fucking CEO of two different tech startups. They both have tons of money, although my dad always tends to eventually lose his shirt somewhere down the line. But it's not like we couldn't afford an upgrade, you know? Imagine! ME! Living in a house built in the 70s. Fucking green carpet and paneling everywhere. Shit was barely even cable-ready when we moved in. What do I look like? A hipster? And you can forget about us cutting the cord and streaming shows, too. We might as well be telegraphing e-mails with the quality of Internet we get out there.

So I get bored, you know? I need fresh and new. Fast. Exciting. You get it. I see it in your eyes. You know where I'm coming from. You want the same thing, except you want it sexy. I saw it in your hard-on. Ha!

I can see what you're thinking now, though. You're scared, and you're horrified because you think I allowed my mom to die because I didn't love her or because I don't like where we live. I suppose I can see how you got that impression. That's not the reason I let her die, though. I seriously think I was just bored. Bored. Out. Of. My. Mind. Fuck, we'd been living in that place for a good four years, and in all that time we hadn't even so much as moved a chair to a different spot in the living room, you know? Last time anything changed in that house was when Daddy walked out.

I am so Bee. Ohh. Arr. Eee. Dee!

Honestly! Look at me! Was I not put here to be somebody? Maybe I'm destined to put all the mediocrities out of their misery. Maybe that's why I'm so good at the killing. Or not. I'm still not sure.

Seriously, I haven't figured all this out yet. Still working it through in the old noggin, you know? I thought I might just be getting a thrill from the power trip when my mom died while I sat there and watched. So that's why I went to my daddy's house afterward. I figured I'd kill him too, just to see where it led. See if it really was just a bored power trip or if it still felt just *right*, you know? Like something I'm supposed to be doing. So I did. And OMG was it ever easy. Too easy.

See, the thing about my daddy is that I already have a shitload of power over him. He never says no to me. People think I'm spoiled because of that, but it's not true. It's not his fault that I'm this way. Seriously. How can be "spoiled" if you're aware of your own spoilage, you know? Being spoiled implies that you haven't checked your own privilege, right? That you can't tell when what you're asking for is an inconvenience or a showing off. See, I know all that. I'm not spoiled. I'm just a hot little bored privileged bitch. And I'm entitled to be. Ha!

Anyway, I knew I couldn't overpower my daddy physically. He might be soft-hearted for me, but he's never been *soft*. So I figured I'd just bat my little eyelashes and wemind him dat I'm his widdle gurl. Then he'd just lie down and let me strangle him. Ha! My daddy always knew he was a

5

mediocrity anyway. Oh, yes, he's the CEO of two different tech startups. That's true. What makes him a mediocrity is that he's never been able to take anything *past* the startup stage. Told you he loses his shirt all the time. If I'd let him live, he'd be broke in a year or two and back looking for that Next Big Thing. I figure that's why my mom divorced him in the first place. The man could sell an investor on anything, but he couldn't keep them interested. Not when they finally realized that he didn't actually have any kind of plan. Mom just decided she had a career of her own and really didn't need a two-timing glorified pitch man for a husband. Daddy got bored easily. Like me, I guess.

The difference between him and me is that I think my boredom might have led me to a real purpose.

Whoa there, buster! You just sit your ass back down, or I'm going to have to put a hurt on you. Guess I should've pulled that seat belt tighter, huh? I just didn't want to get that close to your junk. Ugh. But I'll tell you now that struggling against those handcuffs isn't going to do you any good. They're the real deal. I stole them and that ball gag from my mom's own dresser drawers before I left. Ha! Yeah. Apparently, mom liked to get a little kinky with the odd maintenance guy from time to time, just like the little porno fantasies guys like you like to jerk it to I'm sure. I don't know whether that was before or after daddy left, but I don't blame her. What's good for the gander, right?

Oh, and I didn't wash or disinfect either of those things before I put them on you. Ha! Not that I would expect you to care, considering that nasty little place where I picked you up. Ha Ha!

So, I went over to my daddy's place to kill him next. Know what the first thing he says to me is when he sees me crawling out of this wagon with that crowbar that's laying under your feet? He says, "Well hi, sweetie! Something wrong with your car? Looks like your front tires might be going a little bald." Ha! There I am strolling up to my daddy, grinning ear-to-ear, with a giant crowbar that I borrowed from my neighbor's garage in my hands and he thinks something's wrong with the car.

Oh, I didn't break into the neighbor's house, if that's what you think. Idiot leaves his garage door wide open. I thought about killing him for it, but I wasn't sure he was actually home and I sure as hell didn't want to set off any alarms. Guess I'm assuming he was smarter about the rest of his house than he was about the garage.

Anyway, what'd he think I was going to do with the crowbar? Beat the motor with it until it ran again? My daddy. He knows—uh, knew—about pitching a startup business for investment capital, but he didn't know shit about cars. Dumbass.

I strolled right up to him pretty as you please and went upside his head. Used both my arms and all my strength to do it. Then, while he was rolling on his back in the driveway, howling about his broken face, I jammed the straight end of that crowbar into his right eye. Ha! I told you I make mistakes. I mean, what was it I wanted to do? I wanted to see if I got the same thrill over killing a powerless man that I got from watching my mom die. I wanted to watch his eyes when it dawned on him that his widdle gurl was the one who killed him.

Once I realized I'd screwed up, I doubled-down on the butt of that crowbar. Sent it right on home into his brain, I think. I don't know. Anatomy isn't my thing. Yours either, by the look of you. Ha! Either way, I made sure that I didn't damage his left eye. Would you believe I actually had to pry the lids open on it so I could watch when he died? Like I told you before, the eyes relax when you go, but he had that left one squeezed tight before it happened. I was afraid it wouldn't open in time for me to see. So I just stuck my little fingertips in there and held his lids open firm as I could. Sure enough, there it was again, that smidge of awareness just before the time came. It wasn't the same power I felt when my mom went, but it still felt good. No, I take that back. Not *good*. It felt *right*. So I started to think that maybe I wasn't really just bored, that maybe—unlike daddy—I'd found purpose. My goal was to get rid of all the mediocrities.

I couldn't just decide that on my own, though. I live in the age of STEM, you know? Or maybe you don't. You look kind of redneck. Did you stay in school past third grade? Anyway, like any good STEM student, I had formed a theory, and now I needed to put my theory to the test. Oh, don't look so surprised. You think because I still have this high school cheerleader body well into my first year of college that I'm not smart? I like science. I like to experiment. Duh! *Obviously*. So, I figured that my next kill should be someone who is decidedly *not* a mediocrity. Someone famous, if possible. If not someone famous, then someone who was at least influential in the community.

So I yanked the crowbar out of my daddy's head. Oh man! You should've heard the sucking sound it made. I didn't even bother to clean the goo off it. See? I think you got some of his brains on your big toe there. Then I drove the wagon over to the parsonage, where daddy's pastor lived. Neither of my parents was churchgoers, but my daddy attended every now and then. Pastor Bev operated this post-divorce workshop out of the church once a week. She's become sort of a hero in her parish—is that the right word?—for being able to get the old broken single people back on their spiritual feet, I guess. You know her? Yeah, you know her. Everybody knows her. She also volunteers with the homeless shelter all the time. She's all over the place whenever some poor doofus accidentally burns his house down. Rings the emergency bells loud and long, that one. She's just your basic good soul; highly respected. She was the first person to come to my mind when I decided I needed to kill somebody important.

See, if my purpose was to kill only the mediocrities, the way I would know that for sure was to figure out if I got the same buzz from killing someone who isn't a mediocrity. Hell, if my purpose was to kill mediocrities, I might not even be *capable* of killing Pastor Bev. But the only way you can know is to try, right? What's that old saying? If it at first you don't succeed, smash and slice and stab and fuck 'em over again? Ha!

I drove right up to the parsonage as pretty as you please and jumped out of the wagon and started banging on the door like the devil himself was after me. Ha! You should've seen the look on her face when Pastor Bev opened that door and saw me splattered head-to-toe with my daddy's blood and brains. It was priceless. I could see in her face what she was thinking. She thought I had been attacked by somebody or something and I was covered in my own blood. That one little pause while she tried to process what she was seeing was all I needed, too. I swung that crowbar around from behind my back, raised it high above my head, and brought the hook end down square between her eyes. It made this totally legit sick sound like I'd just smashed it into a thick wet melon or something. Maybe not. I don't know. I have people to carve melons for me. Ha!

Well, that blow sent Pastor Bev reeling backward, flailing her arms and everything, but it didn't actually seal the deal, you know? She landed on her butt and hit the back of her head on the leg of this little table she'd stupidly put right in the entryway. I mean, for real, lady. If you need somewhere to put your keys, hang a damn hook on the wall, for God's sake. That's what mom always did. Probably the only thing the bitch ever did right in her life.

Well, besides having me, of course. Ha!

Oh, yeah. Speaking of "for God's sake," I never heard anybody invoke the name of their God more than Pastor Bev did while she was going down. She was screaming "Oh Lord!" and "Lord help!" over and over while I just kept bringing that crowbar down on her head. "Oh Lord, stop! Oh Lord, help me! Oh Lord, why?" Ha! I must've hit the bitch seven or eight times before she finally shut it. It was like when you're trying to kill a cockroach by smashing it with your shoe, and the damned thing just keeps on crawling like you never even landed on it, you know? Well, actually, I don't really know. I guess I must have heard that somewhere. I'm sure my daddy might have killed a cockroach or two in his day, but mom and I had a pest control guy come by and spray once a month. No way those things were getting anywhere near us.

So once Pastor Bev had finally shut up and was laying still on the floor, I crawled on top of her and peeled her eyelids back. I had the crowbar right beside me, just in case, which was probably a mistake because it was only an inch or so from where her right hand was stretched out on the floor. If she'd been in any kind of shape to fight at that point, she could've grabbed it and knocked me backward. I told you I make mistakes sometimes. If I was to advance my theory, Pastor Bev is the one kill where I needed to be careful. As luck would have it, though, she didn't go for the crowbar, and I was able to watch as all the life in her eyes finally drained away.

It's so weird, the way that works. They say the eyes are the windows of the soul, you know? Maybe there's some truth to that. Well, not a soul, really, but they're definitely the windows of whatever consciousness we have. Think about it, what do we do when we go to sleep? We *close our eyes*. We shut off the lights. But when you die, and your eyes are open, it's like someone turned off the lights in the house while you were standing outside under the windowsill. Only dull darkness is left.

You might be wondering now what I learned from all that. From killing Pastor Bev, I mean. Turns out I didn't learn anything. Ha! Killing her felt just as right as killing my daddy. I liked watching her life disappear as much as I liked watching my mom's life slip away. So, I guess mediocrities and the not-so-mediocre are all the same in my book. Who knew, right?

So then I said to myself: "Self, what if you just killed someone random? Someone you don't know from Adam? What if you just picked up a stranger somewhere and slaughtered him for the hell of it? Would you feel the same way? Would that still feel right to you?"

I couldn't answer that, so I decided to find out. And that's where you come in, buddy-boo, my fine flabby friend. I'd never even heard of that little dive bar when I dropped in on you back there, so I was pretty sure I wouldn't know anybody inside. And ho boy! Did I ever get the eyeballs when I walked in! Well, who could blame you good old boys, really? I bet I look like that girl you weren't good enough for back in high school, don't I? I'm the one all you guys (and maybe even some of the girls) wanted that you couldn't have because you Just. Aren't. Good. Enough.

I guess you're wondering why I picked you out of all those guys, huh? I don't know. Maybe it's because you were the drunkest guy closest to the door. I really didn't want to have to haul your hairy ass all the way out to the car from the *back* of that place, did I? No, not so much. By the way, guy: back, crack, and sack, you know? Shave that shit!

Your face *kind of* looks like you're close to being in my league if I squint a little bit and you're in the right light, even if the rest of you is a bit—ugh—*wanting*. So, you stumbling out of there and leaning against my shoulder to do it didn't look far away from legit. And you were drunk enough to really think you had some kind of chance with me, I guess. Ha! I just hope nobody noticed the good reverend's little blood stain on the hem of my sleeve there. I sure didn't know it was there at the time! Ha! I thought I took care of all that back at her place. I cleaned up after that job, figuring I might have to go out on the town to get my next test subject. I also went through her closet. That's where I found this surprising little low-cut number. I don't know whether I'm more surprised that it fit me or that she even had something like this. Seriously, Pastor Bev? Where would *you* wear something like this?

Anyway, I must have still had some of her blood on me when I slipped this little number over my head. But, hey, I told you. I sometimes make mistakes. Not that they matter too much. People tend to overlook my screw-ups because, well, they're mine! Ha! They overlook a lot of other things, too. Nobody at the bar even asked me for ID when I sashayed in there. Isn't that illegal? I thought for sure I'd have to wait outside and nab one of you fellas as you fumbled around for your keys.

Are you listening to me?

Oh, my. What's wrong with you? Your face is all wet and shiny. Well, then. Guess you've finally figured out that I'm serious about this. Look at the big bad bar boy babbewing wike a widdle baby. Awww, don't cwy widdle baby. If it hadn't been you, it would've been some other random guy who's talked himself into believing that his life has some kind of meaning. Now, judging by the widdle baby tears rolling down your face, I'd guess that your life actually doesn't have any meaning, no matter what you tell yourself when you're laying in bed jacking it at night. The thing is that I don't really know, though. You could be some senator's son or some reality star or some YouTube sensation that I can't watch because I don't have the bandwidth.

But that's the point, isn't it? You don't mean shit to me and you never will. In fact, from tonight forward, your life won't mean shit to you or anybody else either. Because life goes on after we die, doesn't it? Life just moves forward. The world never came to an end because one person's life was lost. I'm sure someone will find your iPhone wrapped up in your undies in the garbage at some point, but I imagine they will have stopped looking for you by then. Oh, I turned it off before I tossed it. Untraceable. Ha!

Huh. Well, that's new. I can't remember ever seeing a man of your size tremble like that. It's hard to tell in the dark like this, but I'd swear you're turning blue, buddy-boo. You're sweating, too. Making a sick mess out of my seat. Guess I should have put a towel down before I sat your nasty ass down on it. Ha! Jesus, what's the matter with you?

Oh.

Oh no.

No no no no no. You don't get to do this, you fucker. You don't get to go this way. I'm pulling over right now. Don't you fucking die in my car. You don't get to go on your own. It'll screw up my experiment. Just hang on, all right? My daddy made us all take CPR lessons back when he and my mom were on good terms because we'd lost gram right before our eyes at Sunday dinner and nobody knew what to do. I still remember how to do it. Besides, I'd always heard a drunk's body was too relaxed to have a heart attack. Or maybe that was to die in a violent car crash. Shit,

I don't remember. Whatever. Oh, you're fading fast, huh? Can you hear me? Hellooooo?

Alright, let's get you out of the car, then. I'm gonna pull the gag out and uncuff you. Guess you're not really able to move too far on your own right now. Ha! Let me just get my elbows under your arms there. I should be able to drag your lard ass over to the shoulder here.

Phew! OK, good. Ever hear of antiperspirant, guy? How am I going to wash your pit stink off my arms way out here? Now, let's see. How did that go? I put my hand under your head and tilt it back, pinch the nose to open the airway and—HEY! OW! What the Hell, guy?

HEY! COME BACK HERE! SERIOUSLY? WHO THE HELL DO YOU THINK YOU ARE HEAD-BUTTING A FUCKING GIRL?

Asshole! Ow! That fucking *hurt*. I bet I'll bruise.

Well, there's a funny sight. I can't say I was expecting that. A bare butt jiggling down the road as fast as it can go. Out of view of my headlights now. Ha! Shit. Tiffany, you do make your mistakes, don't you? Gotta remember that if they know up front that I'm gonna kill them, they're probably gonna be trying to come up with a way out of it. I would.

But you're not going to get very far, are you asshole? No sir. Not far at all. I've still got my car, and it didn't even occur to you to jump in there and try to haul ass out of here before I had time to come after you. Ha! I might make my mistakes, but it looks like the heavens are smiling down on me in some ways tonight. Or maybe the hells are smiling up at me instead. Ha!

No, heavens. It's the heavens smiling down. I'm not a bad girl. I'm just a little bored. And a girl's gotta have her fun. Fun with a purpose. So, I'm just gonna put my little ass-wagon here back into Drive and chase you down. Hell, maybe I'll run over you instead of using the crowbar this time. Wouldn't that be fun? I've always wondered what that would look like from this side of the steering wheel, you know? And what it would feel like. Right, foot on the gas and here we go.

Oh.

Shit.

Shit, shit, SHIT! *Really?* Did you *really* just die on me, ass-wagon? What the hell? Start! Why won't you start? Oh. Well, there's your problem right there. The gas tank's empty. I never even thought about filling 'er up before I stripped the asshole down and tossed him inside. There you go, folks. Tiffany and her thoughtless mistakes. Ha! Ugh. This sucks.

Oh, well. The night's not over yet. I've got a good hour until sunrise, I think. It's getting cold out here, but I'm wearing clothes, I have my cell phone, and I can use it as a flashlight. So I'd say I still have what you'd call the advantage in this situation. Ha!

I gotta say, though, buddy-boo. I misjudged you. I frankly thought a random asshole (especially a drunk naked random asshole) would be the easiest kill of them all. Honestly, I was afraid it was going to be boring. Ha!

Now that I've shut off the ass-wagon, I think I can see the faint glow of some lights on the horizon up ahead. Maybe we were coming up to a town, hey? I was going to kill you at the edge of the desert because, I don't know, it just felt right. But I guess I can kill you in another town. The change of scenery might make it even that much more exciting. I can't remember ever having been to this side of the desert before. I'm betting it's a small town, where everybody knows everybody else. Over there, I'm just a wayfaring stranger with blood in her eyes. Ha!

But I'm also a pretty girl.

I'll probably get bloody sand all over my hands, too.

Well, I guess I should start walking.

I just might have some fun tonight after all.

Bedside Manner

There's no such thing as ghosts, at least according to mommy and daddy. So no one was more surprised than Jake the night he rolled over and discovered the aural lady with the blank expression and hollow eyes standing right beside his bed. She floated there, glowing an icicle white and blue, like the strobes cast from television static when all the house lights are doused. Her arms hung too long at her sides, their bony fingertips stretching nearly to her knees. Or where her knees should have been, had she visible legs beneath her billowing nightgown.

Entirely conscious and no longer the slightest bit sleepy, Jake considered himself lucky. Although he might have thought his first instinct would have been to gasp, or to yank the covers over his head, or to wail for the company of his parents, he had not actually physically reacted to the (ghost?) entity. However, he did suddenly realize that he was holding his breath. He allowed his lungs to deflate slowly, an approximation of what, he thought, might be the long exhale of a sleeping body.

The thing in ghostly female form did not appear to have noticed that he was awake. The face that hovered over her body was slack, its hollow eye sockets staring straight ahead, as if over Jake's body, at the wall behind him. On the other side of that wall lay his mommy and daddy, in their own bed. At that moment they might as well have been in another country.

Now and then, Jake thought he saw something glisten and—he would swear it—move behind the thing's eye sockets. Then something wet and shiny in the glow of the creature's own aura slid from the right socket and fell toward the floor. It evaporated in the ghostly convalesced fog of the thing's gown just before it hit.

Jake thought it might have been a worm. He surreptitiously scanned what he could see of the floor beneath the figure, but could detect no evidence of whatever had crept from her eye socket.

He also could not see the Mickey Mouse clock on the wall behind the floating thing, so he had no idea how much time had passed. An eternity later, it faded from his view. Gratefully, Jake noticed that the shape's head and those hideous writhing eye sockets were the first to go, followed by its shoulders, its waist, and eventually the cloud at the floor on which it had seemed to hover.

In the spot where its head had been, both of Mickey Mouse's white bubble-shaped glove hands were pointing to the giant number three, so it was three fifteen in the morning.

Jake shivered in spite of the double blankets his mommy had piled atop him the night before.

He thought he might never sleep again.

Then he did.

***

The sun came up, as it always eventually does. In the warm light of a crisp autumn morning ride to school, Jake was able to chalk the night's incident up to his own back-to-school nerves and imagination. By the ride home that afternoon, he had all but forgotten the strange and frightening visitor from the night before. Until it was once again time for bed.

His drained energy from a full day of school and homework—not to mention his mommy's hearty cooking followed by a warm bath—had Jake nearly asleep less than one minute after his head hit the pillow. He drifted away to the sound of his parents watching the ten o'clock news on the living room television set. Mickey Mouse reported that it was ten twenty-five. If he stayed awake much longer, he would hear the booming voice of Ed MacMahon introducing Johnny Carson on *The Tonight Show*. Sometimes he listened to Johnny Carson's jokes before he drifted off, but tonight he didn't think he was going to make it that far. The image of the thing from the night before briefly appeared at the fore of his mind, but he managed to push it away with little effort.

"There's no such thing as ghosts," he murmured as he drifted down to sleep. "Mommy and daddy said so."

But that was little comfort when his eyes later fluttered open in the darkness to find the aural lady standing before him again. As on the night before, he had no idea what time it might be. There was no longer sound from the living room television set. There were no footsteps in the hallway, and there was no chatter from mommy and daddy's bedroom behind the wall. There was only the silent floating visage before him.

Something was different this time. Tonight a wide rictus spread across the lower half of its face. Its formerly mostly empty eye sockets were entirely alive now with squirming, glistening gray rolls of those worms he'd thought he'd seen the night before. The thing maintained its glare at the wall behind him rather than at him, at least as far as he could tell.

Jake caught himself holding his breath again and let it out. On his next inhale, he smelled something horrible, something that he had not noticed the previous night. It was like a mixture of the egger farts he sometimes produced when he had a milkshake tummy ache, and the damp freshly turned earth that his father tilled for their miniature homesteader garden every spring. Only it was not spring now. And he had not slurped down one of his favorite McDonald's chocolate milkshakes since July.

Daddy once told him to say something if he ever smelled an egger that didn't come out of his own body. If you smell that kind of egger and it didn't come out of your bum, it means that there's a gas leak in the house somewhere. Jake couldn't be certain, but he suspected that it wasn't a gas leak this time. He thought the egger he smelled was probably coming from the aural lady who was standing beside him and grinning her wicked grin.

Almost as if she had heard his thoughts, the glowing phantom in front of him raised her arm, her skeletal fingers curling themselves into a pointed fist. It looked like she might be about to point to something over his head, or behind him on the wall. But before she had finished the gesture, she started to fade again. First, her head went, then her shoulders. Then she was a misty after-image against his retinas. Then she was nothing at all.

Mickey Mouse informed him that it was three fifteen in the morning.

The following evening, Jake fought his bedtime. His room didn't feel like his room anymore. It was a stranger's place, an uncomfortable place he no longer wanted to be. He was careful to avoid it, doing homework at the kitchen table instead. Mommy and daddy seemed not to notice the change in his behavior, except when Daddy commented on the number of stray Hot Wheels that had mysteriously made their way into the living area from their usual place by the plastic racetrack on the floor of his room.

"I just wanted to spend some time with you guys," Jake had replied. "I think something's wrong with my room. I thought I smelled an egger in there last night."

His Daddy grinned at that.

"Been hitting the milkshakes, have you?"

Jake shook his head. "No, sir. It wasn't me. I don't know where it came from."

Daddy pursed his lips in that thoughtful way Jake had come to know as his "serious" face.

"Do you smell it now?"

"No. I smelled it for a minute during the night, and then it was gone, and—"

Mommy, who had been listening from her place on the sofa, piped up then. She was also wearing her serious face.

"And what, pumpkin?"

"And there was something else there, too. It looked like a lady. A weird glowing lady with no feet and worms for eyeballs."

Jake swallowed. His face felt hot. Saying it out loud like that made him feel a little silly, but he pressed on anyway.

"I don't want to sleep in there anymore."

His Daddy rolled his eyes and laughed.

"Johnny stop it!" Mommy scolded. "You're upsetting him." Then she turned to Jake. "Are you sure you weren't asleep, sweetie? Are you sure you didn't just have a bad dream?"

"It wasn't a dream," Jake replied.

Mommy gently stroked the mop of brown hair head back from his forehead.

"Do you want to sleep with us tonight?"

"Oh come on!" Daddy raised his voice, not quite to a shout. "I have to be at the hospital at four tomorrow morning. That means I need to be up by three at the latest. How am I going to be able to concentrate tomorrow if little Jumpin' Jake here is punting dream footballs against my shins all night?"

"Johnny, he's scared!" she said, wrapping her arms around Jake and pulling him close to her.

"Yes, Sheila," Daddy said. "I know he's scared, Sheila, but I can't risk a botched surgery because I didn't get enough sleep. You remember what I went through, right? The Johnson lady?"

Mommy glared at him. Jake didn't see her glare at him, but he could see daddy's expression through mommy's fingers, which she had instinctively used to cover his eyes instead of his ears. That was the face daddy always got when mommy made him feel ashamed.

"I remember all too well," she hissed. "But we don't talk about that. Not in front of our son. I'll sleep in Jake's room with him so you can get your rest."

Jake pried himself loose from his mother's arms. "No! We can't sleep in there. What if the lady gets us?"

"Shhhh, sweetie," Mommy cooed. "I promise you. No one's going to hurt you or your mommy. Mommies have a special sixth sense when it comes to their little ones. We know when there's danger. If the bad lady shows up again tonight, we'll shoo her away together. Then you won't be scared anymore."

She ran her fingers through his hair again and kissed him on the forehead. "Okay?"

Jake nodded. "Okay."

"Great!" Daddy shouted, but not without some humor. "I'll just amble off to our bed on my own and be cold all night."

"You keep that up, and you'll be cold every night," mommy replied.

Daddy laughed at that, then directed his attention to Jake.

"Son, your mom's right," he said. "You know I don't like to admit that, but there you go. No one's going to bother you or her or anyone else in this house. You're safe as you can be, and you'll see that after tonight.

"And now that that's all over, I'm going on to bed. I'm wiped out and tomorrow's going to be a helluva long day."

19

"Johnny!"

"Oh. Heck! I meant that it's going to be a heckuva long day." He grinned sheepishly, although Jake figured that was probably just for show. "G'night folks!"

Jake grinned too, in spite of himself.

***

"Mommy? What did daddy mean about 'The Johnson Lady'?"

Jake was curled under his bed covers, resting his head on his pillow. His hands were folded together under his chin. His mommy sat on the opposite edge of the bed, his longtime favorite bedtime story—*Harold and the Purple Crayon*—closed between her hands. The last time Jake had glanced at Mickey Mouse on the wall it had been nine o'clock. How many hours then before mommy would finally know what was happening in his room at night? Two? Three? Six? Part of him wished that there were not so much time.

"Why do you bring up the Johnson lady?" mommy asked.

Jake shrugged. "I don't know. Both of you got kind of upset. Did daddy do something bad to the Johnson lady?"

Mommy sighed.

"I really don't think it's a good idea to talk about this right before bedtime. I really don't think it's a good idea to talk about it at all. So don't worry about it, okay? Sometimes, when a person is very young and just learning, they can make mistakes. Most of the time, those mistakes are no big deal. You learn from them, and you move on. But every now and then, there's a mistake that just sticks with you. I guess you could say it haunts you, because it's something you feel bad about and that you know you can never make right.

"Do you understand?"

Jake nodded, his eyes wide. *Haunts.*

"Now, there. You see? I've said too much, and you're scared. Listen, honey, just don't worry about it. What happened with the Johnson lady was a very long time in your daddy's past. He's done a lot of brilliant things since those days.

"And you know he didn't mean to snap tonight, right? It's just his strong work ethic. He wants to make sure he never makes that old mistake again, you know? The best way for him to make sure it doesn't happen again is to be good and rested so he can always be at the top of his game. Right?"

Jake nodded again.

"Okay, then. Let's hit the hay. You'll wake up in the morning, and nothing bad will have happened over night. I promise."

She raked his hair from his forehead and planted a kiss there.

"And if anything bad did happen, I'd be right here to make it all better. Good night, pumpkin."

***

But something did happen that night, and mommy wasn't there.

Jake awoke to find himself face-to-face with the phantom lady and her glistening worm-filled eye sockets. Instinctively, he launched himself out from under the covers and backward across the bed. He reached behind himself, feeling for mommy's form, to shake her awake if he needed. His hands met only the fabric of the sheets atop the firm springiness of the mattress beneath them.

"Mommy?" he managed softly. Then louder, "Mommy!"

There was no reply.

The thing was grinning at him now. Staring at him, not the wall. He'd finally made his rookie mistake and let the thing know he was awake and aware. Had it taken his mommy? Some foul, shit-like odor wafted from the thing's open maw to Jake's rapidly flaring nostrils. He gagged and covered his mouth and nose with his right hand, not taking his eyes off the figure floating before him.

"Mommy?" he called again.

"Mooommy?"

"MOOOOOOMMYYYYYYYY!"

Then he heard the slap of running footsteps from down the hall, heavy falls between longer pauses (those were probably his daddy's) followed by lighter ones at quicker intervals. Mommy. Thank God! The thing floating in front of him began to fade away once again. By the time the lights dangling from the overhead ceiling fan flooded his room, the thing had vanished completely.

Mickey Mouse reported that it was three fifteen in the morning.

Jake only glanced at the clock then fixed his eyes on the spot where the ghost had appeared. They stung, his eyes. Then his vision became blurred

21

by tears. They streamed down his face when he cut his eyes to the open door of his room, where both of his sleep-addled parents stood staring at him, pillow creases still etched across their faces.

"Where WERE you?" Jake shouted at his mother. "WHERE THE HELL DID YOU GO? YOU SAID YOU WERE GOING TO STAY IN HERE WITH ME ALL NIGHT! YOU SAID NOTHING BAD WOULD HAPPEN. YOU SAID SHE WOULDN'T GET ME! WHY DID YOU LEAVE ME?"

"Jake, watch your mouth." His father. Unmoved. Irritated. "Do you know what time it is? I've got—oh my God, I overslept. I need to get going! I've got a Cesarian to do."

Mommy dashed past him, shooing him away as she did so, as if he was a fly buzzing in her ear. "Go!" She landed at Jake's side and cradled the top of his head against the left side of her face. She hugged him with her left arm and stroked the top of his head with her right hand. Jake could feel his own body trembling against her touch.

"Sweetie," she said softly. "Sweetie, I'm sorry. I just woke up a little while ago, and I couldn't get back to sleep. You were sleeping so soundly, I thought it was safe for me to go back to my bed because daddy was going to be getting up soon anyway.

"I'm sorry," she repeated. "I'm so sorry."

"You said you'd stay with me," Jake said. "You said you'd stay with me so nothing bad would happen."

***

In spite of his protests later that morning, mommy would not allow Jake to go to school. At first, she would not explain why, and that mightily frustrated him. Jake didn't care so much about missing school, but he also wasn't particularly thrilled about staying in the same house with that thing all day. His mommy spent the majority of the morning behind the closed door of her study, making phone calls. Jake couldn't make out what she was saying, but there was an urgency to whatever it was, to whoever was on the other end of the call. She never shouted from behind that study door, although Jake wondered if her restraint might be merely for his sake.

She appeared at his side at lunchtime, just as he was settling in front of the local independent television station for an unusual afternoon dose of obnoxious animated lunacy. The smile on her face was warm, empathetic, but there were heavy bags under both her eyes. The end of her nose was red, as if she had a cold, or had been crying.

"Mommy?" Jake said softly. "Mommy, are you all right?"

She sniffled. "I'm fine, sweetie. I've made us some soup and grilled cheese sandwiches for lunch. Let's go sit down and talk a little while we eat."

Mommy turned off the gas to the eye on which the steaming pot of soup sat and poured them each a bowl of creamy tomato. Both bowls sat on plates that just barely accommodated them along with half of the grilled cheese, which mommy had sliced hot from the top of the griddle that sat on a rear eye of the stove. They ate the first part of the meal in silence. When Jake was two bites into his half of the grilled cheese sandwich, Mommy finally spoke up.

"Sweetie," she said, "I'm worried about you. And I want you to know that I would never allow anything to hurt you, okay?"

Jake nodded and reached for his glass of water. He was still chewing that second bite of grilled cheese, and it didn't want to go down. Several toasted crumbs of bread tumbled from his lips and into his soup. His mommy smiled at him.

"Okay. I want you to think back to last night, and any other night before last night, and tell me exactly what it was you saw in your room. I want every detail you can think of. I know it might be hard for you to describe it, or even to think about it right now, but your daddy and I need to know what's happening to you at night. If you don't think you can talk about it, just answer me with yes or no, okay?"

Jake nodded.

"Is a stranger coming into your room at night, Jake?"

He swallowed and nodded again.

"Do you remember what he looks like?"

"She," Jake corrected. "Yes. I do."

Mommy inhaled and straightened up in her chair. "Okay. She, then. Can you tell me what she looks like?"

Jake buried his face in his hands, his elbows propped on the table in front of him.

"Do I have to?" he pleaded.

"Please, sweetie? We need to know."

He shuddered and dropped his hands away from his face. Tears welled in his eyes, and he could feel a quivering glob of snot trying to escape from his left nostril. He snorted it back.

"She's awful, Mommy!" he cried. "She's scary! I think she's a ghost!"

Saying it out loud did not feel so silly this time. It felt good, and somewhere inside him, it opened a door that made him free to spill the rest of the details.

"I don't know what time she comes in," he said. "But I always wake up to her kind of floating right beside my bed. At first, she never looked at me, but last night when I woke up she was right in my face!

"She's just this floating lady. She doesn't even have feet, it's all some kind of cloud or mist down there. And she has these things where her eyes are supposed to be. They're all wriggly. They look like a bunch of worms all tied up in a ball. One night, she even reached out! And her fingers were like bones, mommy. I thought she was going to touch me, but she just pointed at my wall and then disappeared."

He paused and looked at her. If mommy had any feelings about what he was telling her, her face did not reveal them to him. She was still listening, though, so he continued.

"Her breath is the worst part, though," he said, twisting up his mouth and nose. "At least I think it's her breath. If it is her breath, it's horrible! The other night I smelled it. It smelled like poop, or an egger fart, like somebody took a big diarrhea dump and didn't flush it. It was gross! I thought I was gonna be sick!"

Mommy was no longer looking at him. She instead appeared to be lost in thought, staring at the empty space just above his head.

"What was she wearing?" she asked him.

Jake shrugged. "I don't know," he said. "Some kind of dress or gown, I guess. It was hard to tell."

She focused on him again.

"What color was her hair?"

Jake thought for a moment. "I don't know. I guess I haven't been looking at her hair. White, maybe? *If* she had hair, I think I might remember it being white."

Mommy nodded.

"Have you ever seen her anywhere else?" she asked. "Any other rooms in the house? Or outside?"

Jake shook his head. "No, but there is something else I noticed. She always disappears at the same time. My clock is always pointing at both threes when she goes away. I don't know what time she comes in, though. I guess I'm never awake when that happens."

The loud jangling and crash of a ring of keys against the entryway table in the front hall startled them both. Mommy yelped and whirled in her seat. A second later, daddy came ambling toward them from the hall. His face was a mask of rage and shame that comically transformed to surprise when he saw the two other members of his household seated at the kitchen dinette.

"Jesus!" he said. "You scared me. I didn't know you were home."

"I was about to say thing same thing to you," Mommy said, not without some ice in her voice.

Daddy slid into a chair beside mommy, propping the elbow of his right arm on the dinette and his forehead on the palm at the upright end of that elbow.

"I'm sorry," he said flatly. "I've had a bad day, okay? I've had a bad day. Not only did I get to the hospital later than I was supposed to this morning, but then the chief, Baxter, took one look at me and decided he couldn't trust me in the surgery alone. I don't know what it was. Maybe my eyes were bloodshot. Maybe he could just see how nervous I was after getting up late. I don't know." He made eye contact with mommy. "It was humiliating, Sheila. Standing in that operating room with those—those judgmental eyes on me, looking at me like I'd never touched a scalpel before.

"And what was I supposed to do? Tell him I'm fine? I'm not fine. Obviously, I'm not fine. If I had been fine, that woman would've had her baby and been in recovery before Baxter had even finished his first cup of coffee.

"DAMMIT!" He pounded his fist on the table, causing both mommy and Jake to jump in their seats. "Why did I have to oversleep today? Of all days! Today!"

He sighed, then leaned against the back of his chair and rubbed at his eyes with both palms.

"Johnny. It was only fifteen minutes," mommy said. Daddy went on as if he hadn't heard her.

"Maybe Baxter's right, though," he said. "I mean, who knows? It might have been the Johnson lady all over again."

"Daddy? Who is the Johnson Lady?" He hadn't meant to say it out loud, but Jake was unable to prevent the question from escaping. Mommy shot him a horrified look. "How could you ask that right now?" that look said. Jake flushed, although part of him felt relief that the question was out there.

"Was," Daddy replied. "You mean who *was* the Johnson lady."

"Johnny!"

Daddy dropped his hands from his eyes and folded them on the table in front of him. His face was red and bloated. His eyes, bloodshot, were wet with unspilled rage. They sat behind large purple bags.

"What?" he replied. "What, Sheila? Maybe it's about time he heard this story. I mean, the kid's been haunted by imaginary monsters his whole life. Maybe it's time he learned what a real monster is, you know? What it *really* means to be haunted." He turned to Jake. "Son, you can't spend your whole life being afraid of things that go bump in the night, especially when there are so many real world problems that can fuck—I'm sorry— *mess* you up in a big way."

Mommy placed a hand over daddy's folded ones. "Honey, please—"

"No, Sheila. I'm talking." He slid his hands out from under hers. Mommy's lips screwed up in anger. She leaned back in her chair and eyed him balefully. "You're only going to scare him more," she said. Then she folded her arms beneath her breasts and directed her gaze toward the kitchen window as if it had become suddenly more interesting than the conversation at the table.

"Jake," Daddy continued. "Son. Your daddy made a big, big mistake when he was a lot younger than he is right now. Making mistakes is something people sometimes do, and that's okay. The problem comes when people don't own up to their mistakes and try to cover them up. That's what I did, and I've regretted it ever since."

He sighed.

"A long time ago, there was another woman who was going to have a baby."

"The Johnson Lady?" Jake interrupted.

Daddy nodded, his lips spread sideways in a rueful smile. "That's right. The Johnson lady. Anyway, your daddy already had lots of experience with those kinds of pregnancies because he'd spent his residency in a relatively high-risk women's hospital. See, the Johnson lady was quite a bit older than a lot of women are when they have babies. Her hair was almost completely white. But there were other complications, other abnormalities, too. When I saw those indicators—uh, symptoms—I thought her baby had probably made a little poop while it was still inside her. That can sometimes happen if the mommy is still pregnant way past the due date or if the mommy has other health problems that put stress on the baby while it's still in the womb."

"Like being old?" Jake asked.

"Getting older is not a health problem, Jake," mommy spat from her spot outside the conversation.

Daddy smiled again but shook his head. "Well, a woman has a prime, the best time in her life to bear a child," he explained. "But in this case, I thought the complications were because the baby had pooped before coming out of its mommy."

Jake swallowed thickly but didn't say anything. Although he knew that people carried poop inside them until they squeezed it out on the toilet, he also knew that the poop had a specific place that it was supposed to come from. He had never considered that a baby could even produce a poop while it was still inside its mommy. There was something about the thought of having another living creature inside you that could perform acts as mundane as pooping that filled him with disgust. He shuddered involuntarily, but neither daddy nor mommy appeared to notice.

"The poop that a baby has before it's had any food from outside the womb is called meconium." Daddy wasn't looking directly at him now, but somewhere above him, as if he were reciting some text by rote. "If the baby produces meconium while still in the womb, it can end up breathing a mixture of amniotic fluid—the protective stuff that surrounds the baby while it's in its mommy's belly—and meconium. That causes something called meconium aspiration syndrome, which can be very bad for the baby if it's not caught and treated."

Jake shuddered again. Babies can also *breathe* before they're born? He hadn't known that, just as he hadn't known about the poop. He'd once had a nightmare about his mother frying a small dead white fish in a pan on the stove while he watched. The fish, its head and eyes and all intact, had been tossed directly into an iron skillet that was popping with butter or lard or some other kind of cooking grease. A few seconds after the fish had been tossed into the pan, its sides began to bloat and deflate, bloat and deflate, bloat and deflate. It was breathing. The dead fish was breathing, suffocating and being fried alive.

That was the image that a baby breathing in a fluid-filled bag inside its mother recalled to his mind. He knew it was a ridiculous comparison. He knew women carried babies all the time. He was once a baby inside his own mother's belly, and he couldn't remember struggling to breathe at all. He couldn't remember being inside his mother's belly either, although it obviously hadn't killed him. It *was* a ridiculous comparison, but he could not un-think it.

"The Johnson lady's baby was already past due when she came in. I don't know or really remember all the particulars before that because I wasn't her regular doctor. I looked at her chart, but I don't remember seeing any unusual history. Her regular doctor had just been hit with a malpractice suit. The hospital had suspended his privileges there while things were being sorted out. I just happened to be the one on-call when the Johnson lady came in to be examined. And then there were—other complications."

Mommy, whom Jake had noticed had been nervously bouncing her right leg as it lay crossed over her left, barked one syllable of sardonic laughter. Daddy cut his eyes toward her, then focused on Jake.

"Listen, son. Before I go any further with this, I think you should know that your daddy would never, ever hurt anyone on purpose. You know that, right? I would *never* put anyone in harm's way intentionally."

Jake nodded.

"Okay, then. When I saw that Ms. Johnson was already well past her due date and then saw that the techs had recorded the baby as having an erratic heartbeat, my mind immediately went back to medical school and picked up meconium aspiration. It's not the easiest thing in the world to diagnose, but at that point, I had both a symptom and probable cause, so I was pretty sure that the safest thing for both the mother and the child at that point would be to induce, to go ahead and deliver the baby."

Here, Jake's daddy swallowed audibly.

"Well, I should have had one more look at her chart before we went ahead with that plan, Jake. But I was tired. I'd been up for most of the night before. Back in college, that was a common thing. You stayed up all night: partying, studying, whatever. You're young and full of energy. It's not that big of a deal to work long shifts and still make time for your social life. When you're out of school, and you start getting older and building a better life for yourself in the real world, all that changes. It changes whether you want it to change or not. I should have known better by then. A grown man needs to sleep sometimes."

He sighed.

"So, I didn't look at her chart again. I thought I knew what I was doing and the sooner we got started, the better. So we induced labor. Part of that process meant that I had to manually puncture the little sac—the amniotic sac it's called—that contains the baby, to kind of kickstart the process.

"But I didn't know, son. Oh, my God, I didn't know.

"I was so tired. My hands were trembling. And when I went to puncture the amniotic sac, my hand slipped. It slipped! It slipped and stabbed the uterus."

Jake wasn't entirely sure what the difference was between an amniotic sac and a uterus, but he didn't want to ask. His daddy's eyes had welled up with tears, and his shoulders heaved in gigantic circular motions as he sobbed. It wasn't a good time to ask questions.

"She'd already had a Cesarean," he continued when he had hold of himself again, "which you might have heard called a C-section, around a year and a half before she got pregnant with this baby. A Cesarean is when we have to literally open up the mommy's belly and cut into her uterus and remove the baby instead of allowing it to be delivered naturally. But I didn't know she'd had one before, or I didn't remember it from the chart, or something. I don't know. Either way, having had a C-section before meant that this pregnancy was a higher risk pregnancy because the wall of the uterus was probably weaker from the previous surgery. See, your insides, just like your outside, develop scars when they heal from cuts. Those scars are weaker than the original tissue and can be more easily damaged or reopened.

"But I didn't know. I didn't know, and I accidentally punctured her uterus. It's all a blur from there. She started hemorrhaging. Badly. And I couldn't think anymore. I couldn't order anything I needed to help her. I think I must have been in shock. I just stood there, watching her bleed out. I might—I might have even seen some of her intestines starting to spill out from between her legs—"

Mommy slammed the palm of her hand on the table, startling both Daddy and Jake. "JOHNNY! That's enough! Look at him!"

Jake was staring wide-eyed at his daddy, each of his hands gripping the seat of the dining table chair in which he sat. Daddy saw him trembling and, mercifully, cut short the rest of his story.

"Ms. Johnson and her baby both died," he said. A long sigh escaped his lungs, underscoring the finality of the words. "I couldn't help them. I couldn't help them because I was in shock. I shouldn't have been in shock. I knew what to do, but I didn't do it. I was in shock because I had come to work too tired to think straight. That cost both Ms. Johnson and her baby their lives."

Daddy shuddered.

"I was lucky, though. I was lucky on several counts. The whole thing happened before sunrise—I think I might have actually started induction at three o'clock that morning—and, for some reason I've never known, there was no Mr. Johnson anywhere around. I have no idea whether a Mr. Johnson even existed. The few people who were in the room with me all felt as guilty as I do, and we all wanted to keep our jobs (it was a bad economy, after all). Ms. Johnson's previous doctor had already been hit with that malpractice lawsuit. We didn't want to take any chances.

"So we doctored her records. We changed some of the data we'd taken when she arrived. We made it look like her water had already broken by the time she got there and that a natural delivery was already in progress. That the natural delivery process was what actually ruptured her uterus and caused the whole thing.

"Basically," he added, "we blamed the baby."

Mommy gasped. She stared at Daddy with wide eyes and a mouth so far open that it made her look like one of those water balloon clowns at the county fairground midway. Jake wondered whether she had ever heard that part of daddy's story before.

"How could no one have caught that?" Mommy said. "What about the procedure? What about the medical examiner? How did you explain the dead baby, for God's sake?"

Daddy scoffed. "Babies die during traumatic pregnancies. That one was easy. It turns out that I wasn't entirely wrong about the meconium aspiration. At least, I don't think I was. The baby was probably too far gone to have survived even if the mother had.

"We worried about the M.E., though. Turns out he wasn't much to worry about either. The guy was a sot and was probably three sheets to the wind during most of his procedures anyway. And who'd care, right? They're dead bodies. It's not like he could screw them up much more than they already were.

"My guess is that there are a *lot* of unsolved murders from that era, though."

"Murder?"

"Sheila, I don't know, okay? I don't know what I'd be charged with if anybody ever found out about this. But the good news is that the only people who know about it are me, you, and now Jake here. Everybody else that was in that room that night is either dead or have advanced so far in their careers that they don't want to put them at risk by coming clean. And Ms. Johnson's records have been long in the archives.

"Besides, you've never told anyone about this. If you did, you'd be an accomplice by now for keeping it secret so long. And Jake's not going to talk, right Jake? If both mommy and daddy went away, you wouldn't have anyone to take care of you anymore. Right?"

There was a look in his eye, an angry, needy look. Jake felt his stomach twist into a knot.

"I won't tell," he said softly. Then he had an epiphany. "I won't tell because you're sorry, daddy. You're sorry that it all happened and you've been trying to make up for it ever since. Right? When someone says they're sorry, you have to accept it. That's what they taught us in Sunday school back when we used to go to church."

Daddy leaned back in his chair, looking relieved. "That's right," he said. "That's right, buddy. I'm so, so sorry that all that happened. That's why I always need to get good sleep at night. I want to be sure that something like that never happens again.

"I've never forgotten it," he added softly. "I've never forgiven myself for it. I'll never forget looking at the clock that night when I finally gave up and called her time of death.

"It was three fifteen in the morning."

There was a lull.

"I'm sorry," Daddy said finally. "I need to go wash up and lay down. I feel like shit." He pushed his chair back from the table and stood up. "By the way, Sheila, you left the gas on under the griddle. You trying to kill us?" He shut it off as he walked past, dousing the little ring of blue flame.

***

That evening dragged by, with only snippets of conversation between them. Although Jake did learn by listening that it had been Daddy that Mommy was on the phone with earlier in the day, that she had called him to talk to him about possibly getting some psychological help for Jake. Mommy said she was afraid that daddy's work stress and bad attitude were having a negative effect on Jake's psychology. Daddy had apparently shouted at her or blown her off or something like that. Most of the little conversations between mommy and daddy that evening were his apologies.

When it was finally time for bed, Jake did not hesitate. Although she asked, Jake told his mommy that he did not want her to sleep in his room tonight. He said he was a big boy now and he needed to put his childish fears behind him. She had smiled and laughed at that. The grown-ups always thought it was funny when he said things that they thought sounded wise. Later, he heard mommy tell daddy that maybe daddy's trauma was a blessing in disguise because it seemed to have made Jake forget about his own problems. He didn't bother to correct her on that.

Throughout the evening, as his parents went about their own routines, Jake crept to the fridge and nabbed two of the eight-ounce Coca-Cola bottles his father kept in the refrigerator for days when he had to mow the yard. Eight ounces didn't sound like much, but he also knew that drinking a whole eight-ounce bottle of Coke in one sitting on a car trip through rural Alabama had once made him have to pee so bad that he thought the pressure just might float his eyeballs right out of their sockets. He also knew that he wasn't supposed to drink a lot of fluids right before bedtime for that same reason: he'd be up every few hours to pee.

Tonight, in fact, he was counting on that.

At lights out, he grabbed the first bottle from under his bed and twisted it open; he tried to down it. The Coke was still cool, but not refrigerator cold. It tasted sweet on his tongue, and the fizz tickled the back of his

throat. He was only half done when he had to stop for a coughing fit because of a swallow that had gone down the wrong way.

"Jake?" he heard his mommy call from the living room, where a man
on television was talking about soldiers and cold wars and bombs. "Jake,
honey? You okay?"

He took a deep breath and fought the next cough long enough to croak a
reply. "Fine!" he managed. "Swallowed my own spit. Down the wrong pipe!"

There was a pause from the living room, then: "Are you sure?" After a
few more coughs and deep breaths, Jake again replied that he was fine, that
she didn't need to come check on him. That seemed to satisfy her. She told
him to come get her if he needed anything. She followed that offer with
her sweet motherly "good night."

Jake awoke for the first time with an urgent need to pee when Mickey's
short hand was on the twelve, and his longer hand was on the five. There
was no sign of the scary floating lady in white, although the mere thought
of her made him shiver. He was glad that she was not already there. A
small part of him was also disappointed. Ghosts, Jake surmised, only exist
because they want something that they can't get by themselves. Once they
have what they want, they go away. Now, Jake thought, he knew what it
was that the floating lady wanted and how to make her go away for good.

He made sure to not flush the toilet. He was afraid that doing so might
wake mommy or daddy. Quiet as he could, Jake padded back to his bed
and twisted open the second of his two bottles of Coca-Cola. The first
had gotten him to midnight, about three hours from when he went to
bed. He was hopeful that the second one might wake him up in about the
same amount of time, a little less than three hours from now. He downed
the second bottle without incident, then laid his head on the pillow and,
within moments, drifted back to sleep.

***

He next awoke when Mickey's short hand was on the two and his longer hand on the eleven. He had to pee again, and the floating lady was nowhere to be seen. He threw back the covers and dashed to the bathroom. If
he was right, he had about five minutes until she would appear beside his
bed. He wanted to be sure he was back in it before that happened.

He forgot his attempts to be quiet and flushed the toilet anyway. From
mommy and daddy's bedroom, he heard one of them—probably daddy—

groan and roll over, but no one called out to him. He washed and dried his hands with as much speed as he could muster and sprinted with light steps back to his bedroom. He stopped at the door and peered around the corner. The floating lady in white was not there.

Three long steps and a leap, and he was back in bed, his right cheek against the pillow and the shield of the covers pulled up to his shoulders. Their weight was comforting. Then he realized that he was facing the wrong way if he wanted to see when the floating lady in white arrived, so Jake rolled over.

And there she was.

She had knelt beside his bed and was looking directly into his eyes with her writhing, worm-filled empty sockets. Her mouth was open, and his nostrils were once again assaulted by the odor of an egger fart. He thought he could feel her breath on his face as well, waves of damp and gooey warmth that stuck to his skin. Jake opened his mouth to scream, and then stopped himself before the sound could escape. He didn't want to wake mommy and daddy this time. He didn't want the lady in white to vanish before Mickey had a chance to strike three fifteen.

Jake struggled to sit up on his bed, cross-legged so that his feet did not dangle over the edge. He managed to keep his bedcovers about him as he did so. Rationally, he didn't know what protection they could possibly offer him from a spirit visitor in the dead of night, but any protection at this point was a good thing. The figure beside his bed matched his movements so that she maintained his gaze. Her maw remained open, and the stench of her hot breath nearly overpowered what remained in him of his bedtime snack.

For one terrible moment, he couldn't remember why he had gone through all this, why he'd wanted to be awake when she arrived and why he didn't want to call out for his mommy and daddy to come rescue him from the apparition floating before him. Then it came back to him. He closed his eyes, sucked in a stinking draw of air, and addressed the thing directly in one long blast of unbroken thought.

"My daddy's really sorry he hurt you Ms. Johnson and he didn't mean to do it because it was an accident and he was very tired and he wishes he could take it back so much and I hope you find some peace and the grace of our God be with you and your poor little baby amen."

Here he flung open his eyes. He'd hoped that the apology would be enough to send the ghost away. He'd hoped that that would be the end of it. Instead, he saw the face of the lady in white still floating directly in front of him. Her maw was open wide now, revealing sharp teeth that dripped with what looked to him like seaweed, or the wet moss that grew on many of the older tombstones in the cemetery where they had buried his grandmother a long time ago. The shapes of the sockets where her eyes should have been had also changed; they were narrower, angry. As close as she now was to him, Jake could see that the writhing things inside them looked less like worm segments and more like tiny balls of segmented intestines, pulsing in and out as they contracted their tiny loads of shit down to whatever bowels they might connect to.

I might have even seen some of her intestines starting to spill out from between her legs.

Against his better judgment, Jake's eyes followed the trail of the lady in white's face to her neck, down what was visible of her body, to just above the floor where he had before thought that she disappeared into a floating cloud. What he saw there now clearly was not a cloud, but instead appeared to be a nest of writhing intestines, as if the entire figure were somehow made of them.

The ghost stretched one bony finger toward Jake, placing the pointed claw at the end of it directly under his chin. She pressed upward, forcing him to look at her. The claw was hard, cold, and sharp. It felt like it might just break through his chin, impaling his head on her index finger.

"Tell," she said. Her voice was thick and watery, almost as if she were speaking to him through something other than the membrane of air in the room. It echoed and multiplied inside his head. "Tell what happened."

It suddenly dawned on Jake that the thing must know that his father had sworn him to secrecy.

"I—I can't," he said. "I promised. Ms. Johnson, please! My daddy's real, real sorry for what happened. He didn't mean it!"

"Tell," she said. "Tell. Or kill."

Then she was gone.

***

A short time later, Jake heard his daddy's footfalls as he went about his morning routine. On other days, he might have slept through it or not paid the sound much mind. However, Jake was unable to return to sleep that night. Daddy's footfalls sounded like thunder against the bare floors of the house; they rang against the inside of his skull. He lay paralyzed in his bed, covers pulled up to his chin and reinforced there by fistfuls of fabric. He watched silently as Mickey's long hand ticked off the minutes that would eventually force his short hand to the sunrise hour. His mind raced. Tell? He was sure he knew what she meant by that. The aural lady wanted him to tell what he knew, to get his mommy and daddy in trouble so that the policemen would come and take them away.

Jake's not going to talk, right Jake? If both mommy and daddy went away, you wouldn't have anyone to take care of you anymore. Right?

Yes. If daddy was telling the truth, that was right. Mommy had already known most of Daddy's story. She might not be punished as harshly as daddy would be, but most likely they would still take her away from Jake, and that would be bad. Jake had no grandmother anymore, no other family that he knew of or saw on a regular basis. That meant strangers. If the policemen came and took mommy and daddy away, he would be forced to go live with strangers who might hate him or make him do bad things or do bad things to him.

Tell. Or kill.

Was she threatening to kill him if he didn't tell somebody about what daddy had done? Could a ghost kill a person?

Or kill.

Or was she giving him a choice? If he didn't tell anyone about his daddy's secret, did she want him to kill his daddy instead? That would still deprive him of his daddy, wouldn't it? Yes, it would deprive Jake of his daddy.

Kill.

But not his mommy.

Killing Daddy would not deprive Jake of his mommy, who could still keep her secret and would then still be able to take care of Jake. That is, killing daddy wouldn't deprive Jake of his mommy as long as he was *careful* about it.

That was it, then. He had to kill his Daddy. It was the only way he could keep from being forced to live with strangers and stop the aural lady from visiting him.

Kill Daddy.

By the time Mickey's short hand pointed to the five, Jake had relaxed his grip on the bed sheets under his chin and had fallen fast asleep again. Only five minutes after that, his Daddy started the car and left for work.

***

Jake went to school after the sun came up, but he might as well have spent the entire day somewhere else. His teacher's voice in his head was little more than the *waa-waa* trombone of an adult in a Peanuts cartoon. His mind was on other things, like how to do the thing that the aural lady wanted him to do without hurting his mommy—or himself—in the process. If he were going to do the deed himself, he would need to make sure that it looked like an accident.

Daddy was probably right that the policemen would blame mommy—or even him—if they found out about daddy's secret and then found out that he and mommy knew about it but never told. What daddy didn't seem to know was that what he was using as a threat might also be to mommy and Jake's advantage. After all, if Jake was unable to accomplish what the Johnson lady wanted him to do, who was daddy going to tell without incriminating himself?

Basically, we blamed the baby.

Yeah. He'd blame the baby. Jake wasn't a baby, but he was just a kid, a baby as far as his daddy was concerned. However, he wasn't stupid. He knew that Daddy was already experienced with covering up the truth. If daddy knew Jake had tried to hurt him, he'd be sure to find a way to cover himself and punish Jake at the same time. Better for Jake to make sure it looked like an accident, both to the authorities and to Johnny—daddy—if he somehow managed to escape or survive. It had to be an accident. Something that could have happened anyway, at any time, for a careless or maybe even a stupid reason.

Jake searched his memory for something, anything, about everyday life in his house that might be easily turned into an accident. Not just an accident that could kill daddy, but an "accident" that could still look like an accident even if it didn't kill Johnny—daddy. Something even daddy wouldn't know wasn't an accident.

Something believable.

By the way, Sheila, you left the gas on under the griddle. You trying to kill us?

His daddy's voice in his head startled him back to reality. His teacher had just issued a reminder that the poster board project she'd assigned two days before was due tomorrow. They'd known about it since Monday. There was no excuse to not get it done. But mommy had kept him home the day before, so technically he'd only had two days.

By the way, Sheila, you left the gas on under the griddle.

Then he had an idea. He decided to not ask his teacher for an extension on the project. The bell that sounded the end of the school day could not come fast enough.

***

The bus ride home seemed to especially drag that afternoon. Johnny—Daddy—had left for work early that morning. Jake had vague memories of hearing his thunderous footsteps as he made himself ready to go. That meant he'd be home before dinner that evening, possibly was even home already. That might throw a bit of a wrench into Jake's plans, but he might still be able to make it work. Either way, Johnny—Daddy—would most likely hit the sack early again that night, especially if he wasn't already home and did not get an afternoon nap.

He was nearly inside the house before the school bus had even retracted its stop sign. As the front door of his house closed behind him, he vaguely heard the heavy sigh of the brake release when the tired old bus began to trundle its load to the next house. He did not see Johnny's—his daddy's—car in the driveway during his sprint toward the door. So daddy wasn't home yet. That was a good thing.

"I'm home!" Jake called to his mother as he tossed his backpack on the living room sofa and padded into the kitchen for his afternoon snack. His mother replied with a pleasant "Hi, sweetie!" and strode out of her study to meet him.

"Did you have a good day at school?"

"I'm all caught up," Jake replied from around a mouth full of crunchy peanut butter. "Except for the fire safety poster board project I need to have done for tomorrow. The best one in the class gets submitted to a state school fire safety promotion contest. I've got an idea that I think will win it!" He swallowed and added carefully, with just the right amount of shame, "I forgot about it Monday, and I wasn't there yesterday. I just need to get some poster board and some markers to do it. It should be pretty easy."

Mommy sighed and shook her head, smiling as she did.

"Another last-second school project, huh?"

Jake nodded.

"Well, I suppose we can go down to the drugstore after dinner and see what they have. I need to pick up a few things there anyway."

Jake's heart was racing in his chest. He hoped his mommy couldn't hear it. "That's perfect!" he replied. Too enthusiastically, perhaps, because mommy looked a little surprised.

"Excited about a school project?" she asked with mock incredulity. "Well. Who are you and what have you done with my Jake?"

He tittered. "I just have a really good idea is all."

"Okay, sweetie. We'll go after dinner."

Relief washed over him. What he thought might be the biggest obstacle turned out to be not such a big deal after all. No one could blame the baby, or the mommy if the baby and the mommy weren't home at the time of the accident.

Jake cleared his throat. *Sound natural.*

"So what are we having for dinner?"

Mommy smiled at him again. "Didn't you just eat a whole tablespoon of peanut butter?"

"I don't want dinner nowwww," Jake said. "I was just wondering what we're having tonight."

"I don't know. I've been really busy with clients all day. I thought we could do something simple for once, like ham and cheese sandwiches or—"

"No!" Jake said, stronger than he intended. "I mean, can we do soup and grilled cheese sandwiches like we had for lunch yesterday?"

"You want that *again?*"

"Yeah. It was good! Plus it's kind of a cold day outside, and I always like soup and grilled cheese on cold days."

Mommy laughed. "That you do, hon. That you do. Okay. I suppose I can warm up some soup and make a couple of grilled cheese. You gonna help with the dishes?"

Jake straightened his back and crisscrossed his heart with his index finger. "Cross my heart and hope to—uh, cross my heart and hope to skin my knee!"

The front door banged open just then, and Jake heard the familiar dragging thud of his daddy's footsteps down the hall as he approached. When he was particularly exhausted from a long day at work, Johnny—Daddy—adopted a bit of a zombie shuffle walk. He quite literally dragged himself where he needed to go before ultimately collapsing on the living room sofa, just out of sight of the kitchen, and snore away the hour or so before mommy called him to dinner. Being a doctor made a man tired at the end of a long shift. Of that, Jake was certain. Being a doctor who had to cover up a big secret like Johnny's must double that tired on a daily basis.

As if in response to Jake's thoughts, Johnny tossed him and his mommy a half-hearted wave as he slumped through the kitchen and toward the living room, saying nothing. Jake heard the television click on followed by the sound of Pat Sajak telling someone it was her turn to spin the wheel. In a half hour, the evening news would start, and mommy would start cooking dinner. It was enough time for Jake to do what he had to do next.

He shut the door to his room and collapsed on his bed in a heap. He felt a lump in his throat, like he might need to throw up, and feared he might be about to cry. Instead, he crammed his face into one of his pillows and burst into a fit of uncontrollable laughter. He laughed until tears streamed from the corners of both his eyes. He laughed until his sides hurt. He laughed until it hurt him to try to sit up on the bed.

"It's perfect," he managed through steep inhales when he was able to control himself again. "It's perfect. It was meant to be!"

Jake rolled on the bed toward his door and verified that it stood firmly closed, then he examined Mickey Mouse on his wall. Mickey's short hand was on the four. His long hand was on the nine. Mommy would start cooking dinner soon. It was soup and grilled cheese, which didn't take long to fix so he could expect her to call both him and Johnny to dinner by the time the short hand was on the five and the long hand was on the three.

Another glance around at the door, then Jake whispered, "Ms. Johnson?"

There was no response.

"Ms. Johnson, it will probably be a long time before I can see you in here again, but I'm going to say this anyway. I hope you can hear me. I can't tell anyone what happened. It will get my mommy in trouble, and I need my mommy to take care of me. So, I guess what I'm trying to say is that I'm going to do the other thing, the other choice you gave me. I have a plan, but it might need some help if things don't go the way I hope they do.

"That's all I have to say for right now, except that after this is over, I need you to go away from me. I need you to go away and never come back, okay? That's our deal. If I do this, you leave me and my mommy alone for the rest of our lives."

Again, there was no response, although Jake suddenly felt a bit lighter, as if a particularly heavy burden had been suddenly lifted from him. He also smelled something. He couldn't discern from where, but he could swear that in the air he sniffed the faintly tainted odor of an egger fart. He took that as a good sign.

***

Dinner was quiet. Johnny had been difficult to stir from his sofa snooze in front of the television, so mommy was late in calling Jake to the table. Johnny sat at the dinette, a spoon loosely dangling in one hand and a grilled cheese sandwich in the other. His lidded eyes with the purple bags beneath them made Jake think he might at any point fall face-forward in his soup. Some part of Jake hoped he would. Drowning in his soup would prevent him from having to kill his father himself.

Not far into his meal, Johnny gave up trying to stay awake and lumbered back to the sofa, where the first half hour of the local evening news had ended and the next half hour of national news was just about to begin. Jake sat quiet long enough to hear his father's familiar snore, indicating that Johnny had again fallen into a slumber that was deeper than an afternoon nap probably ought to be. Only then did he allow himself to stir the pot again.

"Oh no!" he stage-whispered to mommy, who was dabbing a small drop of creamy tomato soup from the corner of her mouth. "We still have to get my poster board. Look at the time!"

Mommy glanced at the Kit-Cat Clock hanging beside the kitchen entry, and her eyes widened.

"Ooh," she said. "You're right. If we don't go now, it's going to be prime time before we get back. We might miss *Magnum*. Get your jacket on. I'm going to—"

You trying to kill us?

"—check the stove."

"No!" Jake stood, accidentally knocking his chair backward. It clattered loudly against the kitchen tile. From the living room, Jake heard Johnny's snoring cut short. Then there was a loud sniffle, followed by a snort, and it started back again. Jake's mommy was staring at him.

"I mean. Sorry." he said. "I got up too fast. I meant to say that I'll check the stove if you want so you can go get your purse. Then I can do the dishes when we get back, just like I promised."

Mommy grinned at him. "Okay, mister responsible. I'll take you up on that." Then she stepped lightly, but quickly, from the room.

Jake righted his chair and then carried both his dirty dishes and his mother's to the kitchen sink. He considered carrying Johnny's to the sink as well, but then thought better of it and left them where Johnny had left them sitting on the table. Next, he examined the stove and what remained of the pot of soup and the griddle his mother had used to make the grilled cheese sandwiches. Mommy had turned off both the burner under the soup and the burner under the griddle, but he didn't think she remembered doing that, not if she had intended to do as she'd just said and check it before they left.

Jake glanced around to verify that he was alone, then turned on the burner where the pot of soup sat. He started to walk away, but then remembered their lunch from the day before.

By the way, Sheila, you left the gas on under the griddle. You trying to kill us?

He shut off the burner under the soup and ignited the one under the griddle instead. He didn't know what setting mommy used to grill cheese sandwiches, but he hoped it wouldn't matter too much in the end anyway. He set the flame beneath the griddle burning to a medium height and then strode out of the room. Behind him, from the living room, Johnny continued to saw logs like a lumberjack.

Jake then dashed to his room, slipped on his jacket and shoes, and met his mother at the entryway just as she was about to return to the kitchen.

"I'm ready!" he said. He hoped that from this vantage point she would not be able to see the rear burner on which the griddle sat. He smiled at her and quietly prayed that it did not look forced.

"Okay then," Mommy replied. "Let's go! If we get going now, we'll probably be back before your daddy even knows we're gone. I left him a note just in case he happens to wake up and wonder. Told him we had to go in a hurry because your project is due tomorrow."

The note was something Jake had neither planned for nor thought of, but it wasn't a bad thing. In fact, he thought it made his story sound even better. He did not yet know the word *plausible*, but if it had been in his vocabulary, he would have said that his mommy's note to his daddy made his whole story more *plausible*.

He was careful to not glance back over his shoulder as he and mommy walked out the front door and toward the car. He remembered what happened to Lot's wife. They'd read about it in Sunday school once. Jake had never had much use for salt.

***

Twenty minutes later, mommy and Jake walked into the Revco. Jake was distracted. He kept glancing around the store and out the huge picture windows at the parking lot beyond. Daddy had once told him that he had to be careful about how he looked and behaved when he was in a store. "If you act like you've done something wrong," he had explained, "the store employees will think you did something wrong." He hoped his constant glancing about didn't make him look too suspicious, but he couldn't seem to stop himself.

Eventually, Mommy grabbed him by the hand and dragged him along on her trot to the school supplies section of the store, where there stood an upright display of Royal Brite poster board in all colors. Jake had always felt a certain fascination for blank poster board, especially the ones that varied from the standard white. Unfortunately, his teacher said that the poster board for this particular project was required to be that standard white. Even so, there was something about the anticipation of the creative flow or the world of possibilities that the board's blankness presented, that appealed to him in a raw, primal way. The same way some part of him felt excited about what he hoped was happening at his house at that moment. Then there was the duality of the matte. One side of the poster board was shiny, glossy and somewhat reflective. The other side was flat, although he would never describe it as dull. Depending on what markers you were using, the flat side was sometimes much easier to draw on than the shiny side.

Jake carefully pinched the edge of one of the white sheets and slid it upward, out of the display. The shiny side was facing him, and he could see the hard whites of the Revco fluorescent lights bouncing off it as it wobbled in his hands. He held the board out toward his mommy, for her to take. When she didn't, he looked up at her. Now mommy was the one who was distracted. She was facing him, but her head was turned toward the big picture windows at the front of the store.

"Mommy?" he said. "Mommy, I have the—"

"Shhhh!" she interrupted. "I'm trying to listen."

Jake fell silent and listened as well. At first, all he heard was the instrumental music being piped through the speakers in Revco's ceiling. Then, vaguely, he thought he might be able to hear the wail of a siren. A second later, he knew that it was definitely a siren. Not just one, in fact, but a series of sirens all getting closer and closer to the Revco.

Jake gripped his poster board and ran to the picture window at the front of the store, his mommy close behind him. By the time they got there, the first of the county fire trucks was just rushing through the traffic light in front of the shopping center in which the Revco resided. It was followed by another, then another, until four trucks in all had blown past them, screaming and barreling along like they'd just been shot from the barrel of a gun.

"Goodness," Mommy said when she and Jake were capable of hearing again. "You never see fire trucks this far away from downtown. Must be something bad." She absently gripped Jake's shoulder. "They're headed the way we need to go to get home, though. I hope there's not an accident or something blocking our way."

Jake nodded, not prying his eyes away from the world beyond the giant picture window.

He too hoped it wasn't an accident blocking their way. Indeed, he hoped that he and mommy would be able to get all the way home. He hoped that they would be pulling into their own driveway before they saw the first flashing red lights.

He hoped the aural lady had been able to breathe easy over the hot griddle.

He hoped daddy had remained asleep the entire time.

Hoppers

The bump knocked the iPhone right out of his hand. He watched his half-formed text message tumble in slow motion end-over-end through the air, where it ultimately struck the windshield, flickered, and then disappeared into blackness as the device ricocheted off the glass. From there it bounced off the canvas of the passenger's seat and crash-landed on the floorboard, face down and just out of reach of his pudgy right arm.

"Well, fart muffins!" he exclaimed. Not the most creative expletive, but it would do. "Ain't that always the way?"

And so it was.

It didn't matter how many times he diverted his gaze from the iPhone's minuscule on-screen keyboard toward the road in front of him. It didn't matter how deftly he could one-thumb those letters in the proper sequence without having to look down and make a correction. As soon as his eyes left the road long enough to locate the Send button, or to ensure that the dang old auto-correct wasn't messing with his meaning, he'd hit something in the road, and the whole mess would go flying. He supposed it had only been a matter of time before the repeated phone-to-ground impacts took their toll on the tiny electrical circuits inside the device.

"Fart muffins!" he shouted again, smashing his meaty fist into the soft molded plastic of the dash in front of him. "Muffins made of farts!"

He slowed the circa-1990s Saturn SC to a stop, shifted it into Reverse, and guided it onto the narrow shoulder of the little two-lane stretch of state highway that he called home. He flipped the hazards on, shoved open the door, and stepped out into the golden light of the late spring afternoon. The phone could wait. Better to check the car for damage. Find out exactly what he'd hit. Today he drove the Saturn. Tomorrow it might be an F-150. Probably a Mustang on Friday. Because when you hired Mike Bragg to fix a car, you can bet your bum-diggity that he put it through its paces before he'd let you trust your life to it in the tangled mess of suicidal rush hour that defines a late weekday afternoon in Middle Tennessee. Besides, if one of the state's finest happened by while he was out poking along the side of the road, he wouldn't want it to look like he'd been doing something as careless (or illegal) as texting and driving, especially in a customer's car.

Crouching alongside the right front tire of the SC, he balanced his elbows on his knees and ran the thick fingers of his right hand over his stubbly red sandpaper dome.

"Crap on a Ritz cracker."

It was not difficult to surmise what had happened. Crimson drops of warm blood sluiced onto the tire from beneath the edge of the fender well. They trickled down the wall of black rubber and oozed into a thin semi-circle around the edge of the rim. When he decided to drive again, the tire would no doubt create a nice splashy color wheel effect against the lower half of the silver passenger door. Pinched in the groove between the fender well and its chrome custom accessory stripe was a small tuft of brown and white fur. Mike plucked the fluff from where it hung, sniffed it for reasons he didn't quite understand, and then held it up to the bridge of his nose for closer examination. The hairs were short and coarse, the kind you might find on a small dog. An older dog at that.

"Bees in the cheese dip," he muttered, then heaved a sigh. "Cheese on a bee's knees, I mean. Sure hope I didn't kill some big-eyed kid's stupid mutt." The car was neither dented nor scratched, after all. A little elbow grease and it would clean up fine. A child's broken heart, on the other hand, was something an angrier man than he might want him to pay for out of his ass.

He gazed down the long strip of cracked gray asphalt that stretched out behind the SC. A half-mile away, maybe more, a small dark lump lay in the middle of his lane. It was cloaked in the long afternoon shadow of a gigantic red cedar that leaned threateningly into the oncoming traffic as if at any moment it might topple onto some unsuspecting commuter. From this distance, he could see neither colors nor a distinct shape that might indicate what sort of critter he'd accidentally snuffed. He thought it was probably big enough to be a dog, but more likely a cat. Or an opossum. Or a rabbit. More than a few of those last had dashed in front of him as he'd made his way home in the evenings of the past few weeks, all of them just narrowly escaping death by squish. By the hairs of their chinny-chin-chins, in fact.

Until now.

Must be bunny baby baking season, he thought. *Too many of them hoppers around here anyway.*

He wiped his palms on his thighs and then slid back behind the wheel.

Please let it be only a bunny.

He started the car, shifted into Reverse, and backed carefully along the solid white line that marked the shoulder of the two-lane, leaning his jowly head out the driver's window the entire way. As the shadowy lump behind him grew larger in his vision, his heart finally began to beat again, climbing down from his throat.

Ears.

He saw two long ears flattened on the pavement, looking like dried up four-leaf clovers pressed into the family bible. By the time he had closed the distance between himself and the corpse, he could see the tuft of the rabbit's small cotton tail perched on its bottom, which was the only part of the critter that was sticking up in the air. By itself, it might have been funny. Combined with the pool of bright red fluid that surrounded the body and the three stark white ribs that protruded from its middle, the whole scene just felt awkward and sad. Undignified.

One of the bunny's eyes had vacated its socket and lay on the road like a glistening bloodshot marble, still tethered to its stalk. Mike grimaced and averted his gaze.

"Gross! Dumb bunny," he chastised the mangled mass of flesh. "Ought've watched where you was going. Guess you're probably too bruised up to make a good stew, ain't ya?"

He licked his lips and grinned. "Well?"

The bunny did not respond. It only gawked at him from its one escaped orb.

"Ah, poop on a platter," Mike Bragg stated, his voice low and solemn. "Too many of them hoppers around here anyway."

He guided the SC back onto the road ahead of the corpse. A lone fly lit on the point of one of the dead rabbit's protruding ribs but lost its grip in a burst of hot exhaust when Mike stomped his foot on the accelerator. Seconds later, the bunny had once again become a blackened lump in the rear-view mirror.

Then the lump became a dot.

The dot became a speck.

The SC rounded a curve, and the speck became a distant memory.

***

The little brown rabbit startled him at first. It sat on his back porch, upright on its haunches, just behind the middle pane of glass in his back door. Its ears stood fully at attention. Its tiny front paws were clasped together at its chest. Its head was turned in three-quarters profile so that it seemed to be glaring at him from a single coal black eye on the left side of its head. Had it not been for the rapid wriggling and flaring of its nostrils, Mike might have figured the critter for some hunter's trophy, or a child's too-realistic stuffed toy. It was neither of those things. It was a living, breathing brown bunny staring him down from just outside his own house.

"Jumping jacks on a jet plane," Mike huffed. "You scared the ever-lovin' ber-jeebers outta me. Almost had a mess on my hands." He chuckled. "And on the floor."

Indeed, the jolt had nearly cost him his grip on the paper plate full of beef and broccoli he'd been hauling to the couch. His side of microwave mini-cheeseburger still teetered precariously along the edge of the recyclable bachelor china. He righted it and slapped the meal down on the floor in front of the varmint. Then Mike himself flopped down on his knees behind the steaming mass, so that he faced the bunny over top of it.

"Guess you're wantin' my broccoli, eh?" he provoked. "Bein' hungry makin' you brave? Well, ha! You can forget it. This is mine."

The bunny maintained its unblinking stare.

48

Do bunnies even blink? he wondered. He launched himself toward the rabbit behind the glass, waving clumsy thick jazz fingers by his collar and shouting "Booga! Booga! Booga!" in his most startling campfire story punchline staccato. He stuck out his tongue and wagged it at the bunny in a most obscene fashion. But the bunny did not blink.

It did not flinch.

It did not budge.

Mike leaned back on his own haunches and sighed. He grabbed the mound of food from the floor and stood up, regarding the rodent from his full height.

"G'won back to your hole now," he snarled. "You ain't gettin' what I got. Don't care if I did run over your cousin. *Accidentally.* I ain't no hopper hope house."

Then, as if offended by the admonishment, the rabbit finally did move. It opened its mouth wide, splitting the hare lips beneath its nose, and revealing a matching set of wide yellow-tinged upper and lower incisors. They resembled a set of chisels, something Mike might use to "customize" a washer for a bolt that needed to be tightened into a particularly inaccessible location. A long line of glistening vermin saliva stretched out between the two rows of teeth as they spread apart. It snapped in half and vanished as the bunny's maw widened. Just beyond its chopping teeth lay the creature's dark red void of a throat, out of which protruded a thick pink tongue. Both teeth and tongue were surrounded by bulbous, inflamed gums.

Mike sank back to his knees, curious. "What are you do—?"

That was when the thing screamed: a long, gargling, bone-chilling woman's cry right out of a horror movie.

Mike reeled backward, his eyes wide with alarm. His plate of food catapulted out of his hands and went flying over his head. His legs gave way beneath him, and he landed hard on his back, striking the crown of his stubbly head on the hardwood. The impact rattled his teeth and echoed throughout his sinuses like a fart on a metal folding chair. Beef, broccoli, teriyaki sauce, a blackened hamburger patty, and two mini-hamburger buns all rained down on him from somewhere just above his head. A limp piece of steaming hot broccoli slapped him in the eye and then rolled innocently away to a safe spot under a nearby chair.

He blinked, and then rubbed a thick forefinger across his right eye, trying to wipe away the steamed veggie sting. One giant tear crept from the corner of that eye, rolled past his ear lobe, and then splattered in an imperfect pool on the hardwood below. He lay like that for a time, allowing the reality of what had just happened to solidify in his mind, deciding how he should feel about it. He allowed a moment for the blow to the back of his head to throb and recede. Then he sucked a gust of wind into his nostrils, expanding his chest to its fullest width, and blew it out of his mouth in a hot bull snort.

"Aw that's it!" he shouted at the ceiling. "You're one dead bun, son!" He struggled to prop himself up to a seated position, the palms of his hands slipping on the hardwood floor in the slick of teriyaki sauce that surrounded them. He was eventually able to hoist himself up on his elbows so that he could see over his distended abdomen and through the middle pane of glass in his back door.

The bunny still sat on its rear haunches, its mouth now closed, glaring at him just as it had been a moment before. Although now it looked like there were four long furry ears atop its head instead of two.

"Dog food on the dinner table," he mused. "Hit my head so dang hard I'm seein' double."

Then a second bunny leaped into his field of vision from directly behind the first, dissolving the four-ear illusion. The second bunny was nearly identical to the first, except that its left ear sprouted slightly more askew from the top of its head. Its front paws were dirty with something that looked like motor oil. The fur there was blackened and matted into tiny wet spikes that revealed pink bunny fingers capped with equally tiny white bunny claws.

Mike gaped at the cottontail couple. "Uhhh," he managed. He wrangled his legs back underneath him and rose to his knees, his eyes never leaving the two bunnies. Side-by-side they watched him, unmoving and unblinking. When he raised up from his knees, drenching his sock feet in what was left of his dinner on the floor, he saw beyond the duo to what lay behind them.

In a row along the first step down from his back porch were three more bunnies, all staring at him. Beyond them, seated on the grass in the backyard, were five more. None moved. None blinked. From this distance, he could hardly tell if they were breathing.

He took a tenuous, if unwise, step toward the door and scanned the full width of his backyard.

They were everywhere.

Each bunny sat on his rear haunches, its tiny front paws clasped in front as if in prayer. And each bunny stared at him. *Only* at him. Not one ear twitched. Not one critter bent to gnaw on a blade of grass. Not one of the cantankerous capons diverted its gaze from his own.

He swallowed hard.

"Conies in the corn field," he whispered, his voice quavering in the back of his throat.

He looked down at the middle pane of glass in his back door. The bunny that had screamed was turned full face toward him now. The dark left eye that had been glaring at him protruded from the side of his head in the way of any normal rabbit. Its right eye, on the other hand, dangled alongside its cheek, hanging by its stalk from an angry red socket. Three white points, probably ribs, protruded from just in front of the thing's right flank.

Mike drank in the sight for less than a second.

Then he bolted for the gun cabinet.

***

"Hoppers!" he shouted breathlessly on his way down the hall. "Too many of them hoppers. Come to get me!"

He heard a distinct and disheartening thunk against the glass of the back door as he dashed down the hall to his bedroom, where his collection of shotguns, rifles, and ammunition sat behind the clear glass door of an antique oak cabinet. The sound was similar to the one a bird makes when it flies head-first into a window pane. It was followed a second later by another, louder thunk. Then a third. Then he thought he heard two or three simultaneous thunks against the glass. More. Too many now to count, like giant kernels exploding in the world's largest microwavable popcorn bag.

"Hair in a biscuit!" he shouted. "They're trying to break in!"

He grabbed hold of the brass handle on the gun cabinet's door and tried to turn it. It was locked. Panic wrapped a skeletal hand around his heart and squeezed hard. He ran his fingers along the cabinet's rough, unfinished top. The tip of his middle finger brushed against something smooth and metallic, then promptly knocked it backward when he tried to snag it. He heard what had most likely been the key bounce between the rear of the cabinet and his bedroom wall as it tumbled to the hardwood floor below.

"Gizzards and giblets!" he howled. Then, from elsewhere in the house, he heard the unmistakable sound of breaking glass.

"Broke the pane," he said. His lips quivered against the words. He tried to suck a long draw of stabilizing oxygen into his lungs by way of his mouth, but it was like trying to suck a milkshake through a coffee stirrer. He closed his mouth and tried again, inhaling through his nostrils allowing the captured air to then escape slowly from between his lips. He felt his fear dissolve, replaced by anger.

"Broke the dang pane outta my back door," he repeated. "I reckon two can play at that."

He cocked his left arm and thrust his gargantuan elbow through the pane of glass in the door of the gun cabinet. It instantly shattered into large, jagged shards. One long and pointed icicle loosed itself from the top of the cabinet door and fell straight down, lodging in the tendon between the last two toes of his left foot. He screamed and hopped on his right foot, shaking the left one in mid-air until the shard worked free and was smashed into smaller pieces on the hardwood. Crimson blood roses surfaced on his sock, seeping across the toes and mixing with the brown of the teriyaki sauce. Mike collapsed to the bedroom floor, rocking to and fro on his ample bottom and cradling the injured foot in both hands. His teeth were clenched vise-like in his head, his eyes strained shut against the hot pain from the ragged wound between his toes.

He wanted to scream again.

He wanted to swear.

Nothing came out.

When the fire in his foot finally started to cool, he opened his eyes. Warm tears streamed from the corners of both of them and clung to his eyelashes. He blinked away the blur, then gingerly set his injured foot on the floor in front of him. He blinked thrice more to clear away any remaining impairment and cocked his head high over his shoulders, listening.

Quiet.

Too quiet.

He craned his neck over his left shoulder so that he could view the hall-way beyond the open door behind him. In a row just outside his bedroom door sat five brown bunnies, each of them frozen erect on its haunches and glaring at him with cold eyes. Except for the middle one, which was glaring at him from one cold eye and at the floor from the eye that dangled by its stalk from the socket.

Beyond the first row of rabbits sat another.

And another.

And another. Beyond that row, and at the end of the full length of the hallway, he saw more bunnies pouring in through the broken glass in his back door. They hopped single-file through the jagged opening in the pane, seemingly unconcerned about the danger to their own flesh, and then spread out to carpet the hardwood between Mike's bedroom and his potential escape; tiny long-eared soldiers facing down their enemy over a demilitarized zone the width of an interior door frame.

"Sweet Lazarus in his wraps," Mike breathed. His mouth hung slack. His now wide-open eyes ached. "Hoppers come to get me."

He swallowed thickly. His mouth was dry. His tongue felt like a damp sponge mop swiping across the roof of his mouth. Warily, fearing that any false move might provoke a stampede, he rolled off his butt and lifted himself up onto his hands and knees, directly facing the battalion of bunnies in the hallway of his home.

None moved in retaliation.

None blinked.

He rose up on his own haunches, similar to the way the bunnies all stood in front of him, and waited.

There was no response.

Finally, Mike laced his fingers on his plump right knee and pushed himself up, so that he stood at full height before the multitude of tiny brown rodents. His left foot screamed in agony against the pressure from his full weight. He winced, clenching his teeth against the white-hot pain, and shifted the bulk of the burden onto his right side to compensate.

"Come to get me," he repeated. The words came out between the short gasps for breath caused by the waves of pain crashing over his foot. "You? Come. To. Get. Me?"

He sucked in another long breath and let it out through his teeth. Wisps of whatever remained of his saliva escaped his lips and evaporated into the snowy dust that cascaded down the length of the rays cast through the windows by the setting sun.

"Leapin' lizards on a hot plate! *I'll* show *you* whose gonna get who!"

***

He reached into the busted oak cabinet behind him and pawed at its contents blind, ultimately closing his fingers around two thick cylinders of cool steel. He didn't want to risk taking his eyes off the horde of hares in his hallway long enough to put any thought into the selection. He could tell he'd wrapped his hand around one of the double-barrels, most likely his side-by-side 12 gauge. He could feel the groove between the twins pressed against his palm. Alas, he also knew it wasn't loaded. That was an easy prognosis because none of his shotguns were ever loaded.

He suspected that it wouldn't have mattered anyway. Too many bunnies in the hallway now to take them out with only two rounds from a scatter, and he was pretty sure that even if he had been able to squeeze off a couple, he would never get the chance to reload.

"Here, bunny bunny," he taunted, concentrating his gaze specifically on the one with the dangling eyeball. The muscles in his elephantine left forearm tensed, tightening his grip on the gun. "Come and *GET IT!*"

He swung the shotgun out of the cabinet by its barrel and grabbed hold of the business end of it with both hands. He brandished the forearm and stock sword-like over his head so that its butt was pointed at the ceiling and its barrels were aimed at the ground. At that instant, the bunnies broke their statue-like formation and launched themselves across the transition between the hallway and the bedroom. The lead bunny's right eyeball repeatedly bounded off its face and flailed in mid-air as it loped toward him, wailing its shrill woman-like charge in unison with its battalion. The sound was like ice-cold knives in Mike's brain. He fought the urge to let go of his weapon and plug his fingers in his ears.

"BANSHEES ON BROOMSTICKS!" he boomed against the discord. "I THOUGHT YOU CRITTERS WERE S'POSED TO BE SHY!"

He arced the shotgun scythe-like through the air, sweeping from above his head toward his feet just as the lead bunny closed the distance from the bedroom door and leaped at him, its maw wide open to reveal its chopping teeth. The stock of the 12 gauge connected broadside with its target in mid-air. There was a loud *thwack* that echoed throughout the room, and the bunny went flying. It splattered against the eastern wall of the bedroom like wet spaghetti and slid downward, coming to rest against the baseboard. It's dangling eye lay pupil-down on the hardwood.

"FORE!" Mike shouted, as his rightward swing reached its maximum length. He couldn't be sure the bunny was dead. He couldn't be sure it was unconscious. All he knew was that it was no longer moving, and that boosted his confidence in his ability to plow through the rest of them.

He squeezed his shoulder muscles taut and changed direction, forcing the gun into a leftward arc with all his might. He connected at the midpoint with two more bunnies. One of them smacked the western wall. Mike thought he heard the sound of its backbone snapping in half when it hit. The other rabbit tumbled violently across the hardwood and rolled into the baseboard, but quickly recovered itself and crouched down on all fours. It sat stunned and trembling for a second, just like the baby bunnies he was suddenly, vividly, able to recall terrorizing in the wild backyard rompings of his rural upbringing. Then the critter appeared to shake off its fear and again leaped toward Mike, burying its chisel-like teeth deep into his blood and teriyaki-flavored sock, not to mention the hamburger tender flesh of his injured left foot.

Mike howled in pain. He slammed the butt of the 12 gauge down on top of the attacking bunny's tiny head, which split open down the middle, revealing a mass of cracked white bone and dark red gelatinous matter that might have been muscle. Or brains. He didn't know. Didn't care. He shook the bunny loose from his foot and launched its corpse across the hardwood, where it again landed beside its buddy who had hit the wall.

He glanced at his left foot. It was a sopping, bloody mess. However, the pain was almost nonexistent now, replaced by a racing heart and his own desperate need to survive. Another bunny launched itself, teeth bared, directly at the mangled foot. Mike jerked it away just in time and the bunny went sprawling. It slid across the floor and smacked head-first into the foot of the gun cabinet. It rolled over on its side and lay there, stunned. Mike followed it with another powerful swing of the gun stock, connecting hard with the rampaging animal's ribs and shattering them.

His eyes alight with rage, his teeth clenched, and his lips split apart in a maniacal grin, Mike Bragg began to limp his way out of the bedroom and into the hall. Though the pain in his left foot had dulled, the function of same seemed to have been dramatically impaired by the attacks. He could put weight on his heel and use that to lumber forward, but every time he landed on the ball or anywhere on his toes he nearly crumpled. He tried to ignore the handicap, choosing instead to focus on his goal: the back door.

The bunnies had stopped pouring in through the broken glass there. Perhaps that meant that they were all in his house now. Perhaps his back-yard was free from homicidal furball rodents intent on chewing off his left foot. And if his backyard was free, then so was the carport where he parked customer cars when he test drove them overnight.

The SC.

He needed to get to the SC.

Dragging his left heel over the hardwood and through some of the teriyaki-flavored footprints he'd left in the wake of his mad flight to the gun cabinet, he confronted the bunnies as they leaped at him. Each time he was approached by a new critter, he smashed it away with the stock of the 12 gauge. He didn't bother to check whether the ones he swept aside were regrouping behind him, nor did he want to. He had to stay focused.

An agonizing number of seconds later, he reached the end of the hall-way. He slapped away two final hoppers as he stepped into the warm sun-light that yawned across the hardwood through the glass panes in the back door. Next, he chanced a glance back down the hallway from which he had just emerged. There he froze, his right hand on the doorknob and his left clutching the 12 gauge.

The bunnies were not giving chase as he'd feared they might have been. Instead, they were lined up along both sides of the hallway, two columns on the left and two columns on the right. Two long lines of ears traced the path from the mouth of the hallway all the way back to the bedroom door, where a lone hopper silhouette stood erect on its haunches between the ends of the two columns. He couldn't tell for sure because of the dimness, but he figured it was probably glaring at him.

Then it moved.

One hop down the hallway.

Two hops.

Three.

Faster.

Toward him.

Into the light spilling in through the door behind him.

Mike's eyes widened. He could see the points of three white ribs extruding from the thing's right side as it moved. They made sawing motions in its flesh, ripping ever widening gashes in its skin with each leap. Its right eye dangled crazily from its socket, bounding and rebounding off its body as the thing shambled toward him. Stunned. Slower than before. But still coming.

For him.

"Zombies in the zoo," he uttered.

Then he started screaming.

He screamed until his throat was too sore and his lungs too depleted to maintain the sound.

Then he sucked in another enormous lungful of air and screamed some more.

***

Frantic, he grabbed the back door's knob and twisted it. He jiggled it and tugged on it with his right hand while he held the 12 gauge outstretched in his left as if it were a talisman that could ward off the bunnies in the same way a crucifix sends Dracula packing. The door knob turned freely, but the door would not budge. Still screaming in fits and starts—as much as his panicked lungs would allow—he glanced away from the approaching leader of the bunny brigade and examined the deadbolt just above the door knob.

It was locked.

He grabbed the thumb turn and slid the bolt open, then twisted the knob a final time and yanked on the door.

It opened effortlessly.

Without bothering to check on the progress of his pursuer, Mike lunged over the threshold. He stumbled more than ran down the short set of stairs that led from the back porch to the earth, tossing the 12 gauge away so he could grab the hand railing for support. He hit the spongy springtime soil of his backyard hobbling as fast as he could. The gun landed flat and without fanfare on the soft grass beside the steps. Mike did not stop to retrieve it.

The carport, which was little more than four posts supporting a metal roof, stood only five yards away. The SC was parked under it. The gleam of the slowly setting sun glinted off its silver metallic front bumper, simultaneously beckoning him and blinding any view he might have of the bunny leader's guts on the front passenger fender well.

Maybe it wasn't as bad as I remember, he reasoned, glad that he was not able to see the mess on the front passenger side of the car. It might have been too much of a reality check. *Maybe it was just stunned, not dead after all.*

Mike huffed his way the full distance to the vehicle in a matter of seconds, in spite of his inability to put any helpful amount of weight on the ball of his left foot. His heart pounded in his ears and temples, pushing its limits against the walls of his massive chest. He crammed his right hand into the front pocket of his jeans and retrieved the Saturn key fob, repeatedly hammering the unlock button with his thumb even though he could clearly hear the keyless entry system's beeping reassurances that the doors were already unlocked. He yanked on the driver side door handle, threw the door wide open, and stuffed himself behind the wheel just before the door rebounded on its hinge and slammed shut. As a quick afterthought, he pounded his index finger on the driver's side door lock button. Relief washed over him when he heard the *clunk* of the locks settling into place.

He next tried to shove the key into the Saturn's ignition but struck the steering column instead. His hands were trembling. He tried to steady them long enough to get the key into the slot and breathed a sigh of relief when, after three failed attempts, it finally slid home. He fired the engine and then chanced a look through the windshield. Bunnies flowed out the open back door and down the porch steps like lemmings over a cliff. The one with the dangling eyeball held on to an awkward, shuffle-hop lead. It was almost as if the others lagged behind him on purpose, letting him lead the same way an obliging parent might allow a very young child to win a game of checkers.

"Runts on a rampage," Mike cursed, revving the Saturn's engine. "Let's see what you got now!"

He switched to the brake with the soaked and now grass-stained foot, intending to shift the SC into Reverse, and yelped in pain when the tender toes of his chewed-up left foot were mashed under the pedal as it fell flat to the floorboard. It had gone down too easily as if the brake lines had been cut or bled. His memory flashed on the image of the bunny at his back door, the one that had what looked like motor oil dripping from its front paws. Or had it been brake fluid? The image of a tiny rabbit in mechanic's coveralls trying to bleed the SC's brake system flashed across his mind. He grinned but shooed the thought away. No time for funnies. How the brakes got broken was a matter for another day. At that moment he didn't care about being able to stop the car anyway. He wanted to escape. To go. Fast.

He released the brake pedal and revved the engine twice. His right hand found the shifter and yanked it hard into Reverse. The car immediately lurched backward, and Mike eased off the accelerator, choosing to idle out of the carport instead of mashing the gas, which could cause him to lose control and bring the whole thing down on top of his head. Ahead of him, the bunnies appeared to have all exited his house and were slowly closing in on the carport. He waggled his fingers at them in a taunting good-bye, then craned his neck to peer between the seats at what lay behind him.

There, too, he saw bunnies. Seven of them. Sitting as still as Terra Cotta warriors in the back seat of the SC.

Glaring.

At him.

Mike yowled both in rage and surprise. He shoved the SC back into Park, skidding it to a halt in the rutted crush and run that served as his driveway. The jolt sent three of the bunnies reeling off the back seat and into the floorboard. The four that had not gone flying hopped in turn from the backseat onto the center console then sprang from the console onto him. One rodent landed in his lap and immediately drew blood from his thigh, digging into the flesh there with its upper chisel. Another attacked his right arm, scratching and clawing at the meat of his forearm as if it were Bugs Bunny tunneling his way to Albuquerque.

Mike flailed wildly behind the wheel of the SC. He managed to shake the one from his forearm. He batted at the one on his thigh with both hands as if he were trying to douse a flame, but it would not let go. From somewhere on his right, one of the other bunnies latched onto his head, the claws on its back feet cutting deep gashes in his right cheek; its front paws slicing the upper flap of his ear in two as it clawed its way to the top of his head.

Screaming, he balled his hands into fists and laid down one-two punch-es on the bunny on his thigh. He heard its back snap and felt it go limp on his leg. He quickly brushed it into the passenger side floorboard. He then snatched with both hands at the one that sat atop his skull. That one leaped away before he could snag it and, he would swear, laughed at him when it landed on the driver side door control panel. One of its back paws struck the unlock button. Mike heard the distinct *clunk* of the door locks being released. The critter then leaped from the door control panel onto the dash just behind the steering wheel and crouched there, its eyes trained on him.

A heartbeat, and then it opened its mouth to scream.

"Oh God," Mike whispered. "Oh no. Don't."

***

What happened next felt like a biblical plague come to life.

Small brown rabbits suddenly sprang from everywhere in response to the wail. They crawled over the passenger seat and over his head, claw-ing their way up from the back seat floorboards. They seemed to fill the floorboards from somewhere beneath the front seats as well. The one he thought he'd killed suddenly hopped back to life and leaped from the passenger floorboard onto the seat beside him. It now sported a bi-zarre U-shaped dip in the center of its back. More bunnies crowded the dash around the screaming one, all coming from God knew where. They popped one-after-another out of the center console like trick rabbits from a magician's empty top hat. For a moment he thought he even saw angry bunny eyes glaring at him from behind the shutters of the dash heat and air vents.

Mike sat in stunned, irresolute silence as the screaming rabbit's cry fi-nally petered out. His eyes were wide, scanning the fur-filled automobile in which he sat. His jaw hung slack.

"Son of a banshee," he said.

Then they converged on him.

He screamed. He kicked. He flung his arms in every direction, grab-bing fur and bunny scruff by the fistful as they latched onto him like river leeches. There were too many of them to fight. They bit, clawed, and tore through his clothes and into his flesh. Three of them clung to his face. He had time to see the shiny wet red tonsils of one of them and to smell its rotted earth-scented breath before it closed in on his right eye. Then pain. Hot searing pain and blackness. He thrust his left arm toward the driver side door, desperately slapping at the molded plastic there. His fingers found fur, a tooth, and what might have been a cotton tail before they eventually closed on the latch release. He pulled at it frantically. The driver door sprang open, and Mike tumbled out of the car. He rolled onto the gravel driveway below, feeling the tiny bodies of the attacking bunnies crunching beneath his bulk.

He could not see for the balls of fur in his face. He could not hear, except for a chorus of shrill woman-like wailing. He could not think.

So he rolled.

He rolled over the crush and run until he thought he could feel bunnies letting loose and falling away from him until he thought he could hear their banshee cries diminishing both in number and volume. He rolled until the last of the bunnies fell away, and he finally lay face-down in his own gravel driveway, his right eye burning and non-functional, his left foot aching, and the rest of his body torn, bruised, and stinging with the burns of hundreds of animal bites. When the screaming finally died out, it was replaced by another sound: a loud rumbling sound that at regular intervals became louder and faster and then wound down again.

It was the sound of someone revving an engine.

Mike raised his head from the gravel as best he could and turned his face toward what he thought was the direction of the sound. Through blurred, red-tinged vision, he could see the front bumper of a circa-1990s Saturn SC. The setting sun's reflection in the windshield prevented him from seeing who, or what, sat behind the wheel. The car rocked a little on its springs each time the unseen operator mashed on the accelerator. For an instant, it looked surreally like a two-dimensional cartoon version of the machine he'd driven home earlier that day. Then the engine revved again. It wound up. Higher.

Higher.

It did not come back down.

Mike felt something like a brick splash into the pit of his stomach.

"Oh sh—" he started.

And then the car was racing toward him.

***

Some undetermined amount of time later, he swam into consciousness.

Pain wracked his entire body. His left eye, the one that still worked, fluttered open. In the distance, the sun had disappeared from the horizon, although it couldn't have been very long before his awakening because he could still make out the distinct shapes of trees and the edge of his house against the backdrop of the purple twilight. He rolled the working eye around in its socket, scanning.

He did not see any bunnies.

He did not see the SC.

He tried to move, but his limbs and torso would not cooperate. He couldn't feel his legs at all; they were either numbed or dead, unresponsive. He also was not able to lift his head from its horizontal position, his sliced right ear pressed against the ground. He could move his left arm, although not without a considerable amount of pain. His right seemed to be trapped beneath his own massive torso. Wincing, he ran the fingers of his left hand as far along his own body as he could reach, testing. He wanted to know what was still there and what was still working. Along his side, he felt what might have been bones, probably his own ribs, protruding through his skin. He yanked his fingers away quickly from the sensation as if he'd accidentally touched hot pokers.

Mike started to cry. Large tears ran from the corner of his good eye across the bridge of his nose. He tried to blink them away and discovered that his right eye—the one the bunny attacked in the car—no longer seemed capable of blinking. He could sense the upper and lower eyelids trying to squeeze together, but it felt like something in his eye was preventing them from doing so. He rolled the good eye toward his nose, trying to see what kind of object he might have hit or landed on that had penetrated his injured eye.

He couldn't see anything.

Not without some effort, he stretched his left hand up to his face and softly patted at the earth that lay just in front of his useless eye, searching for a stick. Or a rock. Anything that might have become lodged there after he was struck by the car. What he felt instead was wet and stalk-like. He followed the strange thing all the way to its end, which seemed to be only a couple of inches in front of his face. There he felt a soft spherical object that could only have been the remains of his own eyeball.

At that moment, from just above his field of vision, a solitary figure leaped into view. Dominant in its silhouette against the evening sky were its two long ears. There was something strange about the shape of the right side of its head. A bizarre looking bulge dangled there as if the thing's eyeball had come loose from its socket.

Mike's remaining good eye widened in panic. He opened his mouth to scream.

The last of the waning sunlight vanished from the springtime sky.

Dislike

William Dennison

Well, that's all folks. She finally up and walked out on me. About time, I say. Don't let the door hit you on the ass on the way out, bitch.

> 2 hours ago
> Jason Berry likes this

Blythe Arnold What the? Jenny left?!?!? I just saw you two together last weekend. You looked so happy!

Cameron Fisk What happened?

Jason Berry Dude, you know she can see this, right? She's still on your friends list.

> Jason Berry likes this

Cameron Fisk LOL! At least he didn't tag her!

William Dennison @Blythe: Anybody can pretend to be happy given the right circumstances. @Cameron: She's a bitch. Hate her. That's what happened. @Jason: Do I care?

> Jason Berry likes this

William Dennison

Popping a top again. Might as well celebrate my newfound freedom in all things the RIGHT way. Queue up a Kuuuntry Saaawng on Spotify or something. Feels about right.

2 hours ago
Jason Berry likes this

Jason Berry So THAT'S why you don't care! How many tops you popped so far? Ha ha!

Jason Berry likes this

William Dennison Not nearly enough to work up the courage to do what I want to do, man. Getting there, though.

William Dennison

Well, now. Bitch just tried to call me. Didn't answer. Probably wants some money now. Not that I have any. Shoulda been stuffing it under my mattress instead of buying her bracelets and brand new cars.

2 hours ago
Jason Berry likes this

Jason Berry Good riddance to bad rubbish.

Jason Berry likes this

Blythe Arnold Probably just as well that you don't talk to her yet. You're obviously angry, and it sounds like you're drinking. Maybe after some time passes a cooler head will prevail. Let her go, Bill. Better things are around the corner.

Cameron Fisk likes this

William Dennison Like I want a cool head. She had no business dropping this bomb on me today of all days. I hope she dies in a fire. And what are you, my counselor? No one really believes all that happy slappy positivity motivationy crappity crap they're always posting on here, you know. They're only trying to fool themselves into thinking BETTER THINGS ARE AROUND THE CORNER. Pfft.

Jason Berry likes this

Blythe Arnold Sigh. You and Jenny are both good friends of mine, Bill. I don't like to see either of you hurting.

William Dennison Hurting? Didn't you see my first status? I'M GLAD THE BITCH IS GONE!!!! Just wish it didn't happen today.

Jason Berry likes this

Jason Berry Good riddance! Hope one of those new cars gets a flat in a shark tank.

Jason Berry likes this

Blythe Arnold What's different about today? And please stop calling her that. I'm sure there's more to this than any of us realize, and a public social network isn't the appropriate place for all this rage.

@Jason Berry: I don't know who you are, but you're not helping anything here. Flat in a shark tank? What does that even mean? And what's with the liking your own comments?

Cameron Fisk likes this

Cameron Fisk Blythe, Bill lost his job early this morning too.

Bill, you should seriously consider taking Blythe's advice and going offline. You can call me if you want to rant. I mean, who do you think will get blamed if Jenny DID suddenly die in a fire?

Blythe Arnold likes this

Jason Berry No fire. Shark tank. Puh-leaze, you can't take shit seriously when it's said on social media. Kill 'em all!!! Rot in Hell!!! Jesus was really the devil, and we've all spent the last 2000 years actually living the REVERSE of God's plan!!! AHHHH!!! Bill's just blowing off some steam. So what if people see it?
Let him be.

Jason Berry likes this

William Dennison Cameron and Blythe, it's a free country. I'll rant if I want to. As for the job, fuck 'em. Kicked me out for saying what everybody else was already thinking anyway. What did they expect me to do, just sit by and watch old Asleep at the Wheel Tony steer the company ship right into an iceberg? That ship's sinking anyway. In a few more years no one will have a job.

Jason Berry likes this

Cameron Fisk That's not how I heard it, Bill. You went nuts in the staff meeting, banging on the table and knocking shit off the walls. Scared the bejesus out of Emily and Rob. I work in sales. I see the numbers. There's nothing wrong with where we are headed as a company.

William Dennison How the hell would you know? Don't our meetings usually happen during your lunch hour, say from 9 to 3?

Jason Berry likes this

Cameron Fisk Oh ha ha. Yes, I am out of the office a lot on client meetings, but I happened to be walking by the conference room this morning when you started to blow your gasket. Guess I left right before the shitstorm, though.

Look, Bill, I popped in here to try to be a friend to someone who doesn't seem to have a lot of them right now. If you'll just calm down a little and stop trying to antagonize everybody, we can work through the job thing. I might not be able to help with Jenny, but that's not the end of the world either.

Call me.

Blythe Arnold likes this

William Dennison Right now you can all just fuck off.

Jason Berry likes this

Cameron Fisk *eyeroll* Ok. Whatever, man. Have fun drinking alone. Just remember that anything that sounds like a good idea in a drunk's head usually isn't. Don't do anything you'll most likely regret come tomorrow. You've already terrified a conference room full of innocent people today. If I were you, I'd just go offline and sit in front of the safety of the television for a while.

William Dennison

OFGS, she left a voice mail. Stuffing a sock in my mouth to keep my drinks down while I listen to it.

An hour ago
Jason Berry likes this

William Dennison

I KNEW IT! SHE'S PREGNANT!

About an hour ago
6 people like this

Julie Whiffle Congratulations!

Jason Berry Ummmm, six people like that? "Congratulations?"
Are you folks even paying attention?

Jason Berry likes this

William Dennison

Let me sum it up for you nice and tight, people. Long story short and all. Jenny's gone. Ain't coming back. Don't want her back. The baby ain't mine. She left me for the daddy. Says she wants there to be no hard feelings. Guess she only likes hard feelings as long as they're not mine, huh? Not that she ever put out that much for me anyway.

Also, I got canned today for doing nothing more than telling the truth. All of them can burn in Hell.

> 55 minutes ago
> Jason Berry likes this

Julie Whiffle OMG! Dislike! I'm so embarrassed! Her baby is not yours?!?!?!

William Dennison Uh, no. Matter of fact, I haven't even been able to get it up in over a year. Had a vasectomy two years ago. Been pretty much impotent ever since. Dammit, WE DIDN'T EVEN WANT KIDS! She said herself that she DIDN'T WANT KIDS EITHER. Burn, bitch. Burrrrrrrn.

> Jason Berry likes this

Jason Berry TMI, bro!

> Jason Berry likes this

Cameron Fisk Bill, I'm sorry about all this. I really am. I'm going to ask you again to step away from the social networks until you've sobered up, though. I'd recommend deleting all these entries, too. You know, before someone who shouldn't see them sees them.

William Dennison Ha! Hey, Cameron! TOO LATE, DUDE! Looks like she already saw it all and blocked me! I'm figuring she didn't see it on her own, though. Which one of you little tattletales pointed her here, huh? Which one of you turned on me first?

Oh, well. Now I have even more freedom to rant, right?

William Dennison

Is thinking about suing a certain nut-cutter for malpractice.

50 minutes ago
Jason Berry likes this

William Dennison @Jason: WTF? You like EVERYTHING?

Jason Berry likes this

William Dennison

Six tops on the floor around me. Six men on the court. Court schmourt. I can't sue. All that will do is drain my wallet more than that suck-ass soon EX-wife of mine and my lack of employment already will.

Lawyer would probably screw me over too. That's what everybody does. They screw me, and they screw me some more. And when they can't screw me anymore they just walk off into the sunset like I wanted to be screwed and their job is done.

Well, screw them. I ain't falling for it again.

Besides, I just remembered that I have a 12-gauge in the closet.

Oh yeah, and nobody ever answered me. WHICH ONE OF YOU TATTLETALES TOLD HER ON ME?

> 45 minutes ago
> <u>Jason Berry</u> likes this

<u>Blythe Arnold</u> Oooookay, Bill. Fun's over. You're scaring me now. Call me @ 555.3141

> Cameron Fisk likes this

<u>William Dennison</u> Awww, don't be scared sweetie. I'd never hurt anybody...important. Maybe just some traitors and liars and tattletales. Wait. I guess I'd hurt a lot of people then.

> <u>Jason Berry</u> likes this

<u>Cameron Fisk</u> I just tried to call you, and you didn't answer. You're still posting on Facebook, so you're obviously not busy. Answer the phone. This has gone on long enough. You're scaring everybody.

> Blythe Arnold and Julie Whiffle like this

William Dennison

Old Bessie. Haven't cradled her in years. She still smells like cosmoline. Loving the scent of it all over my hands.

> 40 minutes ago
> Jason Berry likes this

Jason Berry What's cosmoline?

> Jason Berry likes this

William Dennison It's the snob's 3-in-1 Sewing Machine Oil. NOW FOR GOD'S SAKE STOP LIKING EVERYTHING.

> Jason Berry likes this

Julie Whiffle DISlike!

Blythe Arnold I'm calling the police, Bill. I swear. This isn't funny. If you hurt anybody (including yourself) you're only going to make things worse for EVERYbody. Answer the phone.

Please?

> Cameron Fisk and Julie Whiffle like this

William Dennison Tattling on me, Blythe?

Jason Berry Aw Blythie, let the man have his revenge fantasy. Besides, he already told you he's really only shootin' blanks. Haw haw!

> Jason Berry likes this

Cameron Fisk Jason, I don't know who you are, but you need to shut the hell up. Right now. Otherwise, you're an accessory. Bill's already had one nearly violent outburst today. His drinking is exacerbating his rage over his marriage and loss of employment, and now he has a gun. What part of this seems harmless to you?

> 5 people like this

William Dennison He's an accessory to what, Cam? I haven't done anything (yet). Besides, ain't nothing Jason Berry can say that's gonna make me act one way or another. He's dumb as fuck. I'll think for my OWN self, thanks very much. That's more than I can say for that little twat EX-wife of mine and her brand new clump of baby cells built from the spooge of the man she was cheating with.

> Jason Berry likes this

Jason Berry Wait. Dumb as fuck? Dislike! DISlike!

Jason Berry likes this

William Dennison about time you disliked SOMETHING.

Jason Berry likes this

Julie Whiffle None of this makes any sense Bill, and I can't sit here and watch this anymore. Unfriending you. I think anybody who disagrees with the tripe being posted here should do the same. I hope you get help.

Jason Berry Don't let the data byte you on the ass on the way out.

Jason Berry likes this

William Dennison You go right ahead with your bad self, Jules. Ain't the first time I've been betrayed today.

Cameron Fisk For God's sake, Bill. No one's betraying you. You're not Jesus.

I just talked to both Tony and John. They're willing to discuss what happened at work today. I don't think you'll get your job back, but they might be willing to help you out a little bit until you find work again. I know a few counselors who can help with your personal stuff, too. They're good people, Bill. So are you for the most part when you're sober. Don't do anything stupid.

Please?

Call me, or call Blythe, or don't call anyone. I don't care which way you go. But sitting in front of a computer screen with a drink in one hand and a gun in the other isn't doing you any good right now. Trust me. You might feel a whole lot better tomorrow if you just shut everything down and sleep it off. There are lots of jobs in our line of work, and there are lots of fish in the sea.

Jason Berry Not to mention a lot of clichés in this thread.

Jason Berry likes this

William Dennison

There's something satisfying about the sound of a shotgun shell sliding into place. All these years and I still don't like the TASTE of cosmoline, though.

> 30 minutes ago
> Jason Berry likes this

Blythe Arnold Oh, please. Enough. Just, enough.

Cameron Fisk Bill. For God's sake. Stop it. If all this IS a joke, it's not funny. I'm sure Jenny and your job meant a lot to you, but nothing is worth your own life.

Blythe Arnold This stops now.

William Dennison You don't get to tell me what to do. I make up my own mind. Right now I'm making up my mind to pop another top. Who knows? Might even get the guts to pop my own top after this one! LOL!

> Jason Berry likes this

William Dennison

ALL RIGHT! WHICH ONE OF YOU ASSHOLES DID IT THIS TIME?

BLYTHE?

15 minutes ago
Jason Berry likes this

Jason Berry Uh oh. What's going on now? *grabs popcorn*

Jason Berry likes this

Blythe Arnold Damn right I did. I told you this stops now. If we can't get through to you, maybe the police can.

William Dennison You BITCH! I didn't DO ANYTHING!!!

Jason Berry likes this

Jason Berry WHAT'S GOING ON?!?!?

Jason Berry likes this

William Dennison I've got a bunch of blue boys pounding on my door. That's what's going on. You having some trouble following along on this one Jason?

Jason Berry likes this

William Dennison STOP LIKING EVERYTHING

Jason Berry likes this

William Dennison

Count of three. That's all. If my walls still are painted with blue lights by then, I'm blasting holes through the door. I think they know it too. Ain't one of 'em tried to bust in yet.

This is your fault, Blythe. Always remember that. Yours, that ass of an EX-wife of mine's, and good old former boss Tony's. All of you can BURRRRRN. And if you were here Blythe, you little traitor bitch, I'd take you out too. You had NO RIGHT.

> 10 minutes ago

Blythe Arnold BILL DON'T BE AN IDIOT. JUST PUT THE GUN DOWN AND SURRENDER. LIKE YOU SAID YOU HAVEN'T DONE ANYTHING YET AND YOU CAN STILL TURN THIS AROUND.

> Cameron Fisk likes this

Jason Berry Dude, you OK?

William Dennison You didn't like anything in this entire post, Jay Jay. Somethin wrong?

William Dennison

That's a count of ONE. This little piggie went to limbo...

8 minutes ago

<u>Jason Berry</u> DISlike, man! DISLIKE!

<u>Cameron Fisk</u> Bill, PLEASE give it up!

<u>Blythe Arnold</u> likes this.

William Dennison

That's TWO. Think I just saw one of 'em trying to sneak by my window here. This little piggie went to Heaven...

6 minutes ago
Jason Berry likes this

Jason Berry Ha ha. Ok, you got us, Bubba. This is OBVIOUSLY a joke folks. I know Bill. He does NOT have it in him to REALLY do something like that, and the little piggies thing means there has to be a punchline coming.

Jason Berry likes this

Blythe Arnold THIS DOESN'T HAVE TO BE THE WAY IT ENDS, BILL! DROP THE GUN AND GIVE YOURSELF UP!

5 people like this

Jason Berry Oh, let it go, Blythie. He's yankin' us and yer fallin' for it. We'll have a big laugh about it over beers tomorrow night.

Jason Berry likes this

William Dennison What was it you said before Blythe? There are better things to come, right? One door closes another one opens? That how it's supposed to work?

Or maybe it's the opposite. If I just throw open my front door right now, maybe another door will close. Maybe all my traitors will be behind it.

Jason Berry likes this

William Dennison

THREE!

4 minutes ago
Jason Berry likes this

Blythe Arnold BILL DON'T DO THIS!!!

Cameron Fisk IT'S NOT WORTH YOUR LIFE YOU IDIOT! ANSWER THE DOOR AND TALK TO THE COPS!

Jason Berry ROFL @ all you gullible peeps. Alright, game over, then. Come on, Bill. Let us off the hook.

William Dennison

See you all in Hell.

2 minutes ago
<u>Jason Berry</u> likes this

<u>Jason Berry</u> Annnnd, the end. Ok, Bill. Come on back and laugh at the babies.

<u>Jason Berry</u> likes this

<u>Jason Berry</u> Ohhhh Beeeeeeilllllll!

<u>Jason Berry</u> likes this

<u>Jason Berry</u> Come on, dude.

<u>Jason Berry</u> BILL FOR GOD'S SAKE ANSWER ME!

Safety First

Matt's heart sank.

No one—not even Matt—could accuse his mission partner Grant of being a lousy shot. The smoke encrusted black hole in what had been Matt's PTT, his sole remaining link to Mission Control outside of the lander, was proof enough of that. The tangy odor of the electrical burn singed the hair in his nostrils, even inside the thin environmental suit he wore.

That was bad news.

His suit was probably punctured as well, which meant his supply of oxygen was dwindling at a faster rate than it normally would. What he didn't have time to inhale was pouring out of the hole in his suit and into the moon's atmosphere, where it was of no use to him. It wouldn't be long before the moon's poison atmosphere crept in and entirely depleted the supply. That meant he didn't have long to live.

That was worse news.

Earth scientists had guessed that the thin atmosphere of this desert moon contained carbon dioxide as its primary compound so explorers would not be able to breathe in it without an external supply or manufacture of oxygen. There also was, they thought, strong evidence of some other yet-unknown molecule swirling about in the dust storms that scarred the moon's surface on a regular basis. Thus the environmental suits. The

WGPSN eventually named this place Psamathe, because they didn't want it confused with the other moon called Nereid, even though this one fit the description of the mythical figure better. Matt typically just referred to the place as Neptune's butthole.

Technically, all he and Grant needed to move about on the moon's surface was an external oxygen supply or a way to manufacture it from the moon's CO_2. The atmosphere was thinner than Earth, but there was enough of it and enough gravity to prevent the duo from being crushed or floating away. The suits themselves should not technically have been necessary. They mainly wore them as an extra security measure against whatever untold havoc that mystery molecule might wreak against their vulnerable human bodies. The problem, then, was that the oxygen supply system was built into the suits themselves, to make them lighter, instead of using tanks and mouthpieces like SCUBA divers used to wear, or a massive backpack-style CO_2 scrubber.

The lander was a good quarter-mile away from him now, he and Grant its only crew. His partner's enraged, grimacing face shone down from the top of the sheer cliff wall above him. Grant's right arm dangled over the drop as well, his silver-gloved hand still gripping the weapon that Matt had smuggled along on the trip. Unfortunately, Grant had discovered the blaster before Matt himself could make use of it. The older man's cheeks were red, and Matt thought he could see droplets of perspiration drooling down the plexiglass face of his helmet.

The chase across Psamathe's landscape had been long and painful. In spite of Grant's favor with the brass who had handed him this mission, Matt knew his old frenemy really wasn't in great shape these days. A few too many burgers and fries and far too little exercise had taken a toll on the once golden boy. Matt, who was no one's golden boy, had managed to keep after himself, however. Even these fifteen years after he'd graduated from the Academy. It had probably been twenty years or more since Grant had strode across the stage in his cap and gown. Matt had easily outrun him over this harsh, dusty, and deserted landscape, and had known from the start that he would.

Then he'd had that moment of weakness when he'd looked back over his shoulder. And then that misstep along the crater wall—

Now here he stood, trapped on a small ledge just an arm's length out of Grant's reach, the memory fresh in his mind of the edge of the shelf breaking away when he landed there, the rocks at the precipice crumbling away beneath his feet and tumbling end-over-end into the crater before him. He could escape another blaster shot in a fashion similar to that rock, he thought, if he didn't care to live through it. In fact, there was nowhere to go *but* the depths of the crater, the bottom of which he couldn't even see from this height. And his suit was bleeding precious air.

Great.

Just perfect.

Okay, so maybe he'd brought this on himself. Maybe Grant had suspected all along that Jill was planning to leave his fat ass for Matt when they finally landed back at the station hidden in the asteroid belt between Mars and Jupiter after this years-long excursion into the outer reaches of this dusty red wasteland. Was it really worth Matt's death to him? Not to mention Grant's own court martial and dishonorable discharge that would inevitably result from the murder?

Perhaps it was.

At least that was what Matt thought he could read in Grant's red-rimmed and bloodshot eyes, which glared down at him from above the crater, above the ledge. And if that wasn't enough, there were his angry, laborious breaths, fogging his visor like smoke from a dragon's nostrils. Wait, fogging his visor? Maybe Grant's suit had been punctured as well. The moon's rocks were jagged, and some had been sharpened to razor edges after eons and eons of superstorms with no vegetation to cull the winds. He'd taken pictures of some of them for Jill's solar system geology art collection that she curated back on the station.

Jill.

Jill didn't know any of this was happening. She fully expected both Matt and Grant to return safely to the asteroid belt in a few years, where they would resume their little love triangle until everyone felt comfortable enough to bring the awkward situation to an emotional head. Neither she nor Grant could have possibly known about the blaster when he'd smuggled it aboard. Matt's plan had been to sneak up on Grant while he was digging in the moon's soil or squatting to take a shit. He'd pick up one of the jagged moon rocks, and slice open the older man's head with it, make it look like Grant had simply taken a tumble and banged his noggin on the wrong end of one of the moon's sharp rocks. Matt would relay the report of what happened to Mission Control, who would instruct him to bury the body and continue alone if he could, or abort and start the long trip home if he could not. It's something every explorer knew was a possibility when they signed up, although it had only ever happened once before. And no one had questioned those circumstances.

He'd only brought the blaster along as a backup, in case the time was never right, or he lost his nerve, or he was somehow magically overpowered by Grant. It might be harder to cover up a blaster shot as an accident if future missions happened to uncover Grant's body, but at least the job would get done. And it might be a good decade before they sent explorers out this way again. Support for these types of excursions had waned among the public way back on Earth over the years. They were more interested in using taxpayer dollars to clean up their own drinking water sources than finding possible new places to live. Sometimes he wondered if some wingnut new president might pull the plug on them from the home world and just leave them stranded forever in that asteroid belt.

Matt had set his standard issue explorer's bag right next to Grant's identical one at the foot of the lander's entry ramp while they were unloading for the day's work, but he'd forgotten to stow his camera the day before. It was still sitting by his bunk, so he went back to the lander to retrieve it. His short absence meant Grant had been the first to start searching a bag for tools. Grant must have opened the wrong bag first. He must have seen the blaster, put two and two together, and grabbed it for himself. That didn't explain how he'd known about Matt and Jill in the first place. Maybe Matt had been talking in his sleep again. Or maybe Grant only suspected because of the puppy-like way Matt and Jill had been behaving around each other before the mission. But none of that really mattered now. He would never see Jill again.

"Grant!" Matt screamed the name inside the insulated globe of his helmet. The word echoed in his own ears but did not carry. It was like screaming into a giant vacuum filled with cotton. "Grant! Stop this! Help me, for God's sake!"

The air.

He was wasting his air.

He stretched his right hand upward toward Grant's hate-twisted face. His fingers groped for purchase just an inch or two below the business end of his former blaster. Grant's lips spread open behind his visor in a broad, Cheshire grin, and Matt thought he saw a genuine twinkle in the middle-aged explorer's pale blue eyes as it dawned on him that Matt was pleading with him for his life. Still grinning, Grant shook his head deliberately. Then he made a slow slicing gesture across his own throat with the hand that was not holding the blaster. Hot rage balled up in the center of Matt's gut like seething coals of a bonfire.

"Bastard!" he yelled, although he was sure Grant couldn't hear it. He hoped the old man could read his lips. "I'll get you for this!" The grin on Grant's face faded a little at that. Then it resurfaced, and he shook his head at Matt again, mocking him.

The back of Matt's neck suddenly felt as hot as his gut, as did his cheeks. He breathed in quick, raspy gulps of air, some of which left a decidedly sour taste on his sandpaper-dry tongue. The image of Grant above him wavered a little, and he felt unsteady on his feet as if his knees and hips might give up on him at any moment. That was the exhaustion, no doubt: that particular drowsy feeling that comes from the slow drain of breathable air from one's environment.

Fine.

Just perfect.

Maybe, if he were lucky, he'd go to sleep there on the ledge without feeling the sting of that blaster again. Grant was a great shot, but he had managed to only knock out Matt's communication with that first blast. He supposed he was lucky that the PTT was manufactured from a substantive compound that proved to be somewhat impact resistant, especially from a blaster set on stun, which Matt's had been before Grant got hold of it. It was enough to protect him from the blaster's ray, even if it couldn't protect the sensitive electrical equipment inside the PTT. Too bad the environmental suits weren't made of the same stuff. If not for the PTT, he might already be dead. Grant could have stunned him first, then killed him as he lay there unable to move. It occurred to him then that Grant had perhaps fired at the PTT on purpose.

On the way to retrieve his camera, Matt had stopped to take a shit. "One should always ensure that one's bowels are sufficiently evacuated when one plans on going for an extended exploration," his former Academy commander had always intoned with forced gravity in his voice. Funny or not, that particular piece of advice had always stuck with him. There was that counseling and the other more valuable information that he handed to all the testosterone-filled young men who seemed to be applying to the Academy in those days.

"You're here to be an explorer and a scientist, not a hero," went the other. "We don't send you to space to die. We send you because we want information. If you're somewhere where danger is imminent, hole yourself up like the scurrying little mammals we all used to be and wait it out. Safety first."

Matt and Grant had both heeded that advice just yesterday when they scurried back to the lander after noticing one of the moon's surprise tornado-like dust storms forming in the lower atmosphere.

"Good thing we looked up," Grant had said.

That next day, after his visit to the shitter, Matt was just about to radio to Mission Control that he was on the moon's surface and waiting for his partner when he noticed that Grant was already there, waiting for him. What he didn't pay much attention to at the time was how Grant was not holding his standard issue tool bag by its straps in his right hand. Instead, he was hugging it against his chest with his left arm, his right hand buried inside it. Matt nodded his "good morning" and pressed the latch button that raised the lander's ramp and locked it into place. They usually closed up the lander when going out to explore. Not for security reasons (there were no thieves on this moon to fly away with their transport), but to keep as much of the moon's dust and atmosphere out of their temporary shelter as possible. It was also great protection against those storms.

With the ramp secure, Matt bent to pick up his own tool bag. He rummaged through the bag, intending to obtain his excavation tools and ensure that the blaster was still safely stowed. The digging tools were easy to locate, but the blaster was gone. That was when he stood and turned to face Grant, who had dropped his own tool bag and now stood, legs apart and right arm extended, pointing Matt's own weapon directly at him.

"Planning something?" he heard Grant's cracked voice say through his suit's earpiece. The PTT had a short-range component that enabled an unending stream of communication between explorers nearby. You only had to physically press the device if you wanted to communicate with Mission Control in addition to your partner. Matt's right hand immediately went to his chest to tap the PTT. He had, in fact, already formed the words he was going to say.

"X314 to Mission Control, my partn—"

The sting of the bolt from the blaster against his chest knocked him backward and stole his breath before he could finish. It wouldn't have mattered anyway because he'd started speaking before his fingers had been able to reach the PTT. He supposed he had just been trying to get as much information out as possible before the inevitable, or what he thought was going to be inevitable, occurred. He tried to catch his breath, wincing against the pain of the impact on his chest. When he opened his eyes again, Grant was standing over him, looking pissed. The blaster was aimed at Matt's head. He could've killed Matt right then, as he lay paralyzed on the moon's dust if that's what he'd wanted. But he hadn't. He had paused long enough for Matt to recover and then sweep Grant's legs out from under him, nearly causing him to drop the blaster as he fell to the ground. Matt had watched him fall. Grant's right rib cage struck one of the jagged moon rocks. Matt then scrambled to his feet and launched himself on a full-fledged run across the desert landscape. There was no time to press the button and wait for the ramp to come down again. No way to get inside of the lander in time to save himself from being shot again. Instead, he'd had to run and hope for the best.

He didn't actually want to kill me outright, Matt now thought as he watched the eyes of the man above him, the man who was his partner and who appeared to be struggling to breathe behind that fogging visor. *He wanted to torture me first.*

Surreally, Matt thought he could see dust clouds twisting in the lower atmosphere over Grant's head. If that were the case, a new storm would be forming soon. Those things seemed to funnel out of nowhere in an instant, just like tornadoes on Earth. "Tornadoes with a purpose," Grant had once said of them because unlike the random trails of destruction tornadoes leave in their wakes on Earth, the dust storms on this moon had lightning-like precision. They funneled down from the sky, destroyed whatever was beneath them, and then unraveled, eventually dissipating as they sharpened the stones scattered along the moon's surface in a strong gust of straight-line wind. If there were a storm brewing directly above them, neither he nor Grant would be likely to make it back to the lander alive. No matter what.

"Go on then," Matt mouthed to the man on the ledge above him. "Go on. Shoot me. At this point, I'd rather just go ahead and get this done than wait on this godforsaken moon to do it for me. Face it. Jill doesn't want you anymore, Grant. She doesn't care about you. Even if you somehow miraculously survive all this, you don't get her back. My bet is that she's filing for divorce right now while you're still six months and a million miles away. That's funny to me. You want me dead because I'm taking Jill away from you, and I'm dying here for sure. But that won't get you Jill back, will it?"

Matt doubted that Grant could hear any of this, but perhaps the gist of it had gotten through. From behind his visor, Matt brayed laughter. He made sure that Grant could see him. His mouth was open. His eyes watered, the lids squeezed together with joy. He made sure that every "ha" he uttered visibly bounded in his shoulders. He stomped his right foot on the ledge below him, slapped his knee, and howled in the face of the man who would be his murderer.

When the hilarity (or his miming of it, anyway) had mostly subsided, Matt looked up at Grant again. He couldn't wipe the tears of laughter away from his eyes, of course, but he blinked away enough of them to be able to see that the man's arm now dangled limply over the side of the precipice. The blaster hung upside down on his gloved index finger, like a hat on a hook. In contrast, Grant's head was no longer visible on the precipice. Matt thought he could see a glimpse of the top of the man's visor gleaming in the light from the sky that was not yet obscured by the oncoming dust storm.

Is he dead? Matt wondered. *Oh God, please let him be dead.*

He waited ten seconds. Twenty. Thirty. Grant did not move. His hand remained limp and just out of Grant's reach. If he wasn't dead, he had at the very least fallen unconscious from lack of oxygen, a fate that awaited Matt himself if he didn't find his way off the ledge and back to the lander. Matt leaped deftly into the air and slapped the blaster from his former partner's dangling fingers. He had a panicked moment when he thought the weapon had gone plummeting into the abyss below him, but he managed to wrap his fingers around the barrel before it had fallen too far from his grasp.

He holstered the blaster in a pocket that was meant for his excavation tool. It was too big for the pocket and projected clumsily from it, but it would have to do. For what came next, Matt would need both hands and all his remaining strength. He already felt light-headed from his escaping air, and falling unconscious on this tiny ledge would probably mean plummeting to his death.

The blaster stowed, Matt scanned the precipice wall in front of him, searching for signs of holes or ledges on which he might be able to make a purchase and hoist himself back to the more-or-less level ground. Holds were slim pickings. What wasn't sheer was either too small or too large to firmly grab. The first outcropping he attempted to put any weight on crumbled away beneath his fingers. Moreover, both the tips of his gloved fingers and the toes of his boots were rounded; no use attempting to claw new places of purchase in the desert moon rock.

All this technology, Matt thought, *and no one ever invented gloves with retractable claws.*

He glanced at the threatening sky. From where Grant's face had previously been glaring at him, a sure-enough dust storm funnel was forming. The swirling mass was oddly localized, just like all the previous events the scientists had witnessed through the high-powered telescopes that were housed in the lab circling the asteroid belt. Beyond the crisply defined circumference of the wide end of the funnel, there were no clouds at all. It was almost as if there was some guidance there, some intelligence or collective mind that coalesced dust in the atmosphere to form these precision downward spirals of wind, red dirt, and mystery molecule.

While Matt watched, the rate of the storm's spin increased, and he thought he could see the first signs of its ground-ward spiral. From his angle, it looked like it was directly above Grant and, thus, directly above him.

So maybe I should just stay right here, for now, he thought. *Maybe I'm safer here until the storm blows away. If it's anything like Earth lightning, it'll direct itself at the highest available object within striking distance. Right now that's Grant.*

As Matt kept watch, the storm descended, picking up speed as it neared its target. There was enough atmosphere on the moon to carry the sound to his ears, even through his protective suit. The funnel made a high-pitched whining sound, the sound of a large turbine, that he was pretty sure was making his ears bleed. Combined with that was the freight train roar of a tornado and what sounded like a swarm of giant mosquitoes, bumble bees, and house flies. Matt's hands clamped on the sides of his head, where his ears would have been if he had not been wearing the suit. He was unable to shut out the noise.

Just before the thing landed on the ground above his head (and, he presumed, on Grant), Matt crouched on his knees. He crammed his body tight as he could against the wall of the precipice and covered his head with his hands. The roaring whine was suddenly drowned by a thunderous crash, so near that it temporarily deafened him. He squeezed his eyes shut, afraid to watch what was happening around him as the funnel struck its target and then peeled apart into a long rush of straight-line wind over his head. He thought he could feel the rush of it, even crouched against the wall of rock as he was, but that might have been only his anxious imagination.

He didn't know how much time had passed before he dared to open his eyes again. When he did, he allowed himself to breathe a single, short huff of relief. His remaining oxygen wouldn't afford him the luxury of a long sigh. He stood and examined the edge of the precipice above him, blinking against the brightness that had replaced the harsh shadow of the dust storm.

Something was different.

The silver glove that covered Grant's dead fingers had split open, revealing the right hand of his former partner within. The division ran upward along the interior seam of his arm. In places, Grant's flesh protruded from the openings, but somehow it no longer resembled human flesh, at least not any flesh Matt had ever seen. Grant's arm had gone from human pink to a deeper crimson shade, similar to the landscape that had surrounded the two explorers since they'd arrived. More than that, it seemed to have dried out, creating cracks and gullies and jagged edges in what used to be Grant's perfectly pristine, if a bit meaty, shooting arm. It looked almost exactly like the dust and rock of the moon's surface as if Grant was becoming a part of the land on which he'd died.

His dwindling oxygen temporarily forgotten, Matt stared, confounded, at the fingers of the hand dangling above him. The thing inside Grant's environmental suit was expanding, or growing, or evolving, or eroding, or something. He didn't know what. He knew only that he could see the rip in the seam widening and that the fingers seemed to be getting closer to him as if the arm was growing longer over the edge of the precipice. The fingers also weren't really fingers anymore. What had been Grant's index finger and middle finger had fused together into a solid obelisk-shaped form. His thumb had dried up and broken off somewhere. Maybe, Matt thought, it had already tumbled into the void below them.

Seconds later, the thing's growth slowed and appeared to come to a stop an inch or more above Matt's head. Grant's glove was long gone, shredded beyond recognition, but the cracked and hard thing above him still bore a smidgeon of resemblance to a human hand, albeit with fewer fingers and sharper edges. Fleetingly, Matt toyed with the idea of grabbing hold of it and attempting to use it as a rope to climb off the ledge. He reconsidered when it occurred to him that he didn't know what the state of his former partner's feet was on the other side of that cliff. They could be flesh still, for all he knew, and anchored to nothing, which meant that pulling with his weight against what had been Grant's arm might end up sending them both tumbling into the abyss. Best to test it first.

He retrieved the blaster from his pocket and examined it. The slider was on its highest setting, the one that only specially (and illegally) modified blasters could achieve. He was sure he'd stowed it at its stun setting, which hurt and might cause temporary paralysis but was not fatal. It was the weapon's only safety feature. Many were the blaster nuts who had accidentally disintegrated themselves or others by attempting to demonstrate the shock, only to discover to their horror that the blaster had been set to kill instead. Grant must have changed it after he'd shot Matt in the PTT out by the lander. There could be no doubt now. He'd meant to kill him.

Matt slid the bolt all the way back to the stun setting. Safety first. Not Grant's, of course, but his own. He tilted the weapon so that he could see the other side of the barrel, the side with the charge meter. He had one or two shots left at the highest setting before the thing would need to be recharged. The stun setting would be less apt to drain all the energy in one gulp.

Matt clenched the blaster by its grip and nudged rock Grant's longest "finger" with the tip of the barrel. The block of sharp red matter did not budge. He tapped it again, harder. Nothing, although a small crescent moon-shaped dent, slightly less red than the surface of the thing, did appear where the barrel struck.

He stowed the blaster again. Then he pressed his back firmly into the wall of the precipice and grabbed hold of the thing's longest finger with his right hand. He wrapped his left hand around what looked like it used to be Grant's pinky. Then, carefully, he picked his feet up off the ground and allowed his back to loose itself from the precipice wall. He hung there by his arms, all his weight supported by what had been Grant's shooting hand, like a butterfly cocoon dangling from the branch of a tree. When it became difficult to breathe, he let go, landing on the soles of his feet, his back again to the wall of the precipice.

Maybe it *was* possible to climb out, then.

Matt allowed himself a few seconds to recover. He was still bleeding oxygen from his suit, but there was no use trying to reserve his breath or strength. The more he sought to save his breath, the more oxygen he lost to the atmosphere, and the longer he waited to get moving on a plan to get back to the lander, the lower the likelihood that he would ever make it back at all. The lander, with its working communication, its practically infinite manufacturing of breathable air, and its ability to get him back to the asteroid belt, is what made his race against time worth running.

Steeling himself, Matt crouched cat-like on his haunches before the thing that had once been both his partner and his rival. He inhaled deeply through his nose, held it, and sprung from the ledge with his calf muscles. He exhaled through his mouth as he flew the distance between the ground and the dangling stone arm. The middle of his torso struck it first. He felt the destroyed PTT in his suit bury itself in the thin covering of flesh over his solar plexus. He thought he felt himself beginning to slide and reflexively knotted his arms around the arm of rock and bear-hugged it. A second after that he actually did slide against the arm and began to struggle to maintain his grip. Panic rose up in him when he realized that a fall from here would most likely send him sailing over the ledge on which he'd been stranded and into the darkness below it. Then, to his surprise, he felt...*something*...cradle him between the legs. He chanced a look down and, for an instant, thought the moon's gravity was playing tricks on him. His perspective was changing as he clung to the arm, from the moon's sky in the distance to the open maw of the abyss below. Then he noted that his legs were dangling wrong. They were no longer hanging vertically from his hips, but at a right angle to them, as if he were laying face-down on a steel girder at a high-rise construction site like the ones in those ancient Looney Tunes cartoons they watched in school. Gravity wasn't changing. The moon-rock "arm" he had latched himself onto was *moving*.

Just like that, as if it knew it had been found out, the rocky Grant arm catapulted Matt into the air. He watched helplessly as the ground on the moon below first went hurtling away from him, and then, following his apex, came back at him like a jungle predator closing in on a kill.

He managed to twist his body toes-down on the descent, landing hard on his feet. He balled himself up like a boxer trying to protect his midsection, and then flattened and rolled on his back, just as he'd learned way back in basic training. Lucky for him, Matt thought, the Academy won't send a person into the air without first teaching him how to get safely down again. He thought he might have felt a twinge in his right ankle when he came down, and he'd definitely heard a ripping sound. It could have been his suit. It could have also been a muscle or a tendon. His adrenaline was pumping too hard to be sure, and there was no time left to focus on such things as physical discomfort or further threats to his oxygen supply. Not now.

Matt scrambled to his feet. His blaster, which had fallen from his suit's excavation tool pocket while he was mid-flight, lay between him and the rock creature that appeared to be clawing its way from the edge of the precipice along the moon's surface. Crawling towards him.

The thing that had been Grant rose to its knees and then stood, shakily at first, on two "legs" resembling pillars from Earth's Stonehenge that had been dusted with red moon soil. At full height, rocky Grant was easily twice Matt's size. The "arm" that had hurled Matt through space a moment before was gigantic and asymmetrical to the smaller and more razor-like rocks that formed the monstrosity's left arm. The left arm ended in something that looked similar to a hand, except with long, sharp fingernails formed of rock.

A glove with claws, Grant thought.

The giant's face bore no resemblance to Grant at all except, perhaps, for the broad, crescent-shaped smile that had spread across its lower half. It was pretty much the same mocking grin that was on Grant's face when the dust storm or sand lightning or whatever the hell it actually was hit him. Except it was larger, more pronounced. And only blackness lay behind it. As far as Matt could tell, the thing had no eyes. Grant's environmental suit was gone, shredded to dust, but the only evidence of his former partner's nakedness was a pointy nub of rock that jutted from between the two pillars on which it stood.

"Guess the molecules can only work with what you give them," Matt said, and then it clicked with him what must have happened to Grant. *The mystery molecules*, he thought. *They're not just any old molecules swirling around in the atmosphere looking for the right conditions to coalesce and strike. They're lifeforms.*

Lifeforms. Not randomly striking targets like lightning on Earth, and not just blowing around like debris in a tornado. Lifeforms. Not trying to destroy, at least not at first. Trying to combine with other things to create new lifeforms. Trying to reproduce. Trying to evolve. Whatever Grant had been before (human, partner, rival, would-be murderer), he was now Grant plus moon mystery molecule. He was Molecularly Moon Grant, and he was just as alive, twice as big, and (out of proportion pecker aside) a dozen times harder than Matt. And that meant that Matt needed to get the hell out of there. Now.

He launched himself at his blaster, looking away from the creature at the edge of the precipice only long enough to ensure that his gloved fingers were wrapped around the weapon's grip and not some random moon rock that was laying on the ground beside it. When he looked up again, the creature that had once been Grant had taken a single step toward him that halved the distance between them.

"One small step for Grant," Matt said as he snatched up the blaster from the moon's surface and bolted in the direction of the lander, "one giant squish for little old me." He squeezed off a single shot from the weapon as he ran. The beam hit its target but appeared to have no effect.

Stun setting, Matt thought. *I just tried to stun a pile of rocks. Safety first. I'm a fucking idiot.*

With his thumb, he slid the blaster's settings bolt to its highest level, the not technically legal one. He then turned his attention to the run ahead of him. He didn't fire again. Not yet. There was no way he could accurately

aim the deadly blast at the monster behind him while simultaneously trying to get away from it, and any shot at the highest setting might deplete
the blaster's charge. He needed to be accurate.

He could feel the thing's thunderous steps shaking the ground beneath
him. It was getting closer. No time to turn and aim, especially if he had
no guarantee that it would slow the thing down. He hoped that the Grant
creature's size and Grant's own historical lack of physique would work
against the creature's ability to close the distance. Sure, it had fewer steps
to take, but the steps it did take would be slower and more lumbering than
Matt's mad dash to the lander. Hopefully. He *had* already outrun Grant
once that day.

A quarter of a mile of moon dust was all that lay between Matt and
escape unless he ran out of air first of course. Or the creature caught
up to him. Or the lander ramp didn't come down fast enough. Or the
creature was able to damage the lander even if Matt could get aboard in
time. Best not to think about all those things right now. A quarter of a
mile: he could run that in his sleep. At the lab, he'd once run a 5K in 20
minutes. Back then he'd done the math and figured that he had averaged
about 6.25 miles-per-hour. If he could get anywhere close to that speed
across this rocky moon's surface, he could make it to the lander in less
than two minutes.

The available air alarm in his suit buzzed in his ear. Two minutes. It
was more than enough time under normal circumstances. The alarm was
supposed to sound when five minutes of air were left in the suit. His suit
had a smoky hole and was possibly breached in other ways by his fall, so
his air was actually bleeding faster than that. He forced himself to assume
that he still had five minutes remaining in spite of his leaking lifeline. It
was easier that way. It made him feel less apt to panic.

The terrain he had to cover was rugged, dusty, and treacherous. It was
like trying to run across a thin layer of sand that had been spread over a
dry bed of coral. The good news was that he'd already figured out how to
make the run without hurting himself. He'd learned that much when he
was running away from human Grant. Keep your head down. Look at the
ground in front of you, not at the horizon or the lander. If you keep your
eyes on the moment instead of your destination, you're less likely to do

something stupid, like trip over your own shoelaces and twist your ankle or cut your boot open on one of the moon's razor rocks.

Or look over your shoulder to see if the thing chasing you is gaining on you and falling over a cliff, Matt thought.

He tried to think of something besides the thing behind him, something to prevent himself from looking over his shoulder. Math, maybe. Like the 5K. If the thing really was twice his size, that meant it had twice his stride length, so it was able to cover twice as much ground in a single step than Matt could. The giant could cover in one step what took Matt two. That was if it was walking regularly, like a human, and not actually chasing some running prey. Scratch all that then.

He felt the ground shake again with one of the giant's footfalls. There was a better measurement, one based on reality instead of guesses about proportions. If he could count the number of steps in a sprint between the giant's footfalls, Matt would be able to calculate whether the giant was gaining on him, losing ground, or keeping pace. The longer his sprints between the giant's moonquake steps, the more likely it was that he was outrunning it. He waited for the next moonquake and started his count as soon as he felt it.

One, two, three, four, five, six, seven, eight, nine—
BOOM!
One, two, three, four, five, six, seven, eight, ni—
BOOM!
One, two, three, four, five, six, seven, eight—
BOOM!

It was gaining on him, no doubt about it. Matt tried to put on an extra burst of speed but found that his breath couldn't keep pace. His heart was pounding faster than he could count and there was a stitch in his side that threatened to double him over. His lungs felt like they were going to explode inside his chest. He suspected that his environmental suit had only seconds of oxygen left. He'd hear the oxygen depletion alarm any time now. He might have a few more seconds of consciousness if he kept running after that. Then he'd be down. He'd be rocky Grant food.

He glanced toward the horizon. The lander was growing large in his field of vision. Good. High in the sky above it, a new dust storm appeared to be forming. Bad. He'd need to be inside the lander and preparing to launch before Grant could squash him *and* before the mystery molecules in those dust storms transformed him into a Rock 'Em Sock 'Em Robot just like his former partner. Just a few more sprints and he'd be at the ramp before Grant closed the gap. Maybe even before the dust storm could start its descent.

The ramp. Shit!

He'd closed it. To keep the dust out.

Safety first.

He was close enough to see the latch button on the lander's leg. Then he was upon it. He pressed it firmly and had to fight to prevent himself from pressing it multiple times, like those types who don't trust the light behind an activated elevator button and need to press it again even though the elevator is of course already on its way. One press on the lander's ramp latch and the ramp starts to lower. If you pressed it again before it had completed its descent, it would stop dropping and go up again, wasting precious seconds.

Helplessly, he watched its slow decline. The muscles in his legs thrummed in anticipation, trying to prepare him for his sprint from the dusty moon to the safety of the lander. Depriving those muscles of the oxygen they needed now was no help. Grant's thunderous steps grew louder, and the ground beneath Matt's feet more tremulous as the moon monster approached. Above him, the dust storm swirled.

Come on! Hurry up!

Earfuls of oxygen alarm interrupted his thoughts. His suit was empty. If he waited, Matt would not have enough oxygen left in his system to run from the Grant thing when it got too close. And it *was* close. It would be upon him before the ramp was low enough for him to climb on it. Out of options, Matt raised his blaster and fired at the Grant thing with the full intensity of its not technically legal kill setting. In spite of his own shoddy aim, the blast hit its target. The Grant thing's "chest" exploded in a volcano-like eruption of chunks of rock and crumbling red debris.

When the dust cleared, Matt saw that perhaps predictably, the Grant thing was not destroyed. It stood against the landscape in front of him looking stunned and confused by the new hole in its body. But it was still very much alive. It was still very much able to get to him.

Matt glanced at the ramp. It was finally low enough for him to touch the lip of it with the fingers of the hand that was not pointing the blaster. He reached for it, pulling on it a little, trying to urge it lower. He was afraid to put too much weight on it. If the sensors detected what they thought was a person standing on the ramp, the ramp would stop where it was so as not to harm the rider. It would neither rise nor continue its descent then.

Safety first.

His suit's oxygen alarm died, giving up on him. Matt thought he could feel himself suffocating. His vision clouded over, and it was getting harder to move. Every muscle in his body screamed for a fresh gulp of air. He raised the blaster toward the Grant thing again, hoping against hope that there was still charge available, and squeezed the trigger. The thing's right shin vanished in a violent avalanche of crumbly rock, and it took a tumble, crashing to the moon's dust and razor rock surface. Still, it was not dead. Matt could see it struggling to pull itself along the ground with its monstrous outstretched arms. The open end of the blaster's barrel fizzled and sparked, a sure sign that it had used up the last of its charge. Matt resisted the urge to throw it at the creature closing in on him.

The ramp was nearly down now. Close enough. Faintness overcame Matt, and he collapsed, falling onto the ramp, his feet hanging over the edge. The ramp immediately halted the remainder of its descent because of the new weight of his body on the conveyor belt. With his last ounce of consciousness, Matt stretched out his hand and pressed the ramp's UP/CLOSE button, just above where his body lay. The conveyor belt started, ferrying Matt to the safety of the lander. When he was dumped off the edge of it, the ramp would detect that his weight was gone and would start closing on its own. Matt figured that as long as the conveyor rolled him off when he got inside, he didn't really need to be conscious for a while. The lander would fill the entry bay with air as soon as the ramp shut. With any luck, he'd still be alive to enjoy it, and the Grant thing would be unable to get to him.

Unless it still remembers that it was Grant, his mind warned. *Grant knew how to push the buttons.*

Below him, the Grant thing continued its slow crawl toward the lander. Above them both, the dust storm had formed its striking spiral. What-

ever new devastation the mystery molecules were planning was imminent. Matt's last conscious thought was his hope that the strike would
land somewhere away from him and the lander. That it would hit Grant
again and maybe complete his conversion to moon dust. Then darkness
fell upon him.

He awoke sometime later, still wearing his broken environmental suit,
and tried to shake off the remnants of a particularly bad nightmare he'd
been having. It was something about Jill, and rocks, and dust. Something
he had to hide from her but wasn't sure how he was going to do that. He
shook his head to clear it, and the dream was gone. He pulled off his helmet and felt the cold recycled air of the lander's interior caress his face.

He glanced at the viewscreen beside the now closed entry ramp. The
image there was of the ground outside. Below him, the crusty busted up
body of his former partner Grant appeared to be slinking away from the
lander, toward nightfall. The dust storm that had formed overhead hadn't
struck him, then. He still bore the same scars of their battle. He appeared
to be unchanged. How long had it been? Matt had no way of knowing.
His environmental suit's life support and other features were completely
dead. Protecting his modesty was its only remaining function. He stripped
it off and tossed it into the refuse that would be collected and studied by
his coworkers in the lab when he returned. He already had his story ready.

He would tell them that Grant, in a jealous rage, had confronted him
about Jill and had tried to kill him, damaging his suit in the process. He
had obviously smuggled a blaster aboard the mission for that purpose.
Matt had run from Grant and made it back to the lander just in time to
see Grant consumed by one of the moon's freak dust storms. He'd waited
inside the lander but could find no sign of Grant. With no way to support
himself on the moon other than the lander, and shaken from the experience, he had aborted the mission and started the ride home.

That's how it happened. Matt thought it would be easy to convince
himself of that on the long trip ahead of him, and that would make it
simpler to convince the folks in the lab when he reported to them. Later.
He'd get back to them later. After he'd had time to get the lander on course
and himself some much-needed rest. His brain still felt foggy. Some side
effect of his oxygen deprivation, he figured. The joints in his fingers and
toes ached terribly.

He examined his hands while he made his way toward the lander's captain's chair, wearing only his skivvies. Were the fingers on his left hand a little longer than they used to be? Maybe. They sure looked like it when he compared them to the fingers on his right. The fingernails on the index finger and middle finger of his left hand looked a bit discolored, too. They were red. Not the pinkish red of fingernails over ordinary flesh, but moon dust red: crimson and flaky. He scratched the surface of one of them with the nails of his right hand. It was like trying to chisel a chunk out of the side of a mountain. Matt grabbed the survival hatchet off the wall of the entry bay as he passed through the door. Perhaps he'd been touched by the mystery molecules in the dust storm after all. Maybe he needed to perform a little surgery before he launched himself back toward civilization. If he could chop off his left hand and toss it back to the moon's surface by itself, he'd return a hero. He'd have prevented a more widespread infection. Jill would be fascinated by that and love him all the more for it. Of course, she would. Jill loved geology. She'd have to love a story about a geological lifeform.

There was antiseptic, suturing equipment, and enough wrapping to make an adequate tourniquet in the First Aid kit hanging on the wall. Matt grabbed that as well.

Guess I still won't be getting my claw gloves, he thought.

Safety first, after all.

Deal With It

There you are, buddy-boo! I knew it was you as soon as the beam from my iPhone bounced off that hairy butt of yours. Well, it's not like it could've been just any naked guy freezing his nuts off out here. Ha! Just laying right there huddled up on the road, huh? Trying to survive the cold? Well, I guess I can't blame you. That sun-baked asphalt is probably the warmest place you could find to go fetal out here in the desert at this time of night. Or morning, I should say. It looks like the sun might be starting to peek over the horizon of that little town in the distance. Caught up with you just in time. I'm glad you didn't decide to bury yourself in some sand to stay warm. Come to think of it that might've been the smarter thing for you to do. I might never have seen you then! Ha!

Oh, but we've already established that you're not the brightest bulb, haven't we? I do wish I hadn't had that weak moment way back there at the ass-wagon before it up and died on me. Faked me out, you and that ass-wagon. You weren't really dying, but it was! Ha! I just wonder now how far you might've taken it if I hadn't believed you were really having a heart attack. I was so intent on you not dying before I could kill you myself that I didn't even consider you could be faking it. Tried to fake it 'til you made it, didn't you buddy-boo? Didn't make it very far, though! Ha!

Look at you laying there naked and shivering. Just something about that makes me want to kick you right in the head. I'm afraid that might get your adrenaline pumping again, though, and I can't risk that. So I guess I'll just close these cuffs around your wrists while you're too weak to head-butt me again. Got lucky and remembered to grab the handcuffs when I walked away from the ass-wagon. Also remembered to grab the ball gag, so let's strap that on real tight too. Can't have you screaming on me out here. You might scare up a coyote or something. Did I tell you that I ran out of gas? That's why the ass-wagon died on me, and that's why it took me so long to finally find you. Hell of a thing, huh? Hell of a thing. I do make my mistakes sometimes, don't I? I think I told you that.

Now here's a problem. I forgot the crowbar. What do you know? Now how am I going to kill you without my crowbar? I suppose I could strangle you. I wonder if I have the upper body strength left for that. Or maybe I could try to snap your neck. I've seen the tough guys do that in all those running, jumping, and fighting movies the boys want to drag me to go see. I wonder if I'm strong enough for that. Tonight's been quite a workout for me already, what with the three others dying before you and me having to chase you on foot half-way across the damned desert. Asshole. What'd you go and run for?

Snapping your neck would be faster, of course, but then I might not get to see the lights go out behind your eyes. That's what started this whole thing, remember? Yeah, let's do a strangle. It's not bloody, but at least I'll get to watch your eyes. Unless you squeeze them shut like my daddy tried to do. You do that, and I'll rip off your balls before I finish strangling you to death. How about that? That enough to motivate you to keep your eyes open while I snuff you out? Ha! I thought so. You guys. You don't give a rat's ass about getting a broken nose, or even staying alive, just as long as you don't feel any pain in the old family nuggets. So funny.

Right, so I'll just wrap my little fingers around your throat here and— uh oh. Say, buddy-boo, you aren't turning blue already, are you? I haven't even applied any pressure yet. No, that looks more like an electric blue flashing in your eyes there. Looks a lot like a police car's flashers, as a matter of fact. Shit. There's a cop coming up behind me, isn't there? Well, I guess they were going to show up eventually, huh? I figured I'd be well into that town over there before that happened, though. Now, you just lay here and try not to die yet. Let me do the talking. Not that you have much of a choice. Ha! Now, you so much as twitch an eyebrow and I'll stomp you to death before Officer Happenstance here even understands what's happening. Got it? Nod if you do. Good. Now just watch this.

Oh my God, Officer! Thank heavens you're here! You have to help me! Please! Whatever you do don't let him loose! Don't let him get me! Okay, I'm sorry. I'm sorry. I'm just so upset. I'll try to calm down and tell you what happened. Please, just keep him away from me! And don't listen to him, officer! He tried to kill me! Look at my face. I'll bet I have a nasty bruise on my head from where he tried to knock me out. See it? Shine your flashlight right here. See? I told you. He hit me with a crowbar way back there in the desert where my car died.

Oh, good. That's a good idea. Go ahead and put him in the back of your car. I feel much safer with him behind locked doors so I can tell you what happened. See, I was on my way home from a friend's house, and I guess I had gone inside without locking my car. I make mistakes sometimes. When I got back in my car to go home, this guy just leaped out of the backseat and grabbed me around the throat and conked me on the head! I think I must have blacked out for a second because the next thing I knew I had been shoved over to the passenger's seat. Well, before I could get my senses together, he leaped into the driver's seat. He took that pair of handcuffs he has around his wrists now and strapped me down. Then he drove off with me! Oh, officer! I was so scared! I've never been in trouble before in my life, and then—out of nowhere—this happens! Look at me! I'm still shaking!

So, anyway, this guy—he never even mentioned his name—he jumps into the driver's seat and speeds off in my ass-wa, uh, my car. Before I know it we're on this empty stretch of desert road. He pulls over and shuts everything down, and then takes off all his clothes! Starts waving his dick at me like he's going to have his way. Well, I totally freaked out at that point. Started having a panic attack just like my daddy used to have whenever he saw the stock market take a tumble. I felt my eyes roll back in my head and I started just shaking all over like I didn't have any control over my own body anymore. That changed things a bit for him, I guess. My freak-out must've freaked him out too because all of a sudden he's smacking my face and trying to get me to snap out of it. The next thing I know, I feel the cuffs come off.

I don't know what he was thinking. Maybe he was just thinking "nevermind," you know? That he'd just dump this crazy bitch out in the desert somewhere and be on his way. Too bad for him, though. When I felt those cuffs come loose, it sobered me up real quick. I punched that sucker straight in the balls. Well, he keeled over real quick with both hands holding his sack. At that point, I just reached over with both my hands and shoved him out of the car. Then I started it up and took off like a bat out of hell. Drove off with his cuffs and clothes and everything. But then—wouldn't you know it—I ran out of gas. We'd been driving most of the night by that point, I guess. I'm surprised we made it as far as we did.

I knew he wouldn't be far behind me, so when the ass-wa, uh, car wouldn't start again, I grabbed his clothes and those cuffs, and I took off running toward those city lights there behind you. What town is that anyway, officer? Clarington, huh? I might've heard of it. Anyway, I threw his clothes out all along the desert as I was running. I figured he might be at a disadvantage trying to catch me or hold me if he had to stay naked and I had easy access to knocking on his sensitive parts.

And oh boy, he caught up to me all right. He must've been a football player or something because he ran up behind me fast! Knocked me right to the ground! Then, while he was trying to climb on top of me and pin me down, I did exactly what I'd planned to do and kneed him in the nuts as hard as I could. That got him off me again real quick. He was rolling all around on the pavement and screaming to beat the band. Do a guy's nuts swell when you hit them? I guess not. Otherwise, his would've been the size of grapefruits after they met my knee. So while he was rolling around, I grabbed the cuffs from where he'd tackled me and slapped them on his left wrist. I don't know where I got the strength, but I somehow managed to get his right wrist behind him along with his left and cuffed it too. It wasn't easy. He really wanted to keep cupping his balls. Honestly, I'm not sure why I put the ball gag in his mouth. I guess I just got tired of him screaming in my face and calling me a bitch. And that's when you pulled up behind me, officer. I'm so glad you're here!

Seriously? You want to get his side of the story, huh? Well, I guess I can understand that. You're not going to take him out of the car to do that, are you? I know he's cuffed, but I don't want him to even be able to walk toward me, you know? Do you think you could just question him from the back seat of your patrol car? Pretty please? I'd feel a whole lot safer if he stayed in there and I stayed out here. I mean, it's not like I can run away. We're in the desert, and we're still at least a half-mile away from Clarington. I won't go anywhere. I promise. You can just bend down and poke your head inside the back of your car there and question him that way. You might want to make sure you have handy access to your gun, too. He's a slippery guy. Very dangerous, I think. Yeah, there you go. Hold onto your gun and just lean into the car a little bit like that. You're so big and strong to do this for me.

Hey! Nice ass! Too bad I have to put my foot in it now. Oof! Ha! And slam goes the door! Well, look at you both now, locked in the back of that patrol car. Oopsie! You even managed to let go of your gun, there, Officer Bumble! I guess I'd better pick that up before you figure out how to get the door open, huh? Now, let's see. How do you use this thing, hmmm? My guess is that all I need to do is point and shoot, right? Oh no, don't try to call for help. I can see that you still have your radio mic hooked to your shoulder there, but if you use it, you're both gonna be dead in two seconds. The naked guy and the police officer. It's such a sweet story. Ewwww, you pretty much landed face-first in his lap, too, didn't you? Gross! I don't envy you there. Lucky me, though, Mr. Officer, because you left your flashers on and your engine running! Oh, and did you leave your keys in the ignition? Yes! You did! Wow. I'd always heard that cops had a special ignition system that let them take the keys out but leave the engine running, so the lights and radio don't drain the battery, but it automatically shuts the car down if someone tries to steal it. Not your kind of tech, huh? Exactly where did you go to cop school? Oh, I know. I know. I'm a pretty girl who looked like she was in trouble. That makes all your quality education and police instincts just melt away, doesn't it? Ha! You might be a cop, but you're still a man. Dumbass.

Now, now. Don't look at me like that. It's a new day, and it's very young. We can have lots of fun together. Now, I'm going to need you to do me a little bitty favor. I want you to take those handcuffs off your belt and clamp one end of them around your right wrist. If you don't do it, I'll shoot you in the face, and I'll do it through the window, so the glass gets all embedded in your skin. Sound like fun? No, I didn't think so. Do it now.

Good. Very good. You're almost as smart as your ass is pretty, aren't you? Now, I'm going to open this door, so I can cuff your other wrist. You try anything funny, and I'll blow your head off. Ready? Okay, here we go. Good! Again with no sudden moves! You really are smart, aren't you? Smart, but with just a little bit of bad luck tonight. I mean, you came up on me just as I was about complete the next step in my grand experiment. I'm starting to wonder now if I was really meant to kill buddy-boo there after all. First, he got away from me by faking a heart attack, then you happen up just as I'm about to strangle him! You know what that means Officer Cute Butt? It means you get to take his place as the random variable tonight! In fact, you're probably a better random variable in this little experiment of mine than buddy-boo ever was because I didn't pick you out of a crowd or out of the bar like I did him. No, you just wandered up to me and saw what I was doing. And since I can't have you stopping me or warning the good citizens of Clarington about the honor of the presence I'm about to bestow on them, I guess I just have to go ahead and kill you.

Oh, yes, I know you don't believe it yet, but you dying out here is pretty much inevitable at this point. Now, let me think—all I really have to do is just point this little thing at your head and squeeze the trigger, right? Or is there some kind of safety button somewhere? That's the question, isn't it? Do you police types walk around with the safety on or do you walk around ready to draw and fire when the breeze blows the wrong way? It's not real easy to see out here in the early dawn, but I can't seem to locate a button of any kind. Wait. What's this? Oho! Looks like it might be a safety to me! So I guess I just slide this little thing back and—shit! Will you look at that? That wasn't a safety at all. It was some kind of ejector button for the ammo thingy.

Shit! Let me just pick that up and pop it back in there. I do make my mistakes, don't I? Ha! I guess it would be too much to ask you, Officer Fine Ass, to tell me how this thing works, wouldn't it? Of course it would! You still think you're going to survive this. Yeah, you do. So, I'll have to figure this out on my own. Hi-ho-what's the dealio? I've seen this kind of thing in those action movies you macho man types drool over on the weekends. I was telling buddy-boo about those when I was thinking about snapping his neck. I think I remember some old shirtless guy running around in the dark who slid the top of one of these things backward like so and—oh!

There we go! My wasn't that a satisfying sound? Sort of a click with a thunk at the end. Now all I have to do is point and shoot, isn't that right? Just like taking a picture? Now, let's see. Where should I shoot you? If I put it between your eyes, I might not be able to see you go. I bet you're wearing one of those bullet-proof vests, too, aren't you? So shooting you in the chest isn't going to be real reliable either. Oh, what the hell. I'll just put it in the middle of your forehead. I've always got buddy-boo there as a backup if I don't get to see you go into shutdown mode, right? Here we go!

Oh. Oh! OH! Wow. That was fucking intense! I felt it all the way up my arm! Got a little tingle in my shoulder. Hell, I can feel it all the way down to my sinuses! Did you see that, buddy-boo? It left this smoking black hole right in the middle of his forehead. Mmmm that felt gooood. Is this what an orgasm feels like? I bet it is. I bet this is it. Well, I think I might just hang on to this little tool. Whoa! Hold up! I almost forgot to watch him go. Bye bye, Officer Buttinsky! I see you going! I'd say see you later, but we both know that's not going to happen. Ha! There he goes. There he goes.

Whew! I can see why guys like you like guns, buddy-boo. It's like your dick is an extension of your arm that can make your wad punch a hole through flesh and bone. I see I got a little of my splatter on your face too. Ha! Oh well. It's not like you're going to be alive long enough to be disgusted by it because, unlike you, I don't have to wait to get it up again. Ha!

On the other hand, Officer Nosey Pants here pretty much completed my experiment for me, didn't he? He was the random one, the wild card. I guess I've proven what I set out to prove, right? I'm here to kill! There's no one I can't kill! Well, except you apparently. You seem to have formed this nasty habit of cheating your own death, haven't you? So where does that leave me now? It just kind of sucks all the fun out of the discovery process to get to the end of my little experiment like that, especially when it wasn't the way I planned it.

The other thing is that now that I know I can kill just anyone, I'm afraid I'm going to get bored again. Seriously, I almost don't even feel like killing you anymore. I mean, what am I supposed to do? Just wander around randomly killing people for the rest of my life? Sounds like something that would run out of meaning real quick, doesn't it? I don't know, buddy-boo. I just don't know. I suppose I've gone too far to turn back now, though. I mean, where would I go? I can't go home. Mommy and daddy are both dead! Ha! Oh, Tiffany, Tiffany, you do make your mistakes.

Except—

You're still here, aren't you buddy-boo? And I really did enjoy seeing the look on your face when I blew out Officer Clueless' brains like that. Maybe the reason I haven't been able to kill you yet is that you're supposed to be my support. My naked flabby sidekick, maybe! Ha! That makes total sense, doesn't it? I guess I've just gotten a teeny bit attached to you after sharing all my night's adventures on our little road trip together.

That's got to be it! I'm just ready to settle down, that's all! Ha! Well, there you go, buddy-boo! You get to live because, well, I guess I kind of own you now. You're my official ear. I mean, I can't really let you go now, can I? And I'm not going to kill you, at least not until I get sick of having the company, I guess. I mean, it would get kind of lonely out here committing murder all on my own forever and ever. You'll be my widdle companion!

The first thing we need to do is uncuff Mr. Police Officer here. Let me see. Ah, here we go. Now I'm just going to shove him down here in the backseat with you, and we'll be on our way. Jesus, it's nice to have a car again! I just need to turn down that squelchy little radio thing and turn on some tunes. Then, my little groom, we're going to head right into Clarington there and find ourselves a little place to make ourselves at home.

***

So this is Clarington. Creepy looking high school over there. I'll tell you what, buddy-boo, it's a good thing it's so early in the morning here, seeing as how we're driving a cop car right through the middle of town with a dead cop in tow. Glad the fucker wasn't wearing a body cam. Hey! You awake back there? I gotta be honest, it looks like you're getting kind of cozy on Officer Nice Butt's shoulder. Didn't figure you for bi, much less a necrophile! Ha!

Not another soul in sight around here, though. That's good. There's more good news, too. Know what it is? I see a shit-ton of for-sale signs all up and down these streets. That means empty houses. Maybe we can hole up in one for a little bit, huh? Get our bearings and—oh, hold on just a minute, look at what we have here. Isn't that just the sweetest little thing? Reminds me a little bit of my daddy's place. Small and stately. Looks like it's been well kept, too. And for sale! I think I even see a garage on the right side there. That'll be perfect for our little paddy wagon here! Sign says it's reduced price, too. My mom always told me that if you see real estate with a reduced price sign, you can bet that they're having a hard time showing it. Maybe somebody died in it. Maybe it's haunted or something. Ha! I'm guessing that means we'd be left alone for a while there, hey? Except that there's not going to be any power in there. And probably no water. And I guess no TV or Internet.

Fuck.

Well, buddy-boo, there's a lesson to be learned here, I think. I'm all grown up now, huh? My mom and dad are gone, and you're probably an idiot, so I guess I have to be the adult and take care of us both. Just deal with it, Tiffany. You do make your mistakes, but there's nothing that says you can't make the best out of a bad situation, right? It's not much, but I do have my iPhone. I'll just have to find someplace to charge it up every now and then until we figure out what's next.

Okay, then, it's settled. This is where we're going to live for a while. I'll be the breadwinner. You be the house-husband. As such, the first thing I want you to do is bust one of those little windows out of that garage door, so we can unlock it and go inside. Can't just park a cop car out here in the driveway, can we? Nope. That won't go over well at all once the sun comes up and people start noticing that Officer Dumbass has been sitting in the backseat by himself for days on end. Now, I'm going to get out of the car and open the door. You're going to step out of the car and sashay over to the garage door and do what you're told. I don't think I want to uncuff you for this, considering you've already run out on me once before, so I want you to get creative. Use your foot or, I don't know, your elbow or your forehead. Just break that glass open. I'm going to keep this gun pointed your way while you do all that. You try anything funny, and I'll blow your butt-ugly little nose right off your face, got it? Awesome. Okay, opening the door.

Come on. Lift your head off of Officer Booty's comfortable little shoulder. Goodness gracious, buddy-boo! Look at that. You *like* being ordered around, don't you? Guess there's not much way you can hide it, you meme you. Ha! All right, get over there and bust that glass. Try your elbow first. Kind of pointy to belong to someone with your gut. Beer much? Okay, get over there and punch it. Oh, come on. You can hit it harder than that. I figured you for a farm boy. Hit it harder. NOW!

There, you see? That wasn't so bad. You're barely even bleeding. Now, now. Let's get you back in the car. Can't have you trying to run away again, can I? Here we go. Hop in. Good! I'll be right back. You just sit there and try not to get any of your old cop buddy's leaking bodily fluids on your delicate skin, okay? Put your widdle head back on his big daddy showdur if it makes you feew aw bettah. I'm going to get this garage door open so we can move the car inside.

***

Look at that, buddy-boo! A perfect fit! We're all snug as a bug in a rug in our own little place. Isn't it romantic? Ha! Well, maybe not. But it's still pretty sexy for you judging by the state of your honker there. Whew! I don't know about you, but all this running around and killing people and chasing naked guys and escaping the cops has me pretty well tuckered out. Now that we're all safe in our new little hidey hole, I think we'd better get some sleep. It's not the Hilton, but it'll have to do, hey? We're just dealing with it. That's what we're doing. It'll be uncomfortable, but maybe it'll be fun, like camping I guess. Although I've never actually been camping. Ugh. Bugs. You know. Shit. I'm just trying to convince myself here, aren't I? Yeah, I'm not happy about this either, buddy-boo. Tomorrow I think we'll just leave Office Butthole's car here and go find us a place with power and a comfortable bed. How the hell are we supposed to sleep here? Come to think of it, how the hell am *I* supposed to sleep here knowing that *you* might not be sleeping? If I happen to drift off before you do, you might find some way to wrangle your ass loose, huh? What to do. What to do.

Hey, you know what my mom used to do when she wanted to get rid of my dad for the night? She'd fuck him. She'd fuck him, and then he'd just roll right over and drift off to dreamland. They thought I didn't know, but I did. They thought I couldn't hear, but I could. I knew what she was doing. Soon as he was out cold, she was headed for a big old bottle of wine she kept in the fridge. I don't know, it was like sex was valium for him or something. I see you're still bright-eyed and bushy tailed (seriously, dude, we've gotta shave that shit). It's adrenaline, I guess. Doesn't look like you're going to drift off anytime soon. But knowing what I know about you now and what you like, I'm going to bet the way to get you to relax and drift off is to consummate our brand new little relationship here.

I know, I know. I told you back in the ass-wagon that I didn't want to have sex with you. I still don't. But it's nighty-nite time now, and Tiffany needs some rest before her busy, busy day can continue. So I'm going to just suck it up and deal with it. Dealing seems to be my new thing, after all. There you go. That's all I had to say. You're already sporting a stiffy again. Ever done it in a car beside a dead body before? Ha! Who am I kidding? You've never done it at all, have you buddy-boo? Well, there's a first time for both of us, then. Here we go!

***

Doesn't that feel good for you? Uhhhhhm hmmmm, I see you drifting. Eyelids getting heavy as all those endorphins race up and down your nervous system. Admit it, you've wanted this all along haven't you? I had a guy tell me one time that his idea of heaven was drifting off to sleep in a recliner with a cold beer in one hand, a cigarette in the other, a game on the TV, and a lady on his cock. Go ahead. Drift on down into the blackness. It's dark in here. Nothing will disturb you. All you want to do is look at the backs of your eyelids. Like this, I'll show you. Close them and drift so that all you'll see is—

All you'll see is—

Why the fuck am I seeing flashes of blue light on the backs of my eyelids?

Oh. Oh no. I can see them through the fucking window you broke. Cops? Really? How the hell did they find us here? Shit. Where's my underwear? There they are. You stay put here, buddy-boo, while I figure out what's going down. Maybe something's happening across the street or something. There's no way anyone knows we're in here. Not yet.

Unless.

Unless Officer Corpsey here isn't really dead. Did you tip off your buddies Officer Corpsey? Hellooooo? Can you feel me smacking your jowly little cheeks around? How about when I punch you in the nose, huh? *Whuff!* That phase you? No, hmm? Guess you must really be dead then. Then how in the hell did they—? Oh. Oh, Buddy-boo, you *didn't*. And after all I've done for you. You weren't leaning on Officer Brainless' shoulder at all, were you? You were leaning on the fucking shoulder mic's button the whole time? Exactly what did you think that was going to accomplish, huh? You were getting lucky! Guess I should have taken that walkie talkie after I put the bullet in his head, but I didn't figure it'd be an issue after he was dead. Well, I do make mistakes sometimes, don't I? Ha! This is the second time tonight that I've underestimated you, I guess. Now I'm sorry I was fucking you because you'd apparently already fucked me first! Ha!

You know what, though? This is okay. Really. It's okay. The old Tiffany from the bar would have probably thrown a fit about this. She would've stamped her feet and whined and complained about how things weren't going her way. But the old Tiffany was still a child with parents and privilege, wasn't she? You know, ever since you whacked me on the bean and the ass-wagon ran out of gas, I've just been sort of rolling with the punches. Playing the hand I've been dealt. I suddenly realized I never understood what those old sayings really meant until tonight, when I had to put on my big girl panties and track your sorry ass. Then I had to kill that nosey cop. I spent all night having to just deal with it.

Maybe I really am a grown woman now, huh? And now I have to deal with this too. Oh well. I'm not just any grown woman, am I? I'm Tiffany! The Clarington PD ain't seen nothing yet, right? You just lay your ass back down on top of Officer Doohickey there. I'm gonna see what neat little war toys we've got in the trunk.

Time to deal.

The Murder of Crows

The back of his right hand fit perfectly over the circle of bright light that beamed down from the sky, but it was not quite enough to clear his field of vision. The rays of sunshine that refracted through the safety glass of his windshield—not to mention the glare from the hood—slid through his fingers like grains of sand scooped from a temperate beach. The light crept into every crevice of the Lexus, unstoppable, creating a brilliant wall of blankness against the windshield that shut out every color.

Except for white.

And maybe a little bit of black.

Along the periphery of the blankness, he thought he could discern the silhouette of a disembodied hand reaching out to him from somewhere within the light, stretching from the ether like so many long-dead relatives along the walls of that tunnel that those freaks on the History Channel always report they've seen while in the throes of a near-death experience. However, this shape neither welcomed him onward nor motioned him away, as said relatives do in said experiences. This shape appeared to be frantically flagging him down.

Then the voluminous branches of a southern yellow pine obscured the over-bright seven o'clock sun, dispersing the glare off the hood of his Lexus and breaking the spell. Before him, in sudden crystal focus, stood a row of startled children, frozen in the crosswalk, their eyes wide. His own eyes, heretofore squinted against the blinding sun, thrust wide open in a perfect reflection of their own. His elbows locked, embedding the unforgiving hardness of the steering wheel in his palms and submerging his shoulders into the back padding of the driver's seat. His teeth clamped down on his tongue.

He thought he tasted blood.

From somewhere outside, he heard the shrill reverberation of a police whistle.

Stop.

Need. To. STOP.

The big toe of his right foot snagged the backside of the brake pedal. He held his breath and forced the trapped foot to the floorboard, sliding it toward him. It came free. He stomped on the brake.

The front end of the Lexus shifted to the left. He fought the urge to jerk the steering wheel to the right; to overcorrect, as they called it in all those police blotter reports he used to compile back in his cub reporter days. The bald left front tire of his Lexus screeched in protest, then jerked to a halt a little more than ten inches from the solid white line that marked the edge of the crosswalk in front of Octavia Academy's Middle School campus.

Suddenly the entire world seemed to have frozen in place.

His pounding heart dropped from his temples and landed in his throat. He rested his forehead on the back of his right hand, which maintained its death-grip on the steering wheel, and quietly thanked God that his reflexes were still strong. A shudder ran through him, beginning at the back of his neck, working its way through his shoulders and down to his hips. He was careful to not allow it to interfere with his right foot's crushing hold on the brake pedal.

When he was finally able to lift his head and look through the glass, the first thing he noticed was the triangular yellow sign adorned with the featureless black image of a walking child. Its sharp, metallic edges glinted accusatorially at him in the brightness of the day. He next became aware of the four children ahead of him. They stood stock still, staring not at him, but at some point below him, presumably the front bumper of the Lexus, that part of the car that had nearly taken them off at the knees.

118

Three of the youths were girls in plaid skirts, each with an identically stricken expression on her face and her hands clasped at the neckline of her blouse. The fourth was a boy, who looked perhaps a year or two older than the girls. He had wrapped his lengthy rail arms around their shoulders. His caved chest and his grip on the biceps of two of the girls at his sides made him look like a mother bird using her wingspan to shield her young. The eyes of the man behind the wheel met the boy's for an instant. There was a shiny blankness to them, like beady crow's eyes. Fitting, he supposed, for a mother bird. Then the youth slowly released the girls and stood erect, relief washing over his face.

The crossing guard blew two short tweets on her whistle and waved the children across. Each immediately turned his and her attention to the task, and bounded the remainder of the distance across the street. The expressions on their faces betrayed no sense of urgency, nor any lingering awareness of having only barely eluded their own untimely deaths at his hands. They really were like birds, he thought. Or squirrels. Or deer. Or some other form of life unfettered enough by the false march of the clock of human existence to be able to live entirely in the moment. One second they're in fear for their lives, and the next they're bouncing around playfully as if nothing had happened.

He felt a twinge of envy for this blithesome little time of their lives.

When the first of the quartet brushed past the Navy blue-clad crossing guard and hopped safely up to the sidewalk beyond, he finally felt comfortable enough to relax his grip on the wheel. The blood vessels under the skin of his strained fingers immediately began to restore the flesh there to its ordinary pinkish color.

"Woo, that was close, Nick." The crossing guard had left her post and was leaning into the open window of the passenger side of his Lexus. The left side of her face was alight, a half moon dangling from the morning brightness that had previously blinded him. Her left eye was a dancing electric blue, its gaze steady. The right eye glaring at him from the shade seemed somehow shiny and darker, more sinister, more interrogative, more predatory.

In that eye was a look Nick Saint knew well. He saw it in the mirror every morning when he shaved.

"I ought to write you up," the crossing guard continued. Nick felt his chest tighten. "But the morning's so bright. I could see you squinting there behind the wheel when I was trying to flag you down. Maybe you should invest in some sunglasses, huh?" She pointed at the visor that was pressed flat against the ceiling of the Lexus. "You know they put those things there for a reason, right?"

He saw the half-smile curl up the sunny side of her lips and nodded. His muscles relaxed under his shirt. Suddenly it seemed easier to fill his lungs with fresh air. He wasn't in trouble.

Thank God.

"How do you know my name?" he asked. He heard no hint in his voice of the fear and panic he'd felt a moment before. That was good.

The crossing guard's eyebrows shot upward, forming an opposing arc to the wide swath of smile on her face. "Doesn't everybody? You're that Nick Saint fella, right? The guy that catches all those famous people doing things they ought not to be doing?" She winked and cocked her finger in a pistol fashion, then pointed it at him. "Yeah, you're him. What is it they always say when they find out you caught 'em? You know, like that one a couple of days ago who'd been cheatin' on his missus?"

Nick beamed.

"'I'm ruined!'" he shouted, popping his eyes wide and dropping his mouth open, as though he'd just witnessed a horrible accident. He mimed the slap of his right hand against his forehead. The crossing guard's eyes positively sparkled.

"They all say they're ruined," he added. "Rich or poor. Famous or not. 'I'm ruined!'"

The crossing guard laughed. "Yeah, that's right. 'I'm ruined!'" She slapped her own forehead with her right hand, popping her eyes wide and her mouth open in mock alarm. It was an entirely successful mimic of the shamed gesture that had become the trademark of his—well, his entire career.

"So," she added, grinning, "who gets it today?"

Nick returned her grin. "I really don't know yet," he said. "That's where I'm going. To work. To find out."

Behind them, a car horn blatted three times in rapid succession. The crossing guard peered over the top of the Lexus at the line of other cars behind it, framing her Navy-clad chest and gold shield in Nick's window.

"All right now," she shouted over the roof of the car, then her face reappeared in front of him. "You be careful out there. And keep the riffraff on their toes, huh?" She smacked her own forehead again. "'I'm ruined!' Ha!"

The crossing guard resumed her place in the crosswalk and motioned him forward. Nick stretched his right hand toward the passenger window and flipped her a wave with as he drove past, mindful of the weight of his foot against the gas pedal. He wasn't sure she saw it. The overpowering sun had emerged from behind the pine tree again, dispersing the solidity of the world before him in its hazy glow.

The speedometer of the Lexus crept up to 24 miles per hour, but Nick wouldn't allow it to cross 25 until he had driven more than a few feet beyond the sign that indicated the end of the school zone. Then he mashed down on the accelerator until he had achieved a comfortable, safe rate of 55.

Most people could get away with driving 57 miles-per-hour, or maybe even 60, along this stretch of highway. Nick had seen more than his share of sheriff's deputies and city cops who turned a blind eye to the drivers in front of him; drivers who were obviously five, six, or seven miles over the limit. Once an F-150 had raced past him, nonchalantly skirting the double yellow line just as he was passing the END SCHOOL ZONE sign. It had practically left him standing still. No one batted an eye, popped open their cell phones, or chased after it. At least not that he could see.

That wouldn't do for Nick Saint, though. Not in his business.

When your whole career is built on aiming a critical eye at wrongdoers, it just doesn't do to become one of them. You have to stay above them. Keep your nose clean. Wash their dirt off your body in the tub every night and then scour the acrylic with a nostril-stinging dose of Comet. Otherwise, you end up like the powerful crooked jailer in every prison movie ever made, the guy who commits all manner of atrocity against the inmates and then ends up among them, getting back everything he gave.

No, when you're the half-bald, slightly overweight, almighty, finger-pointing, bloviating, whistle-blowing Nick Saint, you watch your step on a minute-by-minute basis.

And you keep the riffraff on their toes.

Ha, indeed.

Over time, it had become a source of anxiety for him: always doing the right thing. Or at least trying to ensure that nothing he did could ever be perceived as the wrong thing. It was a new age of ever-watchful judgment, this—a new age of Puritanism born of and fed by constant electronic surveillance and years of constant connectivity to the chronically adolescent culture of the Internet.

It was true, though, what he'd said to the crossing guard. He hadn't a clue this morning as to which unfortunate victim of his own humanity would fall in the shadow of Nick Saint's legion of critical fans and watcher assistants, an unofficial team of informers officially known as Watchtower. Lately, it had become more and more difficult to find folks who were messing up badly enough to exploit, or at least in a big enough way to generate a little hyperbolic outrage on his blog, or his social media accounts, or the online video feed, or his cable talk show. The poor sap that the crossing guard had mentioned—an up-and-coming do-gooder who'd spent most of his days sheltering the homeless and most of his nights cuddling large-chested home-wreckers—had actually been Watchtower's last big bust (no pun intended). That story had first aired way back in May. The crossing guard was either misremembering or had seen it on a weekend rerun of the show. Since then, Watchtower had pretty much been drilling a dry well.

Even Mark, Nick's most enthusiastic Watchtower protégé, seemed to be having a rough patch. One day he was uncovering sex scandals, and lies, and money schemes that spanned a chain of class from a street beggar who panhandles in front of the local mission to the leader of the local Baptist church. The next, he couldn't even find a congressman with a parking ticket.

Nick couldn't help but notice the pained expression on Mark's face during every morning budget meeting, as he first asked Monica, then Jeff, and then every other member of the team what they'd dug up for the day. A few unpaid parking tickets from people who couldn't become congressmen if they were campaigning in a country where their own vote was the only one that counted. Maybe a minor scrape with the law. There just wasn't much available in the way of shocking, outrageous mischief anymore, at least among the noteworthy people, the rich and famous that you see so often in the glossy pages of society magazines.

After all, the Gibsons, the Williamses, the Sheens, and all those types were long in the past. The "Respectable Celebrity Does Bad Thing" headlines weren't shocking anymore. And even if they were, the celebs had all learned to work around it. They'd all learned to be careful. To keep their noses clean. To straighten up and fly right or bury their sins so far down that not even BP could find them.

So Watchtower eventually had to train its sights on more average joes: the people you don't know, but who are still shockingly stupid, the people who never in a million years thought anyone anywhere would ever care about anything they do. They were the three-hundred pounders who blissfully walk into Wal-Mart wearing their Daisy Dukes. They were the people trying to be funny on social media, only to find themselves stepping on sensitive landmine triggers. They were the folks who used to walk around smiling all the time, believing that the private lives that they left at home that morning would never see the light of day. Dropped that candy wrapper on the pavement instead of in the trash bin, did you? No one saw it, so no one cared. And who would *really* know if you mashed just a *teensy* bit harder on the accelerator on your way home that evening, just to see if you could put that squirrel that was racing across the street in front of you squarely under your driver side front tire? Is the guy driving behind you really going to report you for tossing that beer can out the window? Nah. Who'll know?

But if Watchtower got footage of it, you'd better believe *everyone* would know. And not only would they know, but they'd also care, because Watchtower *told* them to care. They'd care enough to tweet about it. They'd care enough to Facebook it, or Instagram it, or whatever the flavor-of-the-month social media verb was. They'd care enough to send you hateful emails about it, to call your employer and get your ass fired. Hell, they might even tell your mommy. They'd get you good, and all because Nick Saint was red-faced and outraged by what you did.

At least he pretended to be.

Everyone pretended to be because that was the entertainment of it all. That great democratizer the Internet had, in the end, created not a marketplace of free thought and ideas, but a simple culture of paranoid sociopaths, a culture in which empathy was dead and the 1980s ideal of "looking out for number one" had congealed and morphed into "I am the only one." The trick was not to get caught being "the only one" by Watchtower or its like so you could continue to sit high in judgment on those who were in reality exactly like you.

For a while—even after folks first started to become aware that their day-to-day activity was being tracked by organizations like the National Security Agency and the fellow who brought that revelation was made a pariah by his own government—the ordinary folks weren't so off-put as to change their natural brutishness. They still picked their noses and scratched their privates in public. They still abandoned shopping carts in the middle of the parking lot instead of doing other shoppers a favor and strolling the squeaky buggies back to the corrals that are provided for just that purpose. They still boxed up squirming, wriggling newborn puppies and tossed them into garbage bins behind their local shopping malls rather than surrender them to a humane shelter. They were also more than happy to record video of their neighbors performing equally outrageous acts that they would then send to Watchtower for distribution.

And that was good.

It was good for Nick Saint and Watchtower, at least.

It kept the machine of public shaming but non-violent vigilante justice fed. It kept people like that crossing guard constantly wondering who was next; always hungry for another mistake, another outrage, *another* unfortunate soul slaughtered and fed to the murder of crows that society at large had become.

Double-park that H2 in front a fire hydrant? The world's going to see your name splashed across Nick Saint's blog, and then across every other online social media as soon as that entry goes viral. And they all go viral.

You're going down. You'll be insulted and harassed and maybe even lose your job because you're an inconsiderate slob. Got in a verbal scrape with your girl in a restaurant over the way you eyeballed the waitress as she walked away with your order? No doubt one of Nick Saint's legions of fans has it on their camera phone. Now the world's going to know you're a scoundrel and a lech. You'll never get another date, and you'll forever be #gawkingasshole on Twitter.

Then, perhaps inevitably, even the nobodies got wise.

The well began to dry up again. The ratings started to plummet. The juicy stories were not as juicy anymore. How many times can the crows feed on a celebrity who kicked a puppy and continue to care about it? How many times can their gleeful crow-black eyes watch an actor have a public meltdown and not surf to something more interesting and out there, like *Ancient Aliens* on the History Channel or *Fat Guys in the Woods* on The Weather Channel?

Once the crows have feasted on everything, there is, Nick Saint isn't such a unique commodity. And he's even less of one when there are others in his business who are just a little less scrupulous about their work, who are willing to take just a teensy bit more license with their hyperbole in the storytelling, or the craftiness of their image manipulation. Suddenly Nick Saint can be replaced by someone more outrageous, more ridiculously hyperbolic, and more willing to use not-so-honest means to provoke the crows, to make them hungry, greedy for more.

It was funny, really. They called themselves journalists, but in the end, he and his kind were just as willing to lie, cheat, and steal to get what they wanted as the "straight news" journalists they so loved to catch in compromising positions and then pick apart for crow food.

Nick's ratings were the Catch-22. Everyone loved his takedowns, but no one wanted to *be* the takedown, which left no one to take down. Which meant lower ratings. Which meant fewer viewers and less vitriol on the social networks. And, of course, that left the door open for those who were willing to lie—or at least stretch the truth—to outrage the masses. If his competitors saw him floundering? Well, wouldn't they just love to take down the great Nick Saint himself? To hoist him by his own petard in a modern ratings war version of that old King of the Hill children's game?

Of course they would.

***

Nick swerved the Lexus into his parking space at KAWW and made his way to the elevator. His own winking mug greeted him on the back wall of the lift. He was smiling in that photo—part of an old ad campaign that never really seemed to go away—and pointing a pistol-cocked finger at the camera, affably reminding the world (reminding himself) that he and others like him are out there. That they're watching. That if you're bad, they're gonna see it and they're gonna *getcha*. That was the caption under the photo, in fact:

GONNA GETCHA!
WATCHTOWER
ON KAWW
EVERY DAY AT 9!

Nick smirked at himself. That particular shot had been taken way back in 2007, when Facebook was still an infant, and the biggest sources of shame and bloviating were still cable television news shows and politics-obsessed talk radio hosts. He looked young and confident in that photo. He looked smug, satisfied that the world was his. The celebrities and politicians of America were still selfish, still visible, and still no damn good. Prime for harvest. He was the shiny new scythe there to cut them down.

Even back in those early days, Nick and his KAWW minions knew exactly who their target audience was going to be. That promo's graphic designer had known it, too. Craftily integrated into the iris swirls around Nick's pupils in that photo were the beady black eyes of a murder of crows. It was what designers and computer programmers liked to call an Easter egg, a hidden feature or message, although there was nothing sacred about them. Not in the slightest.

Nick cleared his throat and turned his back on the blast from the past. He pressed the elevator button for the second floor. The doors closed. He felt the familiar rise in his belly as the little booth climbed upward, ferrying him on his daily ascension into Watchtower. The place was no doubt already buzzing this morning with the clacking of fingers on keyboards as his Watchers surreptitiously combed government databases, the news, social media, street cameras, and viewer submissions for someone to take down.

His own reflection stared back at him from the shiny metal on the back wall of the elevator, contrasting his haggard and exhausted present to his smiling, unrepentant past in the ad on the back wall. Nick cocked his thumb and forefinger at his reflection and winked, imitating the smug, coy charm of the photo. He decided that it looked silly now. Besides, he wasn't that guy anymore. He was older now. And the world had changed on him. More often than not these days, he felt as if he had a bright red target painted on his back.

He balled the pistol into a fist and extended his middle finger at his own aging reflection, then immediately felt a pang of remorse for it. There were security cameras on the elevators, and they might have recorded his little show of self-defiance. Not as bad as, say, punching your fiancée in the face, but certainly not a good impression to leave on any recording media.

He checked the time on his iPhone and made a mental note to erase the section of footage that had been recorded for this elevator between seven fifty-five and eight o'clock. Fortunately, a man in his position had the means to do that type of thing, especially if he got to it first.

The elevator dinged his arrival at the second floor—Watchtower. The doors opened to the soft breeze of men and women in smart business suits. They paced the long row of cubicles that spawned from the elevator and stretched throughout the rest of the floor. The far wall housed a row of offices with exterior windows. Nick's was the largest of those, directly in the center of that wall. Sure, it was an inconvenient walk around the cubicles from the elevator, but it was also his chance to announce his presence, to be sure his Watchers knew that the boss was here and that it was time for them to provide the ingredients for whatever shit-storm he was about to stir. That's exactly how he'd wanted it, at least back in 2007.

First up was Monica, the lead on his imaging team and creator of the crow eyes Easter egg in that old ad campaign. She sat with her back to him, her green and purple Mohawk obscuring the subject of whatever photograph or video she was busy enhancing just then. Monica was the best. If there were dirt to be found via photon, she'd be the one to locate the pixel that contained that dirt.

"'Lo, Mon," he called to her and then jumped backward a bit when she whirled around to face him. She skidded her mouse to the upper corner of her screen and enabled her screensaver. Whatever had been on her screen was now covered by a slow-fade slideshow of skinny, pale men in skimpy Goth attire, many of them cowering in corners with shamed expressions on their faces. Monica's eyes were wide and angry, her nostrils flared. A small diamond in the right blowhole glistened under the light from the lamp that stood in the left corner of her cube.

Then she seemed to recover herself. Her face softened under Nick's startled gaze. "Everything all right?" he asked cautiously.

127

Monica cracked her lips in something that resembled a smile. It looked forced. "Oh, yeah, fine," she said. "All good. You just scared me, that's all."

Nick smiled. "Ok, then." He winked and cocked his index finger at her. "Looking forward to whatever you've got for me today. Must be good if you're hiding it behind a screensaver like that."

"That's harassment," Monica replied sarcastically and turned back to her workstation. Nick noted that she did not disable the screen saver, at least not until he was three or four steps away and could no longer see inside her space. Then he heard the familiar clicks of her mouse.

Nick's next stop was always Jeff, his ace aggregator. Jeff apparently never slept. There were always heavy black bags under his bloodshot eyes and three half-empty cups of cold coffee within arm's reach of his office chair. He was never on time for a meeting, and he always smelled like an all-night bender, but he was by far the best culler of crap from the Internet that Nick had ever seen. If it was dirt and someone posted it on a blog, Facebook, Twitter, or any other pop-up social media sensation, Jeff would find it, sift it, and spin it into Watchtower gold.

"Yo, Mutt," Nick called as he waded through the tangy, slightly rum-like odor that persistently hung over Jeff's cube. "What's hot in the crap-o-sphere today?" He stopped in the cube's entrance. Jeff's bleary head slowly arose from the top of his computer monitor, peering at Nick like a sleep-deprived Man in the Moon over the eastern horizon.

"Nothing," Jeff replied. It was a long, drawn out sound as if he were speaking from somewhere mid-yawn. "I got nothing today."

Nick's eyebrows shot upward. "Nothing at all?" he asked. "I think you're underestimating yourself. You *always* have something."

Jeff shook his sleepy head. A greasy strand of brown hair fell across his left eyebrow. "Yeah, well, first time for everything," he said. "I got nothing."

Nick folded his arms and leaned against the right side of the cube. "Are you all right?" he asked. "You seem a little—I don't know—pissed. Everything okay?"

Jeff's eyes met his own. There was the exhaustion, as always, but Nick thought that he also saw an element of something else in those red-lined orbs. Fear? Anger? Was there a sparkle of amusement, too? It was almost as if his old aggregation machine were hiding something from him.

"I'm fine," Jeff intoned, and then sank again below the horizon of his iMac, out of Nick's view.

"All right, then," Nick said. He tried to keep his voice matter-of-fact. "If you want to talk, you know where to find me. And since there's a first time for everything, how about being on time for the meeting this morning, huh?"

Nick strolled on. In cube after cube, his Watchers sat working, some of them hunched over their keyboards, broadening themselves against their computer screens and obscuring them from his view, much the way that mother hen middle school kid had tried to shield the three girls by stretching out his own body. Others had turned their computers around like Jeff's, so that their backs faced the entrance of the cube, affording Nick a view of each machine's power cord as it trailed through the hole in the top of each desk to the buzzing power strip that no doubt lay on the floor beneath.

By the time he yanked open the door of his own office to retrieve his trusty Bic pen and spiral Steno notepad (Nick had never been able to bring himself to abandon those trusty old staples for an iPad or some other note-taking device), the homey aroma of freshly brewed coffee was wafting into the hall from the large conference room. It was a signal that the Watchers were gathering for the morning meeting, where they would prepare a feast from the corpses of yesterday's news for the crows to circle over while the Watchers continue the search for today's potential kill. Nick sniffed the air as he approached the conference room door. It tasted foul in his throat, and he suddenly felt as if he needed to vomit.

From his seat at the foot of the conference table (the head was Nick's), his protégé, Watcher Mark, grinned at him. It was a grin Nick had seen once before: the time Mark had successfully defended himself against the libel suit by that Johnson lady. She had forced her kid to eat toilet paper as some kind of bizarre punishment for some slight that Nick could no longer remember. Mark had been lucky then. He'd been lucky that Johnson had admitted to the abuse. It had colored the court's opinion of her from the outset. So when she hadn't been able to *prove* that Mark had fabricated a viral Internet piece about some of that TP having been smeared with the kid's own feces—well, let's just say she flushed her shot at redemption down the toilet and leave it at that.

Every seat in the conference room already had a body in it. Nick double-checked the clock on his iPhone. He was not late. Typically, there were always some last-minute scramblers, people who couldn't make the meeting or who were late because they were busy trying to finish up work from the night before. Even bleary-eyed Jeff sat as upright as he could at his place, with both of his hands wrapped around a mug of fresh brew and his eyes downcast at the smooth pool of brown therein.

Every other eye in the place seemed to be on Nick. He scanned them for hints but found only blank stares. It was an unsettling change from the typical vibe he felt in the morning meetings. Something was wrong.

Hot blood crept up the back of his neck.

Whatever they're not telling me, Nick thought, *it's good.*

He reached for the back of his chair. His hand slipped off as he pulled the wheeled swivel from the table, nearly sending him to the floor. He managed to steady himself and then sat down, feeling an almost irresistible need to look at his hands, or cough into them, or something. None of the Watchers' beady crow-black eyes looked away.

There was a time, he thought, when they would have. They would have pretended to not have noticed his slip out of simple respect for his position, not to mention the fact that he gave them their own.

Nick cleared his throat and forced himself to steeple his fingers just under his bottom lip.

"All right," he said. He felt blood pounding against his temples again, as it had in the Lexus that morning. The rush was loud in his ears. He wondered if Mark could hear it, too, from all the way down at the other end of the table. "What's up? Got something juicy for me today?" He addressed them all but looked at Mark, the man who had been his right hand for a while now, the man who, until very recently, always seemed to come through in a pinch, even if he was just a *teensy* bit liberal with the facts. All the heads at the conference table turned their attention to Mark.

Mark's grin did not falter. He kicked both feet up on the edge of the conference table. A black ballpoint pen made circles through the knitting fingers of his right hand. "We got the latest numbers from upstairs," he said. "They're not good. Brass isn't happy. The last few *quote* scandals *unquote* we've exposed on the show haven't amounted to much of anything.

The straight media isn't picking up on them like they used to and none of them are trending on Twitter.

"As a matter of fact," he added, "random people in the Twittersphere seem to be posting more viral content lately than we are. We get some eyeballs by retweeting that shit, but ultimately that just ends up sending people away from our advertisers. It costs us to compete with people who aren't really even in the business."

All eyes returned to Nick.

"That's not a new problem," he replied. There was a jitter in his voice now that betrayed his nerves. "That's why I have you guys. You. Jeff. Mon." He nodded at each of them in sequence. "You're all supposed to be helping me find the dirt that gets eyeballs on us."

Mark's grin widened. "Yeah," he replied. "I don't think the problem is that we're not finding quality dirt." He stopped knitting the pen and made a circling gesture with it, indicating Monica, Jeff, and himself. "I think the problem is that people just aren't buying it anymore. The celebs who would've made great headlines a few years ago have either straightened up or found ways to stay below the radar. The ones that haven't straightened up are just average joes that everybody expects to make these kinds of headlines. They're not *interesting* anymore, at least not coming from us.

"I mean, sure, a YouTube clip about some guy who loses his pants to a wood chipper is funny for a blink, but then it's over. Nobody talks about it anymore. And nobody really gets *upset* about it. You know? There's nothing to keep the fire stoked." He smacked his belly with the palm of his left hand. Then his grin faded.

"People are only going to get outraged if they care, but the human race these days simply lacks empathy.

"Except when it's for kids. People empathize with kids."

Mark paused, scratching his chin thoughtfully. In better times, Nick could have used the lull to regain control of the meeting. At that moment, however, he couldn't think of a single thing to say.

"To keep the fire stoked, we have to create a pariah," Mark finally continued. "And to create a pariah, we have to find somebody who did something really, really wrong. And the victim has to be a kid.

"You know?" he added, his grin resurfacing, "like that bitch who shoved toilet paper down her brat's throat? And to make that pariah the talk of the world, it has to be somebody the public doesn't expect to make that kind of mistake. Somebody they trust. Somebody they look up to." His rictus widened, broad and toothy below suddenly crazy eyes trained squarely on Nick. "Somebody they've always wanted to *be*."

Nick felt gooseflesh spread up his triceps and onto the back of his neck, forcing the hair there to stand up. All eyes at the conference table were still on him. A lump rose in his throat. He tried, without success, to swallow it.

"Just what did you have in mind, Mark?" he asked. His tongue felt thick. His voice sounded far away. It was suddenly very difficult to sit still. "Who can we find that has screwed up that badly? Who do we feed to the crows today?"

Mark's crazy eyes narrowed.

"Well, that's another problem, isn't it?" he said. "Maybe it's time to try another tactic. You know, if we can't find the news, maybe we help make it."

"You mean fake it," Nick intoned. "Playing loose with the facts. Just like that Johnson lady."

Mark chuckled. "No. Johnson was just a feather in the wind. Nobody remembers her." He stretched his arms outward as if intending to hug the entire company gathered at the table. "I mean *we make it*. Let me show you."

He picked up the remote control for the projector that hung above the conference table and pressed a button. The projector whirred to life, shining a brilliant white beam on the surface of the whiteboard that hung on the wall behind Mark. After a few seconds, the Hewlett-Packard logo appeared, along with an indicator bar that showed the time left to elapse before the machine could enter its ready state. Mark took the opportunity to turn down the lights, addressing the meeting as he did.

"In order to kick Watchtower back to the top and drown out all the common voices that are competing with us, we have to have something sensational," he said to the room. "We have to take down someone so high and mighty, someone so untouchable, that to take him down almost looks like anarchy, or cannibalism, or—well, pick your own self-destructive metaphor.

"So, in order to remake Watchtower and take it back to the top, we need to start from within."

On the whiteboard, the image changed from the blue and white HP logo to the image of a Macintosh computer's desktop. A video editing application was running on it, stretched out to fill the width of the display. "We just pushed the button on this little bug at eight o'clock. I think it will be wildly successful, Nick." He turned to face him. "I'm interested to know your thoughts."

All heads turned to the screen. The still preview image within the video app faded from black to a brilliant, blinding white light. Nick blinked, involuntarily squinting against it. A second later, that blinding light also faded to reveal grainy black-and-white footage from what appeared to be the security camera positioned over the crosswalk in front of Octavia Academy Middle School.

On the screen in front of him, his Lexus rapidly approached the cross-walk, where four small children—a boy and three girls—stood frozen in horror. To the car's right, a crossing guard waved a frantic hand in a "halt" motion. She darted into the crosswalk toward the children just as the car screeched to a halt, mere inches from the youthful quartet. There was a soundless pause, and then the guard strolled to the Lexus and bent into the passenger window, appearing to address the driver as the kids contin-ued safely across the street.

From somewhere else in the room, Nick heard the sound of Mark's fin-ger striking a keyboard. The image on the whiteboard froze. At the far end of the conference table, Jeff stifled a cough over his coffee mug.

Nick's throat and nostrils felt suddenly dry as if they'd just been sucked clean by a vacuum. The crows in the conference room all turned their beady eyes to him again, all boring into—*through*—his skin. Even Jeff surfaced from his coffee mug to have a look at the astonished face of the man who had hired him.

"That's," Nick muttered. Then he cleared his throat again. The lump would not go down. It felt larger now, like a golf ball lodged in his esoph-agus "That happened this morning. But, but—"

"Yeah," Mark replied. His voice was dismissive, distant. "Yeah. Watch."

Nick leaped to his feet, sending his chair rolling backward. It slammed into the door of the conference room. From the corner of his eye, he saw Monica flinch.

"The sun was in my eyes!" he shouted. "It wasn't my fault! Besides, those kids are fine! The crossing guard didn't even give me a paper warning for God's sake!"

His breath came in short huffs. He could feel his chest heaving under his shirt. The skin there felt hot, sunburned.

"Mark." He wagged his finger at his protégé. "If you send that out, I swear to God you'll never work in this town again." He looked around the room. "You'll never work in this *country* again." A beat. "*You HEAR ME?*"

Mark waved him away. "Oh, it's too late for that. I already told you we pushed the button on it at eight. It's out there." He grinned again. There was a hint of loss in the eyes over it. "But you really don't have any reason to be upset. Not yet.

"What you just saw isn't the interesting part," he added. "This is just the prologue, the crunchy outer shell covering the meaty center. Honestly, Nick, nobody would fault you for what you just saw, at least not for very long. Everybody's accidentally sped through a school zone at one time or another. And, like you said, the kids weren't hurt.

"People empathize with kids, but they're not going to blame you for an accident in which none were harmed. That story would go viral about as fast as a picture of a paint chip."

Nick cocked his head. "Then what?"

Mark smiled. "Just watch," he said.

Nick heard another click on the keyboard. On the screen, the crossing guard removed her head from Nick's passenger window and glanced over the top of the Lexus at the cars behind it. She then began to back away from the car. At the same time, the security camera began to zoom in on the Lexus. Nick had a feeling the zoom was not the natural zoom of the security camera, but a software zoom applied by Watchtower, probably Monica herself. It didn't *feel* like a hardware zoom.

He glanced at Monica. She did not look away.

On the screen, the rear windshield of the Lexus crept closer and closer, filling the frame. Before the guard completely disappeared off the right side, Nick saw her make a waving motion with her left hand. It was difficult to tell from the angle whether she was waving goodbye to him or motioning him forward. He searched his memory and found he couldn't recall seeing her wave at all.

He looked at Mark, whose eyes were on the screen, and then at the others around him. They were all looking back at him. For perhaps the first time in his life, moony Jeff looked alive. He had a smile on his face. Nick swallowed thickly, turning his attention to the white-board again.

A few more Monica-enhanced powers of two and the frame became filled with the rear window of Nick's Lexus. Then all that was visible was Nick himself in profile, sitting in the driver's seat, facing the passenger window of his own car.

His face looked haggard and old, just like the face he'd confronted in the elevator. The remaining hair on his head was slightly askew, no doubt from the breeze that blew through the open windows of his car that morning. His arm was outstretched in the direction of the crossing guard as if he were tipping her a wave. Had he waved? He couldn't remember.

The view from the security camera then panned along the length of his arm to the end of his hand, which the version of Nick in this image held erect at the wrist, his palm facing him. His middle finger was extended, flipping the bird in the obvious direction of the crossing guard.

There was that sick sound of the click on the keyboard again, and the image froze.

"It's amazing," he heard Mark's voice say from somewhere outside of reality. "It's truly amazing what you can do these days, with all this technology and a little creativity." He chuckled. The last breath of it came out in a snort. "And the killer bit of it is, everything you see in this video actually happened this morning. Every last detail."

"That's your face, Nick. And your bird finger."

On his hip, Nick's iPhone began to chime. He smacked it quiet and felt a twinge in his knee as he did so. His thigh and calf muscles were locked up tight. His eyes stung, and his nose began to run. He wiped at the mucus with the back of his right hand.

"You," he said through clenched teeth, glaring at Mark. "I made you. The only reason you have this job is because of me." He waved his hand over the room. The snot on his index finger gleamed in the ambient luminescence of the projected image. "I made all of you. Watchtower. None of this would exist without me. I made you ALL! YOU! CAN'T! DO! THIS!"

His voice boomed against the stony silence of the coworkers that had gathered around the conference table. To Nick, they looked more like crows than ever, their faces leered over their necks, waiting with perfect patience for his body to land on the table before them so they could feast on it. He recognized that uniform expression on the faces of his staff. It was the same one he'd taught each and every one of them immediately upon hire. When you're faced with a reckless, emotional enemy, you calmly stare them down until they either hit you or sulk away stewing in their own humiliation. Either way, it was a win in the eyes of the audience.

Another wave of panic washed over him. He wanted to throw something at them, at Mark. He wanted to fire them all, although he knew that, by now, the network would simply fire him and rehire them if he did. He wanted to scream at them to pull the plug, to make the public unsee what they undoubtedly had already all seen before he had walked into this alternate reality version of his conference room. Most of all, he wanted to bury his forehead in the palm of his hand. He wanted to scream "I'm ruined!" at the top of his voice, to verbalize in that trademark fashion what his gut was telling him: that his life was over, that he should simply hightail it through the conference room window and hope for his death, that he had been hoisted by his own petard, and that hell was not something he would experience after death, but the facts of his own past returning to take revenge for all the lives he'd destroyed, all those people he had humiliated and hung out to dry.

His iPhone cawed at him again. Nick snatched it from the holster that held it fast to his hip and held it over his head, meaning to hurl it at the wall, at Mark, somewhere.

"That'll be the brass, I presume," Mark said with mock solemnity. "I'm sure they want a word or two."

Nick stared at him.

This was it, then: Mark's coup. This was his protégé's attempt to keep his head above water while the empire Nick had built through the hilarity and popularity of public shaming floundered. It was Nick's worst fear and self-fulfilled prophecy. He closed his eyes and sucked in his breath, holding it for a moment. He no longer felt like throwing the iPhone. In fact, he suddenly felt almost *good*, or at least better than he had in a long time.

Nick returned the iPhone to its holster without bothering to check the caller ID.

"Yes," he replied quietly. "Yes, I'm sure they do, Mark." Then he brightened. "You can go have that word with them for me if you want to. Under the circumstances, I think I should take the rest of the day off.

But I did want to point out one little thing to you before I go. To all of you, really."

On his left, Monica shifted uncomfortably in her seat. On his right, Jeff's moonstruck gaze returned to the interior of his coffee mug. Mark simply looked amused.

"What you've created here today really is cannibalism," Nick said, "to use your words, Mark. You've tried to save yourselves by eating one of your own. Okay, sure, the rest of the press is going to have a field day with this for a while. And so will everybody whose ever wished that that 'smug bastard Nick Saint would get his comeuppance.' I'll be memeified and demonized. I'll probably never get work in this business again.

"But you know what, Mark? Mon? Jeff? It's never going to be enough. Not for the viewers. You can't save yourselves forever by chopping me into crow food today. Who will be next?" He looked at Mark. "You?" Monica. "You?" Jeff. "You, Jeff?

"At some point, each and every one of you is going to be devoured by this. Each and every one of you is going to be ruined."

He caught Mark's eye and smiled. His protégé's jaw was set, but for the first time that meeting, there was an unmistakable flagging of confidence in his eyes.

"Heed my words, Mark," he said. "You're next."

***

Less than a minute later, the elevator doors closed in front of him, shutting him off from Watchtower and reflecting his own face back at him as they had on his way up. He didn't even bother to arrange to retrieve his things.

He felt the rising sensation in his belly as the lift began its descent to the ground floor. The man in the reflection in front of him still looked haggard and old, but the exhaustion, fear, and paranoia that he'd seen in his own eyes earlier didn't seem to be there anymore. For the first time in longer than he could remember, his vision was clear.

There would be the rest of the media to face today, more vulture than crow in his opinion. Terrorism, war, natural disasters, elections: they would all take a backseat to the latest high and mighty man's undoing. Nick was also sure he'd be getting a termination phone call or email or something. Then there'd be the pundits, all the talking heads who had to get a word in edgewise. Of course, he'd have a thousand lawyers lining up to help him bring a case against Watchtower and the network when he gave the press his speech about how he was set up, a speech he and Mark had successfully defended Watchtower against a million times before.

Then there would be the whispering, the chronic public perception of him as Nick Saint, judge turned pariah, the man who flipped off the crossing guard for doing her job of protecting the lives of innocent children. Even if he became the first man to win a case against Watchtower, that perception would live on. The truth is only so powerful against the tide of public opinion and the hot crushing judgment of the media and the Internet.

Even so, Nick was surprised to find himself feeling lighter, feeling good for the first time in a long time. Whatever the outcome, Watchtower was behind him now. So was being the constant angst-ridden monitor of his own behavior.

His deepest, darkest fear—the thing that kept him up nights and always on his toes—had finally emerged into the light of day.

Now that he looked at it, he thought he recognized it. It was his humanity. His imperfection. His willingness to forgive himself.

The elevator dinged, signaling his arrival on the ground floor. Before the doors opened to his new world, Nick Saint pistol-cocked his right hand at his own reflection and winked at the half-cocked grin on his own face.

"I'm ruined!" he said.

Nobody Was Here

He'd never had to pee so bad in his life.

The *whoosh-bang* of the heavy steel door when it struck the tile-covered back wall of the men's room exploded like a shotgun report in his ears. He'd shoved it hard. In its wake came wafts of urine, feces, and a mixture of various types of room deodorizers. Something else hung there, too: a sweeter chemical smell that left a foul taste in the back of his throat. Mold and mildew remover?

He decided that he didn't care.

He grabbed at the front of his pants and had one panicked moment when he couldn't find the zipper's slider. Then the familiar little metal rectangle fell between the thumb and index finger of his right hand. He held his breath and yanked on it, snatching his zipper down with too much force. It made a smallish *rrrrip* sound when he hit bottom. Most likely he'd torn a stitch in the crotch of his threadbare Dockers.

He decided that he didn't care about that, either.

A second later, he completed the launch sequence, narrowly avoiding a drizzle down his own leg. Eight ounces of coffee and sixteen ounces of bottled water ripped out of him like a water jet from the end of a fire hose. He wanted to scream (and nearly did) but the pain of the explosive exit had already subsided by the time the first drops hit the porcelain back of the urinal.

The sound of his waterfall reverberated throughout the restroom. It filled his ears, drowning the mellow and tinkling strains of Robert Plant's "Ship of Fools," which happened to be playing at an equally mellow volume through the little circle-shaped speakers that were embedded in the ceiling throughout the fast food restaurant that called itself Big Burger.

Reed leaned his head backward, resting the back of his skull at the tips of his shoulder blades. He shivered. He sucked a long drag of the restroom air into his lungs and then let it out in a series of three abrupt coughs, choking again on that strangely sweet chemical aroma. Then he opened his eyes and glared at the ceiling.

Damn them, he thought. *Damn them and their damn bellies.*

He had wanted to stop an hour previous when the pressure on his bladder had been urgent but tolerable. *They*—his lovely wife Rita and her spoiled brat Chase—had put up a fight about it. "I'm huuuuungryyyyyyy," the kid had squalled mercilessly from among the trash pile of candy bar wrappers and soda cans he had assembled around himself in the backseat. It was a pile that, Reed admitted to himself, was mostly because of his own bad influence over the boy. But only because Rita insisted on taking these long, cross-country car hauls to the Gulf every year instead of buying a plane ticket.

"I want to eeeeat," Chase squealed. Meanwhile, Reed's sweet understanding spouse bored holes in his skull from her place in the Trailblazer's shotgun seat. She had sensed their drift toward the upcoming exit ramp.

Don't you dare stop here when our baby needs food, her eyes chastised him. *I will not allow him to eat out of a vending machine again.*

"I have to pee, dear," Reed explained. Did he sound defensive? Maybe, and that bothered him. What man never has to pee? He struggled to not sound irritated as well. "Really bad."

Rita craned her neck so that she could see Chase, who sat directly behind the driver's seat. "Daddy needs to go to the bathroom, sweetie," she said in that same sugary baby talk voice she'd used since the lad was born, the one that Reed had asked her to stop using a million times.

He's nine for God's sake! He's not a baby!

"After daddy uses the bathroom we can go find a nice restaurant somewhere," she continued. "You don't need another candy bar."

In Reed's rear view mirror, Chase's lips contracted into a tight little bow. His eyes narrowed. His nose twisted to the right in that all-too-familiar wind-up to another ear-splitting tantrum. "I want to eeeeat NOWWW-WWW," he wailed.

Reed clenched his teeth. His eyes felt like they were bulging out of his head. Rita plugged an index finger into each of her ears and regarded Reed from angry, lidded eyes. Reed gripped the Trailblazer's steering wheel hard enough to create deep stitch prints in the palms of his hands.

"All right!" he shouted. "All right! All right! I'll hold it! We'll find a restaurant! Just shut up already!"

Silence fell upon them. Reed's face felt hot. A prickly sensation crawled down the back of his neck, and he shivered a little in spite of his boiling blood.

He glanced at Rita, who gaped back at him with her arms knitted tightly beneath her breasts, her eyes wide and hurt. He felt a spark of shame struggling to ignite within his heart and squashed it. She rarely smiled at him anymore anyway. Why should he feel ashamed? Just because she thinks he should?

Behind him, he could hear Chase sniffling but could no longer see him in the rearview mirror, which meant that the boy had ducked his head in that sulking way a child does when a scolding parent finally snaps and says something traumatizing or otherwise life-altering. For that, he supposed he *should* choose to allow that guilty spark to kindle and burn him a little. But he didn't.

An hour later, the Big Burger emblem on one of those blue Interstate signs floated into his vision. His need to go immediately became a thousand times more urgent. He veered onto the exit ramp.

Rita, who had been riding with her arms folded, her eyes closed, and her chin resting against her clavicle, suddenly snapped awake. A second blue sign with a second Big Burger icon, this one paired with a thick white arrow that pointed to the left, sped by them. From his peripheral vision, Reed could see Rita glaring at him, her nose twitching.

"Big Burger?" she snapped. "Really?"

He silently vowed not to shout at her. "Honey, I *really* have to go. This is the best we can do." He glanced at her and managed a wry smile. "Hey, at least it's not Snickers joint. Right?"

Rita did not appear to get the joke.

She folded her arms on her abdomen and shook her head in that annoying, patronizing way she had. It was a shaming gesture that Chase had learned to imitate at an early age. There you go, folks. There was the main reason the boy had no respect for him: his mother didn't.

"Right," he answered himself. It came out as a hoarse grunt.

He'd swung the Trailblazer into a handicapped parking space and leaped out, barely managing to snatch the key from the ignition before his feet hit the pavement. He had not bothered to wait for Rita, whom he could barely hear above the sound of his own running feet as she attempted to wake Chase from another sugar-induced stupor.

Damn them, he thought again. *Damn them and their bellies.*

The remaining few drops of his morning beverages splashed with a *poit* sound into the yellow tinted water pooled at the bottom of the urinal. Reed sighed. He waited a few more seconds, squeezing and then relaxing his bladder to ensure that every drop was gone. Blessed relief washed over him.

For an instant after, the warm and sensual aroma of Big Burger fries penetrated and overpowered the reek of the men's room. His stomach rumbled in response, reminding him that he hadn't eaten anything since breakfast. This was as good a time as any for a lunch break, he supposed, especially since Chase was going to eat. Then again, a nice big glob of a BB lunch would require an equally hulking portion of carbonated water and flavoring to wash it down. And that would naturally lead to another intense need to release somewhere down the line, probably at a time that was least convenient for Her Majesty and most whine-inducing for His Highness.

"Maybe I'll skip it, then," he mumbled to the restroom wall. "Rather be hungry than have to deal with that."

From elsewhere in the restroom came a low, drawn-out reply.

"Deal with what, dude?"

Reed started. The sudden movement managed to shake out one more drop of urine before he closed everything up and reached for his fly's slider, which was now buried in the folds of fabric at the very bottom of the crotch of his Dockers. He worked the slider out of the fabric and gave it a quick tug.

The zipper would not budge.

"Shit!"

A burst of laughter sounded from behind the chocolate brown wall of the men's room's single stall, which stood just to the right of Reed's urinal. Suddenly the salted fries aroma was again replaced by the stench of bleach and urinal cakes. Reed gagged and placed a steadying hand against the exterior stall wall. He gave up attempting to zip his fly (*whatever, it's not like anybody's going to notice a balding, pudgy forty-something on a grueling family road trip and say 'hmm, I think I'll check out his package'*) and used his free hand to flush the urinal.

"Whoooosh!" the voice in the stall echoed playfully.

Reed squared his shoulders. He swallowed against his urge to retch and summoned his authoritative voice, the one that used to work on Chase before Rita had managed to strip away any sense of instinctual respect the boy might have had for his father.

"Who's there?"

No answer.

"I said, 'who's there?'"

Laughter again, then: "Nobody, dude. Nooobodyyyy." The last syllable came out in a snake-like hiss. It didn't bounce off the restroom tile so much as it crawled, like the rotten black fingers of a reanimated corpse clawing its way out of chilly October earth. It slithered into Reed's ear, all the way down the canal, and stabbed at his limbic system with bony ragged fingernails.

Next came the thick *clunk* of the stall door's lock bolt sliding out of its keeper, followed closely by the creak and groan of door hinges in sore need of a good dousing of WD-40. Finally, a series of *slaps* beat a leisurely measure against the restroom's ceramic tile floor. It was the sound of a man walking in cowboy boots, perhaps. Or maybe a pair of wingtips.

The footsteps came to a halt some distance behind him. The last mellow strains of "Ship of Fools" from the speakers in the ceiling faded away and were replaced by the grating, obnoxious sound of sinusy shallow breathing.

Damn his fly, his hunger, his newly emptied bladder, and the accusatory sign on the wall reminding him to use good hygiene and thoroughly wash his hands. Suddenly all Reed Reese wanted to do was run.

He spun around, the soles of his Rockports squeaking in protest against the tile. The door. Reed leaned forward and reached for the handle, but had to jerk his hand backward at the last moment, when the tall, tensile figure of a man blithely stepped between him and freedom.

Over his head, Johnny Cash strummed the first few chords of "I See a Darkness."

"Dude."

The first things Reed noticed were his boots. They were not the shin-high brown leather cowboy boots with the Country & Western stitching pattern he had envisioned when he'd heard them clopping along the tile floor behind him. They were shorter, black leather, with no decoration other than a small metal ring adorning each ankle, effeminate biker boots with a rounded toe.

Then there were the arms protruding from the sleeves of his army green T-shirt. Hairless and vascular, the veins beneath his stark white flesh stood out like coils of hose beneath a light dusting of new fallen snow. The skin along the length of them was splotched here and there with angry red spots. Some of them looked scabbed over, old and dark. Others were a brighter, pinkish shade. The lighter types had a sheen to them that made them look like fresh burns. It was as if the cat had spent his entire morning in that bathroom stall, stabbing himself with the lit end of a Marlboro.

His blue roadmap of a neck and gaunt face were covered with similar sores. The one at the left corner of his lips oozed thick yellow pus mixed with some kind of blackness that might have been specks of coagulated blood. The fluid seeped down the edge of his lower lip, splitting into smaller branches amid the prickly ghost of gold colored stubble on his chin.

He regarded Reed from lidded, nearly invisible eyes. The right one sagged wearily on his face. A crop of greasy gold hair similar in color to the stubble on his chin languished askew atop his head, the sides of which he had shaven bald. There was a reddish-black quarter-sized open sore on his right temple. He raised a single bony finger to the wound and rubbed it in a slow circular motion.

"Dude," he repeated. "You a cop?"

Reed gaped at him, searching his mind for a response. Yes? Would that get him out of here? Or would it get him shot, or stabbed with a needle or a switchblade? And what was the alternative? No? Would that get him mugged? Raped? Killed outright?

In the end, he chose to leave his answer vague. "Look, buddy." *Why did I just call him* buddy? "I just want to wash my hands and leave."

"Buddy" continued to stare at him from the slits of his eyelids. Then he slowly nodded his comprehension, as if he'd received the message on a satellite delay. The final nod left his chin hanging low on his neck so that the slits of his eyes aimed more at Reed's middle-aged pudge than his face, which made Reed suddenly, acutely aware that his fly was still down.

"Yeah, yeah," Buddy finally managed. "Wash your hands. Okay, man." Then he held up one finger and tilted his head backward again as if a grand idea had just occurred to him. "Hey, you...*uh?* You... *uh?*" On the *uhs*, he made a swiping motion across his lips with the index finger he'd been using to pick at the sore on his temple. He puckered his mouth a little as he did so, an imitation of Marilyn Monroe applying lipstick. "Huh? You... *uh?*"

It wasn't clear to Reed what the guy was asking him. He thought he might be asking for drugs, in which case he would have no hesitation about providing his answer: "No." He supposed there were other things the lip-swiping motion could have meant, but he chose not to think about them.

"No, buddy." *Dammit.* "I don't do that. Just let me by, okay? My family's waiting on me."

Buddy didn't move.

Reed grew incensed.

"Excuse me!" he growled, and then lunged for the door handle, yanking hard on it. The heavy restroom door swung open an inch, perhaps, before Buddy shoved both of his bony pocked hands against it. The handle slipped from Reed's grasp. He heard the *whuff* of the last breeze of exterior air being shut out of the restroom as the door swung into place.

Buddy immediately positioned himself between Reed and the handle.

"What the?" Reed shouted. "Get out of my way!" The tremor in his voice echoed back to him from the restroom walls. He hated that. The last thing he wanted this bastard to sense in him was fear.

Buddy's eyes were wide open now. He spread his arms at his sides, his palms facing Reed, and cocked his head to the right. His lips parted in a wide, menacing smile that strained the taut skin of his face against his skull. There were four teeth completely missing from the front of his upper row. The others were worn to pointy ragged nubs. His lower teeth were in no better shape. One of them, a premolar, appeared to be little more than a prop for a silver amalgam filling long devoid of its purpose. His gums were shriveled pink and white masses.

"Come on, dude," he said. "Look at me. I'm a handsome guy, ain't I?" He grinned again. Reed caught a whiff of that sweet chemical odor he'd choked on before. It was apparently wafting off the man's breath.

As if to offer proof of his manly good looks, Buddy undid the button of his jeans and slid his fly down.

"You got a faaaamilyyyyy," he hissed. "Faaaamilyyyyy, yeah. You gotta feed that faaaamilyyyyy. I know how you can make some money to feed your faaaamilyyyyy."

Realization dawned on Reed, and his adrenal glands suddenly stomped on the accelerator. His heart raced inside his chest.

I'm not going to call him "buddy."

He straightened his back, set his jaw, and swallowed.

"Look... Nobody," he said through clenched teeth. "*Dude.* I don't care if you're into that sort of thing." He waved a finger at the man's unbuttoned jeans. "Really. It's your business, between you and whoever.

"Me? I have a wife. I have a kid. And I have no intention of touching any part of your nasty drug rotted body with anything more than the front grille of my SUV at 90 miles an hour.

"Now," he continued, "there's only one thing I want, and that's for you to step out of my way. If you do it quick enough, I'll leave without bothering to notify the manager of this establishment as to your *adventures* here in the facilities.

"Stand in my way, and I'll not only knock you on your ass, but I'll have the cops here so fast that you won't even have time to zip up before they slap the cuffs on."

The addict only grinned at him and shook his head. He shook his head in that same annoying and patronizing way that Rita did whenever she knew she had Reed over a barrel.

It was all Reed could stand.

He launched himself at Nobody, plowing palms first into the man's wasted chest. He felt the ribs and flesh under the army green T-shirt give against his hands. Nobody reeled backward and landed on his butt beneath the electric hand dryer. He managed to work himself into a crawling position before Reed struck again. He kicked at Nobody, his right foot connecting directly with the man's blackened chin. Nobody went sliding again down the bathroom wall. Reed, unable to stop the forward momentum of his own right leg, also went flying. He landed flat on his back in front of the bathroom door. His head struck the floor with a wet *smack*.

Hot pain exploded in the back of his skull. The world threatened to go dark. He squeezed his eyes shut and then opened them again, clearing his vision just in time for a fresh burst of stabbing pain in his right ankle.

Reed cried out in surprise. He sat bolt upright and clawed blindly at his screaming ankle, snagging a double fistful of Nobody's slimy hair instead. The monster had sunk what remained of his ragged teeth deep into Reed's flesh. He tore at the lower limb the way a wild dog thrashes a recently slaughtered squirrel or rabbit between its jaws.

Reed wound the fingers of both hands into the strands of Nobody's hair, tightening his grip. Each thrash of his attacker's head threatened to tear his fingers loose, but he managed to hang on long enough to rock backward and slam the sole of his Rockport into the bridge of Nobody's paper thin beak. He heard a satisfying crunch sound as the man's nose collapsed in on itself. A bright red mist of blood sprayed from the wound. Reed let loose of Nobody's hair and wiped the palms of his hands against his own Dockers, his own nose turned up in disgust. Nobody scurried backward to his former position against the bathroom wall, howling in pain. His hands went to his injured nose and covered his mouth, muffling his nasally wailing.

Reed grabbed the bathroom door's handle and hoisted himself to his feet. He leaned there hurt and exhausted, his right cheek pressed firmly against the cool steel of the door. Seconds later Johnny Cash strummed the last chord of "I See a Darkness," leaving only the grating sound of Nobody's caterwauling.

"Shut up," Reed said. Annoyance. Fatigue. But no tremor in his voice now. "I said, 'Shut up.'"

Nobody glared at him over bloodstained fingertips. There was pain in his sickly eyes. And anger. And hate. He cupped his hands around his mouth and let loose a gurgling and defiant scream.

Reed plugged his ears until Nobody ran out of breath. Over head, the voice of Meat Loaf suddenly began to wail that he'd do anything for love, but he won't do that. Reed glanced up at the speakers in the ceiling and laughed hysterically. *Meat Loaf*, he thought. *Perfect.*

On the floor, Nobody sucked in a fresh supply of air and opened his mouth to scream once more. Reed bolted forward, ignoring the pain in his right ankle. He hauled Nobody to his feet by his hair and launched him head-first through the door of the stall. The door, the front of which was painted with the words JOHNNY WAS HERE in thick black permanent marker, slammed open against the interior wall, its hinges groaning only the slightest protest. Nobody banged his shins against the bowl of the toilet and bashed his mouth on the stainless steel top of the flushing mechanism. A bloody oblong rock of silver amalgam dropped out of his mouth, plinking to the floor beside the toilet bowl.

Good, Reed thought. He preferred to see Nobody's teeth lying on the floor rather than embedded in his right ankle.

Nobody landed face down over the toilet. He propped his forehead against his right forearm and coughed. The sound echoed dully against the well of the bowl. Something (more dental work?) splashed into the water below him.

Reed grabbed Nobody's left shoulder and spun the addict around on his hips. He sat compliantly on the stall floor, his legs splayed out and his back against the toilet bowl. The anger and hatred in his eyes had been replaced by fear. Trickles of blood ran from both his nostrils. When he opened his mouth to speak, more blood spilled down his lower lip and onto his chin.

"Please," he said. "Kid. I have a kid. Outside. In car." A lone tear crept out of the corner of his left eye and ran down his cheek. "Please. Leave me alone."

Reed grinned at the man sprawled on the floor of the stall. He grinned and slowly shook his head. "I won't do that," he said at the same time that Meat Loaf belted the phrase through the overhead speakers.

Nobody's eyes widened. He opened his mouth to scream. Reed knelt down between the man's legs and grabbed his throat with his left hand. He squeezed hard, the muscles in his arm thrumming with the effort.

"I told you to shut up!" he screamed in Nobody's face.

He snatched a wad of toilet paper off the roll that hung on the stall wall to his right and balled it up his fist. "You types," he said, shoving the wad into Nobody's open mouth. "All you do is want, isn't it? You want, and you want, and you want."

He followed the first wad of toilet paper with a second.

"You're selfish, that's what you are. You're selfish and lazy. You think the world owes you a high. You think the world owes you an escape from all the hard work and all the *shit* the rest of us have to deal with every day. You think the rest of us should just put our own lives on hold so we can dump our money into your pockets to support your little fantasy world.

"Isn't that right?"

Nobody's eyes rolled back in his head. His chest heaved under his T-shirt. His arms flailed against Reed's ribs, but Reed was only distantly aware of it.

"And then," Reed continued, "when we have to take a break and take care of our own needs, you get upset don't you?"

He balled up a third wad of toilet paper and shoved it inside.

"You get *so* upset that our own lives have to come first, that we can't spend every second of our day finding ways to feed you and clothe you, and pity you, and feel guilty about you, and find some damn way to *help* you.

"Well, you know what?" he shouted. "You know *what*?"

He reached behind Nobody's battered head and grabbed a dripping black turd from the toilet. He held it high above the shaking man. Nobody, eyes shining and full of awareness for perhaps the first time, stared at it in stark terror. Droplets of water shook loose from the downward tip of it and dripped onto his forehead.

"I'll tell you what!" Reed screamed. "SOMETIMES A MAN JUST NEEDS TO TAKE A PISS!"

He thrust the turd downward, shoving it into Nobody's mouth. He crammed more wads of toilet paper in after it until nothing more would fit.

Nobody struggled weakly, beating at Reed's ribs and at the sides of his face without any real force. Reed grabbed the top of the man's head with one hand and his lower jaw with the other, forcing his waste-filled mouth closed. The man's wasted nostrils flared once. Twice. And were still. Seconds later, his stricken eyes glazed over and his gaunt face went slack. His arms fell to his sides against the stall floor, and he slumped forward, dead.

Reed released his grip on the corpse's head. He crouched on his haunches in the stall, his mouth open and his eyes wide and staring.

Dead.

Nobody was here.

Nobody was dead.

Panic wrapped its icy arms around Reed's chest and squeezed, making it difficult to breathe. The air he did manage to inhale was stale and stinking, not conducive to rational thought. He shuddered and backed crab-like out of the stall, allowing the door to close, censoring the image of the dead body before him so that all he could see were the dingy soles of the man's biker boots and the whitish blue of his jeans.

"Oh, God," he whispered. "Oh, God." His hands went to his nose and mouth as if to capture the words. He smelled the stink of the shit there and gagged, thrusting the hand away from his face. He grabbed the rim of the sink with his cleaner hand and used it to pull himself to his feet.

He pumped the wall-hung soap dispenser over the sink three times, capturing a half-dollar-sized glob of burnt orange antibacterial soap in his palm. Once he'd worked it into a lather, he smeared the mixture all over his hands and up each arm to the elbow. He rinsed both arms and then pried his right Rockport off its foot with the toes of the left one. He repeated the cleansing ritual on his right ankle, rubbing the lather vigorously into the seeping open wounds that Nobody's teeth had created there. He found that he enjoyed its stinging burn.

Next, he examined himself in the mirror. His clothes were wrinkled, but otherwise free of stain. What little hair remained on his balding head was only slightly disheveled. However, he thought that his eyes looked too wide, too haunted. He experimented with his facial expressions, feeling them so he'd know exactly what Rita and Chase saw on him when he emerged from the restroom.

When he was satisfied, he chanced a glance at the reflection of the men's room behind him. He felt a stab of guilt at the hint of Nobody's boots he could see at the bottom of the stall. It was a prickly, stinging feeling along the back of his neck. He swatted at it without thinking and then realized that it was a sensation he was probably going to have to live with for a good long while.

As if to underscore his guilt, Nobody's corpse suddenly slid off its prop against the toilet, thrusting the heels of his biker boots just beyond the perimeter of the stall.

Reed sighed. He left his reflection in the mirror and pushed open the stall door. Nobody's eyes were open, and his left cheek had been pushed upward against the toilet bowl, creating a grinning effect, death's imitation of the rotting, mocking smile he'd sported in life. Only instead of ragged stinking teeth and shriveled up gums, the mouth behind that grin was stuffed with shit and bloody wet wads of toilet paper.

Hatred welled up inside Reed, but he managed to suppress the urge to kick the grin off the corpse's face. Instead, he knelt down between Nobody's splayed legs and wrapped his arms around his waist. After two preparatory huffs of stale bathroom floor air, he heaved the dead man off the floor by his hips and flipped him prone, so that his face hovered directly center of the toilet seat.

Next, Reed positioned Nobody's pale, sore-covered arms on either side of his dangling head. He bent the right arm at the elbow so that it formed a right angle across the toilet seat. He formed the right hand so that it looked as if it were gripping the left wrist. Finally, he propped the corpse's forehead on its right forearm.

Reed then made a fist with his left hand and planted it thumb-side directly under Nobody's navel. He covered the pinky side of the fist with his other hand so that his arms were wrapped around the dead body and his chest was pressed snugly against its back. He allowed himself a count of three and then pressed hard into Nobody's abdomen. He heard three objects splash into the toilet bowl. He heaved again at another three count and heard what sounded like one large object *thunk* into the toilet water. It was followed immediately by several smaller splashes. One more heave and Nobody uttered an eerily lifelike groan. *Trapped air*, Reed reasoned, but could not prevent a shudder.

Finally, Reed stood, admiring his own craftiness. Although peculiar, seeing a man kneeling in front of the toilet wouldn't be nearly as suspicious as a man unconscious (*dead*) and leaning against one.

He was about to leave the stall when a glint of silver on the floor caught his eye. Nobody's filling. Reed bent and plucked it, dropping the silver amalgam into the left pocket of his Dockers. Then he slid the latch on the back of the stall door into place, locking it. *Nobody here but me and you, Nobody*, he thought.

Mindful of his handiwork, he crouched down in the stall space between the soles of Nobody's biker boots and the shut door. From the crouch he went plank-like to the floor, his arms stretched out one side of the chocolate stall and his legs out the other. Then he slithered out from under the stall wall and stood again in the wider area of the restroom, Nobody's empty shell now securely locked away behind him.

After a final look around, Reed, at last, wrapped the fingers of his right hand around the handle of the men's room door, swung it open, and stepped outside. The door *whuffed* shut behind him. The breeze of the concussion felt good against the back of his neck.

The restaurant appeared to be empty.

The kitchen was noiseless, no clattering of pots and pans or scraping of spatulas on char-broilers. The dining room was equally silent. The only sound was the final phrase of Meat Loaf's "I'd Do Anything for Love (But I Won't Do That)."

"Hello?" he called. "Anyone here?"

There was no response, so he walked outside.

A crowd had gathered around a rusty light blue sedan that was parked in the far corner of the parking lot. A man in a business suit was wedging an undone coat hanger between the car's frame and the rear driver's side window. A man on the other side of the car barked orders at him: "Left," he said. "No, the other left. That's it. Now down." The others watched from a slight distance around them. Some of them looked worried. The ones smoking cigarettes looked bored.

Reed scanned the onlookers for signs of Rita and Chase and locked onto them at the farthest edge of the crowd. Chase's arms were wrapped around his mother's waist, his face buried in her abdomen. Reed strolled up to them and put a hand on his wife's shoulder.

"What's going on?" he asked.

"Oh." She looked surprised to see him. "There's a poor child trapped in that car, Reed," she said, shaking her head. "A little one. Somebody ran inside looking for her parents shortly after you went to the bathroom." She eyed him. "What were you doing in there so long, anyway? Taking a shower?"

Reed felt in his pocket for the silver amalgam. He cupped it in the palm of his left hand and nonchalantly tossed it into the pea gravel landscaping beside him. It made a barely perceptible *plink* when it hit.

"Kidney stone," he said. "Felt like hell. Ok, you guys ready to get back on the road?"

Rita looked alarmed. "There's a child locked in a car! Don't you think we should do something to help her?"

Reed pretended to examine the situation.

"I don't see anything we can do, hon," he said. "Looks like those two gentlemen have it well in hand. And we don't know the baby, so what good would we be in tracking down her daddy?"

"What makes you think it's her father who left her here?"

"I don't know," Reed said. "Looks like a deadbeat's ride. Let's go. I should probably go see a urologist or something."

Rita shuddered. "Whatever you say," she said. Then to Chase: "Come on, sweetie, let's get in the car."

Chase shot his father an accusatory look. "But I'm huuuun-gryyyyyy," he wailed. "I'm staaaaarviiiiiing. I didn't get anything to eeeeaaaat."

Reed knelt in front of his son. "Chase. Son, your mother was right about the way I've been letting you eat. From now on I'm not letting you put anymore, uh, *crap* in your mouth."

"But..."

"No," Reed interrupted. "Get in the car."

Chase stomped to the driver's side of the Trailblazer, opened the rear door, and climbed in. He sat there with his arms folded across his chest, a long pout on his lips.

Rita looked confused. "What brought that on?"

"You were right is all. The boy's getting a little chubby and a lot more demanding about what he wants to cram down his throat. It's time I put my foot down."

Rita smiled at him. It was the first time in years. "Really. What other revelations did you have while you were in the bathroom?"

"Just that one," he replied, "for now." He grinned back at her, remembering how he'd practiced it in the restroom mirror, hoping it didn't look forced or insane. "Your chariot awaits."

They climbed inside. Reed started the engine and slowly backed out of the handicapped parking space.

The trio had just entered the northern on-ramp toward the Interstate when two police cruisers, sirens wailing, sped by them in the opposite direction.

"They're probably responding to the locked car," Reed said, then realized he'd said it aloud.

Rita looked at him earnestly. "Reed, something's bothering me," she said. "Why didn't somebody just break the window of the car?"

It hadn't occurred to him. Probably hadn't occurred to her, either. Until now.

"They didn't want to get sued," he replied.

Rita nodded, eyes drifting back to the road in front of them. "The manager at that Big Burger was having a devil of a time figuring out who owned that car," she added. "No one would own up to it." She glanced at him again. "Was there anyone in the bathroom with you?"

Reed's grip on the steering wheel tightened.

"Nobody," he said. "Nobody was in the bathroom with me."

Diggum

My Christian name's not Diggum, but that's what most folks around here call me. Doubt anybody remembers the man I used to be. You ask 'em who that old stooped over fella is mopin' around the cemetery, that's what they'll tell you. "That's Diggum," they'll say. "He's the caretaker." Most of 'em don't know much more than that. Not anymore. Not in these hurry up and rush around days.

Hell, it's a wonder anybody ever notices me at all anymore. If they're not flying by me at ninety miles an hour on the highway, then they have their faces buried in those glowin' little smarty pants phones they all carry around now. Heh. If they happen to be drivin' while they're lookin' at them things—well, I reckon I'll be the one buryin' their faces before too long.

I'd be buryin' their faces if there was room left in this old boneyard to do that, anyway. See, this is an old cemetery, and there ain't but one plot in it without a marker now. That one's mine. I claimed it back when I first got this gig in, oh, I guess it's been about forty years. There was a whole lot more community around here and a whole lot fewer wrinkles on this old face back in them days. Sure enough.

There was work when a man needed it back then, too. And boy did I need it. It wasn't then like it is now, where everybody's gotta have a job with some adventure or upward mobility or lifestyle accommodation in it, or however the young-uns are puttin' it these days. It ain't enough anymore for 'em to just find a way to make ends meet. They gotta be excited by what they're doin'. What is that word they use, anyway? *Fulfillin'*. That's it. It's gotta be fulfillin' work. Back in my day, you just wanted to find some way to keep food on your table and put clothes on your back, shoes on your feet. Well, that's the way it was down here in the little town of Lost Hollow anyway. I guess up in bigger cities they cared about upward mobility. It was the Reagan era, after all. Around here it was mostly all small farmers and people who commuted to their factory jobs one town over.

Ends meetin' is exactly what I was lookin' for when I strolled into this little town back then. Sure enough. Lost my wife, my kid, and everything I had in a fire on this little farm I had just west of here. Didn't have no fancy insurance on any of that. Wasn't no going back there and rebuildin' either, not there. Not where my wife and kid had burned themselves to death while I was out plowin' the field. Fat lot of good it did me, plowin' that field. I was just doin' what my daddy taught me to do. Was his farm before it was mine. But by 1984 that didn't matter too much. Everybody was gettin' their produce from the grocery stores who got their stuff from the big industrial farms. Nobody gave a shit about their locally grown stuff anymore.

Took some doing, but I eventually sold the whole lot back to the bank. Sure enough. I reckon they were able to turn it around eventually. Probably turned it into a strip mall or somethin' by now. Meantime, I just tied up my bindle and took off down the road. Turns out the first help wanted sign I saw was this county job diggin' graves in this cemetery. I reckoned back then that somebody somewhere's always gonna need to be buried, and I still had all the calluses on my hands and grit under my fingernails that was proof enough that I knew my way around the dirt. So I applied right then and there. They pretty much hired me then and there, too. Sure enough. I been diggin' holes and fillin' 'em in ever since.

Now you might think a man would get creeped out by takin' on a job like this. Not me, though. I seen my wife and my boy both lyin' there in the ashes of that old house, charred black and flakin' apart like the newspaper my daddy used to use to start the kindlin' burnin' in the old fireplace. I seen all that, and I think I cried my last tears right then and there. They was both too burned up to even put 'em in a casket. Practically cremated, they was. Sure enough. You know what the old timers always said about that, right? If there ain't no body in the ground, it can't be raised up again come Judgment time. Neither one of 'em deserved that fate. Sweetest mother and son you'd ever meet. But if the old timers are right, I reckon both of 'em are lost forever. Haven't wept for a soul since them days. Never since, because if a God whose best two creatures got turned to ashes by a stupid accident can't see fit to bring 'em back around when the roll is called up yonder, why should I bother to give a damn about anybody at all?

I can see it in your face. You think I resent what God did to me. Yeah, you damn right I do. Damn right. He's got no business takin' those two darlins out of this world and not lettin' 'em into the next one. God's plan, the old preacher man'll tell you. God's meanness is what I think.

So I decided right then and there that as long as I had some strength in my hands and some will to live, I wasn't gonna let God get away with it, at least not without me gettin' away with a few things my own self.

This caretaker gig comes with its own little cottage at the edge of the cemetery, did I mention that already? Ain't nothin' fancy. No mortuary or crematorium. All that stuff's back in the city. No, this place is just for buryin' folks and keepin' the man who does it. Folks around these parts, they're superstitious that way. Just like they'll walk in and out of a cemetery all day long as long as old Mr. Sun is shining, they'll allow the old cemetery caretaker to shop and live among 'em for his necessities. And just like how they won't go near a cemetery at night for fear of their own lives, they don't want the old caretaker anywhere around 'em after Mr. Sun yawns his big old evenin' yawn and pulls the sheets over his head for a good night's sleep. So they give me this little house to live in right by the workplace. Sure enough. Sure does make an easy commute.

Turns out that being so close to my "office" at night has other advantages, at least as far as gettin' away with stuff. See, I dig the holes, and I fill 'em in again. Because I dig the holes and fill 'em in again, I can pretty well dig 'em back out again without too many grunts or groans. After the last mourner has dabbed her eyes dry and strolled off to have her supper, I sit in my little cottage and wait for the sun to go down. I don't bother cleanin' the dirt off me. I don't bother turnin' on the old tube to see what else has happened durin' the day. People are born, people die. That's all that ever happens anyway. No. What I do is wait on that old sun to drift off to dreamland. Then I stand up and march myself out to my little tool shed in the back, the one where I keep all my tools and a few gallons of gasoline. You know, for the lawn mowing equipment. I also keep some diesel for the backhoe when it's needed. I grab a pry bar, an ax, and a couple of gallons of gasoline, and then I stroll right back out to the freshest filled-in grave and dig it right back up again. I don't use the backhoe for that. Makes too much noise. I dig 'em up the old-fashioned way, and it's pretty easy goin' as long as I'm careful about the way I tamp down the fill-in in the first place.

Don't go thinkin' any burial vaults get in my way, either. We don't use 'em here. We require concrete grave liners. The cheapest ones don't seal—and cheap is the way most of the dead folks' "loved ones" usually go around here—so all I gotta do is pry the top up to get right at the casket. Yeah, it's heavy, but I built me up some pretty good muscles over all my years of diggin' graves.

The coffins ain't typically much trouble for me either. Folks in these parts can't afford the big old fancy stainless steel ones with the built-in spas and central heat and air. Heh. No, they usually buy the cheap-ass ones. Most of the time, those ones will break right open once the right amount of earth has been piled on top of 'em. Of course, we have them grave liners in place to prevent that. Still, them coffin lids generally just lift right up.

I can see you askin' yourself how I do all this maneuverin' around in the dark. Well, usually I carry a little penlight with me. Keep it in my mouth while I work. Makes it a little hard to see—and it's even harder to douse it if a car happens by while I'm workin'—but I reckon it's less visible than a headlamp or a Coleman. That's what I use. Sure enough. Never fails that when I lift them coffin lids, the light from that penlight falls right on the face of the corpse. Sometimes their eyelids have popped loose by then, and the light shines right in their eyes, so it looks like they're glarin' at me. That'd be spooky if I had any fear about it, I reckon. Don't make me fear nothin', though. If I happen to have my mean-streak on that night, I'll stab an open eye with the butt of my ax before I start to work on the rest of the body. Other times I just press that penlight into the bare earth part of the wall beside me and let it do its job while I get to work on mine.

Once I have a good light showin' on 'em, I heft that big old ax into the air and bring it down with a good swift *thwack* on each of their arms. There ain't much in the way of natural stuffin' left in a body by then, you know, so it's not quite as much work as you might think to chop off a limb. It's more work if some water's gotten into the grave before I get to it. The more water soaks their skin, the tougher it is to cut through with that ax. It'd probably be good to sharpen up that old blade sometime, but I don't reckon I'll ever get around to that now.

First I chop off both arms, then I chop each arm in two at the elbow. Then I chop the hands off at the wrists. Once I've got all that done, I go to work on their legs. They're a bit thicker and tougher to chew through, but I can usually get one off at the groin in two or three whacks. When I've got 'em loose from the body, I cut 'em in two at the knee, then I cut the feet off at the ankles. Ain't too much blood in all this work now, seein' as most of that has circled down the drain and into the county water system at the morgue. Heh. Didn't know you might be drinkin' water that's been filtered through the dead, did ya? Sure enough.

I cut off their heads last, right through the meat and bone where their necks attach to it. Sometimes I miss. Sometimes it's easier to chop 'em off a bit lower than that. Mostly I just want to make sure that the cut is clean enough so that I can balance the head upright on the neck, make it sit up in that hole the same way it would've sat up on the body if it was still alive and kickin' around.

I reckon there are some folks who might do things different, but my daddy always taught me that if you wanted to build a good fire, you really need to make a pyramid. Gotta have some way for the fuel to catch and the air to get all around in there to feed the flames, you know? And since you can't reliably bend a dead man into a pyramid shape, I figure the best you can do is cut off everything you can cut off, use the torso as a base, and the rest as the uprights. A lot of times I can put their heads right in the middle of their torsos and burn the whole body just by lightin' the hairs of their chinny chin chins and lettin' it catch everything else. But most of the time I have to drown the whole structure in gasoline first.

I make sure to get completely out of the hole before I toss in the matches. Usually pick me up a bunch of little books of paper matches down at the Shop-Rite when I go for groceries. I ain't never smoked, but I always pick up a carton of cigarettes along with those matches too, just for show. Most of the time I just toss the whole carton in along with the matches. It's expensive, but if they're gonna burn down there, they might as well enjoy a final toot on the death sticks, am I right? Heh. Sure enough.

After I got the fire good and goin', I just lean back on my elbows and wait. Every now and then a car will drive by the cemetery. Sometimes they catch me off guard, and I've been surprised that nobody calls the cops or the fire department or somethin'. Then again, most of 'em have a little glow of their own goin' on from the driver's seat. Damn phones. Be the death of all of us. If they don't kill us on the road, they'll rot our brains shootin' them damn radio waves into our skulls like that. I'm guessin' if anyone ever paid any attention to the little orange glow from my "camp fires" they probably just figured it was a trick of their peripheral vision or somethin'. Mostly I'm bettin' they just don't care enough to get involved, and their God don't care enough to make 'em feel any guilt about it. All the better for me, I reckon. All the better for me.

Dependin' on a whole lot of things, I might spend a couple hours layin' out there propped on my elbows among the stiffs. They don't burn up real fast, you know, 'cause they ain't all dried up and dusty yet. Guess if I had a proper crematorium it would be a matter of seconds, but I reckon there'd also be a whole lot more work and evidence of what I was doin' out here if that was the case. Whatever, though. I'm a patient man. My work ain't really got no deadline on it. My time's God's time, and I always figured I'd be done whenever I dry up and blow away or whenever God decides to stop me by burnin' up this old world and everything on it. Reckon it's a good thing I don't live in a place with a high water table like New Orleans. Sure enough. Wouldn't ever be able to burn anything at all down there.

Things went on that way for several years. New dead person, new fuel to burn. Was happenin' on a daily basis for a while. Always felt it was a shame that I wasn't able to dig up the ones that was buried there already when I got the job. Let too long go by and the earth is just too hard-packed for one person to dig up by hand, so there was always gonna be a natural limit to fulfillin' my mission. Only way I woulda been able to dig up the older ones would be if I had a partner in crime, but there ain't no way I'd ever be able to trust anybody in knowin' what I was up to. So you can imagine how distraught I was when the county up and hired me an assistant right around December of 1999. Sure enough.

I didn't ask nobody for that, I'll tell you that right now. To this day I can't tell you what was goin' through their damned old heads. I reckon it had somethin' to do with that old computer panic. What did they call it? The Y2K, I think. Folks around here thought it was gonna be the end of the whole world on account of computers not knowin' we was headed into the year 2000 and not the year 1900. Didn't make no difference to me what year it was, but apparently, a lot of folks were thinkin' the nukes were gonna go off all by themselves and the jet planes were gonna fall right out of the sky. I reckon there was somethin' in me that was hopin' it all would happen that way. Then my job would be done. Anyway, I guess the county board figured there might be a few more bodies to bury after midnight on December 31, so they hired me some young punk who need-ed a supplement to his weekly allowance or wanted to save up to buy a car or somethin'. I was s'posed to show him the ropes and then let him take over most of the back-breakin' stuff. Seein' as how he was about thirty years younger'n me, I reckon they thought he'd be stronger.

He wasn't stronger. I can tell you that right now. I did away with him real easy. It ain't as hard as you might think to swing an ax at a live body and separate their noggin from their neck parts, though it's quite a bit more bloody than when you're workin' on a corpse that's already had a mortician have at it. Sure enough. Took me a few sleepless nights and get-tin' a little bit behind on my work to figure out how I was gonna get rid of the little smart-ass. The good news was that he went home at night, so that left me in the caretaker cottage alone, just like before. The bad news was that he liked to tamp the ground down real hard, which made my night work harder. He also had real clear eyeballs, and I'm guessin' he might've wondered a time or two why I was always buying matches and cartons of cigarettes but never stoppin' for a smoke break.

Truth is, I never felt threatened by the dude so much as I felt inconve-nienced. He made it harder to do my job and to *get away* with doin' my job, so I relieved him of his. Bought a gallon of bleach the next day to take care of the mess, and then I had to figure out how to get rid of the damn body. I know what you're thinkin'. You're thinkin' "Diggum, you been gettin' rid of bodies your whole life!" And you're right. Sure enough. But the bodies I've been gettin' rid of already had a little slot in the earth reserved for 'em, so to speak. This little punk had probably never even considered that he was capable of dyin', much less dyin' so young and in such a podunk town. I fixed that, though. I found a spot to dig and cover up the mess, a spot where I thought no one would ever think to look, at least until they tried to bury me in it. By then it'd be too late. I already told you that there's only one plot left in the place that ain't got a marker, but you can be sure it's got remains in it. Sure enough. Burned up his body like all the others, although his took a little longer to get started than most of 'em do.

Didn't nobody really question old Diggum too much about the boy's disappearance, either. I just said he never showed up for work that day. Nobody else said otherwise on account of it just bein' the two of us who worked at the cemetery and, other than my occasional visits to town for groceries or my job buryin' their so-called loved ones, nobody associates with me. County didn't bother tryin' to replace him, either, at least not for a little while. The Y2K had come and gone by that point, and the economy was sure enough headed into a recession, so I reckon they had the foresight to not spend money they didn't have to on a big old field of dead bodies nobody cared about but me.

So the county didn't bother again until sometime around 2004 when the local boys was comin' home from Iraq in body bags. Joe was the new guy's name. He was quite a bit older and stronger than the punk from '99. Smarter, too. Sure enough. A whole lot smarter. He figured out pretty quick that I didn't want nobody else around my work. It wasn't that I was nasty to him. I just come off cold, like I smelled somethin' on him I didn't like. If he asked me for anything, I never answered. Just nodded or shook my head as appropriate. He tried to strike up a conversation a couple of times. Asked me where I hailed from originally, like anybody from these parts is ever from anywhere other than these parts. I could see in his face that he was gettin' exasperated as the days went by and I didn't speak to him at all. He'd glance at me sidelong every now and then while we was maintainin' the grass, like he wanted to try somethin' else but wasn't quite up to the disappointment of failin' at makin' the connection. I figured it was only a matter of time before I could run him off without havin' to so much as lift a finger. Sure enough.

I was also gettin' a bit more patient in my work in those days. The incomin' body count was slowin' down a bit because the cemetery was gettin' full and most of the plots was already reserved for folks who were still livin', just waitin' out their days. Also, we didn't have that many young men signin' up to give their souls to the government's war. The patriotic heat of 9/11 had kind of already died down around here before the whole Iraq mess even started. Reckon the county didn't see it that way, but they also wasn't throwin' no parades when the boys came home alive either.

So most of our days was spent maintainin' the grass, keepin' the grounds clean and lookin' nice for the people who feel guilty about not havin' visited their old ma or pa while they was still alive. That slow flow of incomin' meant that I had time to drive Joe away instead of killin' him like the young punk. Sure enough. I was all too happy to off that little punk years before, but I was afraid more than one strange disappearance by the caretaker's assistant might get me a visit from the po-po, so I got determined to wait Joe out. Figured he'd get bored or pissed off or somethin' eventually and move on to greener pastures. So that's the way things stayed until that one afternoon when he was packin' up his stuff to go home, and he asked me for a damn cigarette.

I'd let him into the toolshed that day on account of the rain. Don't know why I picked that day to be nice after all the sunny days when I'd been off-puttin' on purpose. I reckon even that twisted old fuck Adolph Hitler might've had a second or two when he was decent to one person. However it happened, I let him in there so he could pack up his own equipment in some shelter from the rain while I was puttin' my own tools up, and what does he see sittin' there on top of my overturned water pail but a carton of cigarettes I'd bought forever ago. Hell, it'd been so long since I'd burned a body that I'd forgotten the damn things were even in there. But sure enough there they sat, on top of that upended pail with a couple of dry books of paper matches on top of 'em.

Old Joe, I guess he figured I was in such a friendly mood that day that he might as well ask. He was all stooped over on the floor of that shed, and he eyed that carton of cigs just as he finished packin' up his tools. He sat up on his knees and looked at me all eyeballs like a little puppy beggin' for a biscuit and said: "mind if I have a smoke?"

Well, damn if he didn't catch me off-guard. I didn't nod. I didn't shake my head like I was sayin' "no." I just balls-out loud said it: "Aw, I don't smoke." Then there was this lull, this little slice of quiet between us. I looked around at him, and he was sittin' there lookin' back at me with his face screwed up all in a puzzle. Then he glanced back at the pail with the carton and the matches on it, kind of shrugged his shoulders, and stood up to go. I remember him mumblin' something or other that might have been "okay," and then he turned to walk out the door.

That was when I knew I had to go ahead and kill him. I don't know if he ever would've thought about those cigarettes had I let him live. I don't know if he would've ever put two and two together if I'd been found out by some other means, but I never wanted to take the chance that he'd forget. Memory is a funny thing. It has a habit of throwin' the right information at you at just the right moment, like when you suddenly realize you left the stovetop burnin' right before you back your car out of the driveway. Could be that old Joe wouldn't think about it anymore until some police detective came knockin' on his door and askin' him all the right questions. I couldn't risk that.

So quick as a rip, I grabbed the handle of my old favorite ax, raised the blade up over my head, and brought it down straight between his shoulder blades. I'd wanted to split the back of his head open, but he was a big man and a little too fast when he ducked to get through that shed door, so the wedge fell wrong. It got stuck there in the meat and bone of him, too. I couldn't yank it out of his back to finish the job. Old Joe fell face-first into the dirt outside the shed, all the while howlin' like a damn coyote. Now, I already told you that there ain't that many people livin' around the old cemetery. Nor do you see many people drivin' by, but I worried that old Joe's big mouth might attract some attention. Instead of lettin' him moan on like that, I grabbed one of the shop rags I use to wipe up the motor oil and gas when it spills over the mower intakes, strolled out of the shed, and crammed it in his mouth while he had both his hands busy tryin' to pry the axe out of his own back.

Before he was able to spit out that rag, I stomped a boot down on Joe's spinal column, grabbed that ax handle with both hands, and gave it a swift yank at an angle. It made this weird wet rippin' sound when it came free, and Joe howled from behind that stinkin' rag. I strolled around his body so I could find the best spot to hit him in order to cleanly whack off his head. I could see he was in right terrible pain. His face was purple, and his eyelids was all squeezed together tighter than a new jailbird's asshole. Every time he grunted, more blood poured out of that ax wound in his back. It was gettin' downright messy on the ground right outside that toolshed, and not in a way that would be an easy cleanup.

Finally, I figured it might be best to wait until I got him back on the concrete pad floor inside the toolshed before I finished him off. I tossed the ax through the door behind me and then I grabbed Joe by the thick of his boot ankles and dragged him in backward. He tried to stop me by clutching at the grass in front of him, but he was too weak from pain and blood loss by that time, I think. He ripped up a couple of patches of blades by the root—I'd have to replace those later—but I got him back inside.

After that, things got easier. I kicked the carton of cigs and the books of matches off the top of that upended pail. Then I picked up the pail and shoved it right down on top of Joe's big old melon of a head. It was a tight fit. I imagine it was hard to breathe with the hole in his back, the rag in his mouth, and the pail pressin' his nostrils shut like that, but so much the better for me. Sure enough.

With his head snug in that pail, I reached for my ax. Then I planted my right foot beside him on the concrete pad and my left one at the small end of the pail near the top of his head. I hefted the ax as high above my head as that toolshed would allow and brought it down between my legs with all my might. It struck his neck just over the rim of the pail and went about half-way through. It took me a total of three swings, but I was done soon enough. That pail rolled out from under my left boot and right through the toolshed door, just like some part of old Joe was still tryin' to escape. Except he didn't have to duck to get out that door no more. Sure enough. I just let his old head roll 'cause I figured it probably couldn't get very far by just gravity alone.

Thinkin' back on it, it was almost like I'd planned this whole thing all along, 'cause I already knew what I was gonna do next. I reached behind me and snatched a box of Hefty Extra Strong Lawn & Leaf bags off the workbench. The first one I unrolled and used to cover his bleedin' neck and torso. The second one I put on him feet first so that the mouths of the bags met right about the middle of his body. I tied the whole shebang together with some of that orange plastic weed whacker line. Not the best I probably could have done, but it was handy and easier to get at than the straps I use to lower the bodies into all them holes. When he was good and tied up in those bags, I stepped outside and snatched up the pail. Lookin' around, I discovered that there wasn't much blood on the ground outside. I was lucky, I reckon. Or maybe old Joe didn't have as much blood flow to his brain as I'd thought.

That night, for the second time in my life, I had to bury a body I'd been responsible for killin' and do it without a backhoe. If I'd done it the easy way, it might've attracted attention. Now, you need to remember that I wasn't gettin' any younger. Sure enough. I was still as strong as an ox, but I didn't have near that same level of stamina I'd had about four years before that night. I decided the best thing to do might be to just unearth the grave I'd already dug for the young punk, toss old Joe in there, and burn him up right there in the middle of that old pile of ashes. So I grabbed my pick-axe and my shovel, and that's what I did. I dug up the spot where I'd buried the young punk, at least as far down as the grave liner. Heh. Yeah. I know what you're thinkin'. "Diggum!" you're thinkin', "you mean to tell me that you put a grave liner in a grave that wasn't even s'posed to be a grave yet?"

You betcha I did. See, I had a feelin' that I might have to use that spot again and, if I did, I wanted it to be a whole lot less work for me to get into it. Also, if anyone ever came snoopin' around with legal papers to open up any graves, it wouldn't look like a criminal burial site if they happened to dig there. Well, at least until they got past the liner.

I dug down to that grave liner and popped the top on it. At first, I didn't see much sign of the young punk's remains, but I reckon that was to be expected. He'd been on fire after all. Sure enough. After I had it good and open again, I tore open the lawn and leaf bags and dumped stiff old Joe over the side. I kicked the pail containin' his head in after 'em. Yep. You heard right. I literally kicked the bucket. Next, I tossed in my ax and the carton of cigs old Joe had been such a fool about back in the toolshed.

I felt my knees pop when I hopped in the hole after him, but it wasn't nothin' serious. My back was achin' from all the diggin', and I was tired from a long day of work, but this work needed to be done before the sun come up. I'd never bothered to ask old Joe whether he had any family that might come lookin' for him. Reckoned I'd just tell 'em the same thing I told the police when the young punk went missin'. Don't know nothin' except he didn't show up for work that day.

I stuck my penlight in the wall of earth beside me, just like I had all those other times before, and I commenced to choppin' old Joe into pieces so I could build a proper fire. I was just about ready to set the blaze a goin' when the penlight fell out of its spot, first time ever. I reckon I thought I was lucky that it stayed on when it landed because that meant I could see where it was and pick it back up again. But then I made the mistake of followin' its beam. I stopped mid-stoop to nab the thing from the floor of the grave when I noticed the light had fallen on this little ball of white goo with a blue spot in the middle of it. Didn't take me too long to realize I was lookin' right smack dab into an eyeball, layin' right there in the grave. I snatched the light up real quick and shone it on old Joe's head, which I had perched in the middle of his torso just like all the other ones before him. Sure enough, he still had both his eyes. And they was both brown and still starin' at me with that goofy puzzled puppy look he had.

I couldn't remember for sure what color the young punk's eyes had been, but I was pretty sure that they would've been long gone from this world by the time four years had gone past. It was right then that this old caretaker for the first time felt what you probably consider to be fear. It was kind of a cold chill that run up my back all the way to the neck, makin' me shiver. Sort of like piss shiver, I reckon, if you've ever felt that before. Could've been fear. Could've been excitement. Sure enough.

Well, I don't know how long I stood there lookin' at that eyeball, but I decided pretty soon that I'd had enough of whatever it was. I shored up the remainder of my courage, and I reached down and grabbed the penlight and stuck it between my lips like a cigar. Then I bent down and snatched up that gross old eyeball. I tossed it right onto old Joe's torso and watched as it rolled across it and came to rest up against his chin like it was givin' him a little kiss. To this day I won't swear to it, but in the split second that thing was in the palm of my hand, I thought I felt it vibratin' like it was tryin' to escape or tryin' to bite me or somethin'.

Quick as a lick I grabbed my gas can and drenched old Joe's body. I made sure to get an extra heavy measure of the stuff on the nasty old eyeball and, I'd swear, it looked to me like I wasn't doin' nothin' but makin' it mad. It got all bloodshot and red on the back even though there shouldn't have been any blood in it, then it rolled over, away from old Joe's chin, so that it was lookin' right at me again. I'll tell you that right then and there I decided to fuck all and get the hell out of that grave. I scrambled out of there like the devil himself was after me, then I lit up that book of matches and tossed it down. Old Joe went up like any kindlin' oughta, and it wasn't long before that hole in the ground was glowin' hot.

It didn't occur to me until after the fire had nearly died that I'd left my ax down there. I was in such a hurry to get out, I'd forgot all about it. Well, it was gonna be too hot to go back down and get it then, so I figured I'd just wait for old Joe to turn to ash and then climb down to get it. I also figured it'd be best to wait for the sun to come up, just in case there was somethin' still down there in the dark besides my ax and old Joe's crispy remains. For the first time since I started work here as caretaker, my shovel and I walked away from an open grave, and I left it that way all night long.

I made sure to set my alarm clock, though. I set it for just a few minutes before sun-up. When it blew in my ear the next mornin', I rose up, grabbed my shovel and my penlight, and I headed back outside. I was still a might groggy from the late night before, so I'd already jumped in the hole to re-trieve my old ax before I remembered about that eyeball. Soon as my feet hit the ground and the beam of that penlight struck old Joe's ashes, I saw it again. Sittin' right there in the middle of what used to be old Joe's solar plexus was a white eyeball with a blue iris, unburnt and white as the day it was buried. It was lookin' straight at me. The sight of it actually made me jump backward a bit, and I nearly took a tumble over my own ax handle. I managed to keep myself from fallin' horizontal too early in the earth by grabbin' a handful of the wall as I reeled backward.

When I set myself back to right, I scanned the rest of the grave with my trusty penlight. Most of old Joe's body was nothin' but ashes, just like it should've been. Then, buried just a little beneath the ashes that used to be his head, I saw another little glimmer of white. While I kept a watch on that little blue-eyed bugger that wouldn't burn (I wanted to make sure it wasn't gonna come rollin' at me), I leaned over a bit, filled my lungs full of air, and blew a gust of wind over the little white spot in the ashes. Enough of them cleared away for me to see it was sphere-shaped and pretty much all white, except for an arc of brown that disappeared into the ash that I hadn't blown away.

Yeah, you guessed right. It was another goddamned eyeball. One of old Joe's brown eyes, I suspected. Quick as a fox, I grabbed my ax and tossed it over the edge of the grave. I heard it land safely on the grass outside.

Then I climbed out after it, grabbed my shovel, and started fillin' that hole lickety-split. That was two times in the fire for the blue eyeball and one for the brown one. Neither of 'em was burnt up, so I wasn't gonna bother tryin' again. The logical part of my head kept tellin' me that there was probably just somethin' about the earth in that spot that messed up the burn. I don't know. I ain't no scientist. That's what it had to be, though. Somethin' about that part of the earth that didn't want eyeballs to burn. That's what I thought at the time anyway. So I covered it all up again and put it out of my head.

As the days and nights went by after that, I kept up my bargain to myself about incineratin' the community's loved ones as they deposited 'em with me. For the most part, I managed to do it without re-openin' the hole that I'd dumped old Joe and the young punk into. I probably wouldn't have ever opened that old hole again if things had kept goin' the way they used to be before I offed old Joe. I told you before that I ain't superstitious, but a man still notices when two plus two used to make four and suddenly don't anymore. The night I noticed was the night I dug up and burned the corpse of that old spinster Betsy Pigg.

Now I never called her that to her face, and I know it ain't what the young folks call politically correct to refer to an unmarried woman as a spinster anymore, but if ever there was a spinster, she was it. The woman literally spun wool for years as a kind of reenactment for the county historical society's weird dress-up events, and she never married. Had no family to speak of by the time she died. She must've been nearin' a hundred years at the time, I reckon. I took my time burnin' her corpse on account of the lack of mourners. The county buried her on the warmest New Year's Eve on record. And, if you'll pardon the pun, New Year's Day is probably the deadest day at the cemetery. Ask any small town caretaker. They'll tell you that the livin' are too busy nursin' their sore heads and egos and eatin' black-eyed peas on New Year's Day to bother thinkin' about the dead. I figured I probably had a good five or six hours after sun-up before the first visitor showed up that day, so I didn't bother coverin' up her burnt remains until long after that ball in New York's Times Square had come down, and I'd had myself a good long winter's nap.

Next mornin' was bright and sunny for a New Year's Day, so I went strollin' out with my shovel to look at my work from the night before. I think I might've even grinned up at the sunshine that mornin' before I looked down at what remained of the old spinster. I remember thinkin' it felt good on my face, and I remember thinkin' I didn't often enough feel the kind of peace of mind you feel as a kid when the sunshine is bakin' your skin, and you don't think you've got a care in the whole damn world. I felt like that on that day, at least until I looked down in Betsy Pigg's grave.

Sittin' right there among all her ashes was a shiny white pelvic bone. I could see it plain as the daylight that was shinin' down into that hole. I can tell you right now that in all the years I'd spent secretly burnin' up the remains of the dearly departed, that had never happened before. Sure, there was those two eyeballs that I couldn't explain, but I'd always managed to get those fires hot enough to break up most of the bones, especially the brittle powder-thin bones of an elderly lady. The bits of bone that remained I could usually crush up with a hammer or the end of my old ax handle. Hell, old spinster Pigg had broke her back sneezin' one night in her seventies when she had a particularly bad case of hay fever. I should've been able to burn hers up just by placin' her in front of my oven while I was heatin' up a pizza. And all her other bones were dust now. All of 'em. There was no bones, no eyeballs, no brain, no nothin' except that pelvic bone. I might not be superstitious, but I wasn't about to leave any part of spinster Pigg in that grave for God to reconstitute on the Judgment. I stuck my ax handle through one of the holes in that pelvic bone and hefted it out of the grave hole. I hit that son of a bitch with a hammer and broke it into two pieces. Then I hit it some more. I broke up pretty well, but there was no way I was gonna get it down to ashes by hand. So I just put the pieces in my pail, and I filled in her grave.

When I had that one filled in, I dug up part of the grave in which I'd buried the remains of old Joe and the young punk. I don't specifically know why I picked that one. There was just somethin' in my head, somethin' that said: "this is where the extras go." I didn't dig all the way down to where I burned old Joe and the young punk, just about half way there. Then I dropped in the shards of Betsy Pigg's pelvic bone and filled that sucker in again quick as I could.

After that, I kept a closer watch on the bodies as I burnt 'em up and crushed up any remainin' bone fragments. More often than not there was teeth remainin', but that was to be expected. There'd always be a few teeth.

Teeth are hard and don't burn up good even if you get fancy like the mob movies and dump quicklime on 'em. But more and more I was noticin' that there was parts other than teeth that didn't seem to be gettin' burnt up by the fire. I'd find a femur here or a finger there, maybe an ulna in another place. Every time I'd chop 'em up into fragments and dump 'em into my own grave hole. The time I burned up old John Handle's body, I found the right half of his brain still in the grave, not even slightly singed by the fire. I suppose that was appropriate for old John, though. He was the guy who owned that hippie-lookin' New Age shop downtown. Figures if any part of him was gonna survive it would be the part that's all about creativity and flowers and daydreams and Pollyanna shit like that.

Every single time I found a bit of a body that hadn't been reduced to ashes, I felt that same compulsion to dig out the grave I'd used to burn old Joe and that young punk. Then I'd toss that piece of body in and cover it all back up again. I even got to the point that I started collectin' and dumpin' in the teeth when I found 'em. Things were gettin' weird, and I didn't want to take no chances. I reckon it helped me sleep at night to know that all them extra parts was in one place in the cemetery, that if I could ever figure out how to get rid of 'em for good, I'd know exactly where to go lookin' for 'em instead of havin' to dig up every grave in the cemetery. Of course, if I'd figured back then what all that was leadin' to, that it was just gonna end up bringin' you here, I might've left them parts where they lay.

So here you are now, standin' over me with your cut up boney old arms all gleamin' in the moonlight. I reckon old God got his last laugh on me. Sure enough. I ain't superstitious. I think I told you that already. Rules are rules, and the rule was that if your body was turned to ashes, you wouldn't be able to rise up on the Judgment. But I guess if God makes the rules then God can also break the rules, or at least find himself a clever way to manipulate 'em. I'm bettin' that if I had my penlight with me right now, I could shine 'em on your eyes and see that you have one that's old Joe brown and another that's young punk blue. That pelvis of yours looks all cracked up and a bit womanly to me, too. I'm bettin' that's the unburnt part of the spinster Betsy Pigg that I tossed in this grave a while back.

Oh, yeah, and that's the other ironic, funny thing, ain't it? All I needed to do was give you a hand. And that's exactly what I was doin' out here tonight. I dug up this grave one more time to toss in old Frank Gilbert's hand that wouldn't burn. Old Frank used to work for the railroads back in his young days. He had these big old thick fingers that was always cracked like he'd spent years diggin' trenches in 'em with a pocket knife. Them cracks was always full of black stuff, too. Dirt and oil from his work, I reckon. If you was thin-skinned and dainty, you didn't want to shake hands with old Frank is what I'm sayin'.

Frank died of natural causes, they said. He had quite a few mourners show up for his service, most of 'em big old railroad guys like himself, complete with their own sets of big old gritty sandpaper hands. They lingered around a lot longer than most mourners do. I don't know why. I reckon when a man has worked his entire life with another man they tend to get on like brothers even if they was never blood. It was gettin' late, on around sunset, by the time the last one walked away. He wasn't but around the first bend in the road before I strolled out there with my shovel and my ax and started diggin' up old Frank.

I stuck my penlight in the wall and chopped him up just like I had all those others before him. Didn't pay no attention to his hands then, other than findin' a good spot to chop 'em off at. When you think about it, you'd figure hands on a man like old Frank would've been the first thing to catch and burn, seein' as how dried up they was before he even hit the embalmin' table. Sure enough. So I chopped him up and doused him with gasoline and lit him on fire, then I sat by his place in the cemetery and waited. Didn't feel right to walk away on that one because, see, old Frank's was the last empty plot in the cemetery besides mine. All them other railroaders was gonna need to find some other place to be buried. I waited to toss in the cigarettes in old Frank's case, too. Actually tore the carton open, drew one out and lit it for myself. I reckon I was celebratin'. Took a few puffs on it before I tossed it and the rest of the carton down into Frank's grave. I reckon I figured my work was finally about all done. There wasn't any more I could do in this old cemetery, and I was gettin' on way too old to go lookin' for work somewhere else just to keep havin' my chuckles against old God.

I must've fallen asleep at some point while old Frank's body was burnin' down because the next thing I knew was I that I felt like I was freezin' to death and it was nearin' sun-up. I sat up with my head spinnin' and my bones achin' from fallin' asleep out in the weather, then I peeked over the edge of old Frank's grave and saw that not one, but both of his big old sandpaper hands was sittin' at the bottom of that grave unburnt. The ends of the fingers on both hands was dug into the side of the earth like they'd been tryin' to claw their way out.

Once I had my wits about me, I climbed down into that hole and knocked over the pile of ash that had once been old Frank. I picked up his remainin' teeth and them two hands and tossed 'em in a small trash bag that I tied at the neck, then I climbed out of the grave and commenced to fillin' in the hole. I wanted to have it done and re-sodded before any of them railroaders from yesterday come back to pay some more respects to their brother. Along about sunset, only two of 'em had shown up to sing another auld lang syne. So I figured I was safe to start gettin' rid of the remainders.

I grabbed the little trash bag containin' the hands and teeth and took it out to my own grave, just like all the other remainders. I dug that hole deep enough to pry open the liner again, then I tore open that little trash bag to dump out the hands. Next thing I know, the bag went flyin'—teeth in every direction—and both of them hands had gone and wrapped themselves around my throat and sent me flailin' right to the bottom of my own grave in this old cemetery. Sure enough. It's funny, I reckon. I've been diggin' my own grave here for years, diggin' it out and fillin' it back in, but until tonight I was never actually bein' buried in it.

I wonder, though, whether God could've pulled off all this if I hadn't buried all those unburnt body parts together here in my own grave. I'm guessin' He probably could've. Maybe He even did. I sure don't remember buryin' some of them pieces of you that I see connectin' your head to your neck and your arms to your shoulder blades. Mostly what I thought I buried out here was dental work and the occasional oddly unburnt other part. But I can almost see the whole of you in the bright of the moonlight that's shinin' off the blade of my ax now that you're standin' straddle over me, and you've got it hefted way up over top of your skull like that. Sure enough.

My God you have a lot of teeth.

Diggum
a screenplay

FADE IN:

INT. TOOL SHED - DUSK

A door creaks open, allowing a wedge of light from the setting sun to shine on a gas can. To the left of the can is an overturned masonry bucket, on which sits a pack of Camel cigarettes and a small box of wooden matches. The head of an ax and the spade tip of a shovel lean upright against the right side of the gas can, as if their handles are both propped on the wall behind the can.

In the wedge of light from the open doorway, the elongated shadow of Diggum appears. The shadow pauses in the open doorway.

> DIGGUM (V.O.)

> My real name's not Diggum. That's just what most folks call me.

> Doubt anybody remembers the man I used to be. You ask 'em who that old fella is mopin' around the cemetery, that's

what they'll tell you. "That's Diggum," they'll say. "He's the caretaker."

I don't think I'll be doing this much longer, though. My work's coming to an end. Ain't but one plot left in this old cemetery. That one's mine.

The shadow in the wedge of light grows larger. The thud of heavy footfalls of rubber-soled work boots can be heard on the concrete floor of the tool shed as the shadow completely overtakes the frame, disguising the contents of the tool shed in complete darkness.

DIGGUM (V.O.) (CONT'D)

I'm more than just the caretaker here, though. I'm the man at war with God.

In the dark, the sound of the ax head and the shovel spade scraping against the concrete floor of the tool shed can be heard.

EXT. FARM - A COOL EARLY SPRING MORNING, CLOSE TO NOON

A 40-years younger Diggum drives a tractor with a plow attached through a freshly turned field. He makes a turn to start plowing a new set of rows but pauses the tractor long enough to take off his hat and glance up at the clear blue sky.

He grabs a handkerchief from his back pocket and dabs at his nostrils. The morning's coolness has made his nose run. He returns the handkerchief to the back pocket of his overalls.

DIGGUM (V.O.)

It all started innocent enough, I reckon. I was just making a living doing what my daddy taught me to do. Makin' ends meet and enjoyin' the company of the two greatest loves of my life.

In the distance, Diggum sees his wife Janie and very young son Joe appear at the back door of their home. The boy is holding a toy tractor and making driving motions with it in imitation of his father. Janie is shielding her eyes from the morning sun and waving to Diggum. She makes an eating motion with her free hand, indicating that it's time for Diggum to come inside for lunch.

DIGGUM (SHOUTING)

Be there in a minute, hon! Just want to finish these rows.

He waves to them. Both Janie and Joe return the wave and go back inside the house. Diggum watches them go. From the farmhouse chimney, a thin column of smoke is rising lazily into the sky. Diggum sets his hat on his head and returns to plowing the row, a smile on his face.

DIGGUM (V.O.)

I must have lost track of time, though. One set of rows turned into two. Two turned into four. Next thing I knew, I was smelling smoke.

Thick grayish black smoke wafts across young Diggum's face as he plows. He looks up and sniffs the air. His expression changes from serene happiness to horror as he brings the tractor to an abrupt halt in the middle of a fresh set of rows.

Diggum leaps off the tractor, panic-stricken. His boots tear up the freshly turned earth as he runs toward the farmhouse, which is now fully engulfed in flames.

EXT. FARMHOUSE BACK PORCH

Diggum launches himself up the short set of wooden steps to the back porch. He reaches for the storm door and attempts to open it, but succeeds in yanking it wide for a second. The handle burns his hand. A large column of flame erupts from the door and licks at the exterior of the house above it.

DIGGUM (SHOUTING)

Janie! Joe! Where are you? Where are you?

He glances around frantically at the rural landscape, searching for someone or something--anything--that can help.

DIGGUM (CONT'D)

Help! Someone, please help!

The sound of someone or something collapsing can be heard from inside the farmhouse. From the flames, a tiny metal toy John Deere tractor appears. It rolls out the back door and comes to rest against the toe of Diggum's work boot.

EXT. TOOL SHED/CEMETERY - DUSK

Old Diggum's work boot stands at the threshold of the tool shed door. Diggum is leaning against the door frame, silently watching a graveside memorial service currently taking place in his cemetery. The casket has just been lowered into the ground by the funeral director. The mourners are seated with heads bowed and hands folded in front of them as the priest finishes his prayer.

PRIEST

Good Lord, bless and keep the John Dalton family as John departs this world and enters yours. Allow them the comfort of Your presence in their time of need, and embrace John in Your loving light. In the name of Your Son, Jesus Christ, we pray. Amen.

MOURNERS (TOGETHER)

Amen.

The mourners stand and begin to talk among themselves as they disperse. The priest likewise walks away from the grave. He places a comforting arm around a woman who might be John Dalton's widow as the two talk.

Diggum leaves his post at the tool shed, dragging his shovel behind him.

DIGGUM (V.O.)

After the fire took my wife and son, I decided that I couldn't stay on that farm anymore. I needed to find a new way to make ends meet. That's exactly what I was lookin' for when I strolled into the town of Lost Hollow back then. Sure enough.

EXT. GAS STATION FORTY YEARS EARLIER

A 40-years-younger Diggum, his face still ravaged by his loss, strolls up to the dusty window of a courthouse. Instead of dragging a shovel behind him, he's swinging a suitcase, all he has left in the world. He has just arrived in the small town of Lost Hollow. He is weary and uncertain about how to begin resettling.

As he approaches the dusty window, the camera closes in on a Help Wanted sign. The county is looking for a new cemetery caretaker. Diggum's reflection can be seen eyeballing the sign. He stretches out his hand, grasps the corner of the sign, and tears it from the window.

DIGGUM (V.O.)

Turns out the first help wanted sign I saw was this county job diggin' graves in this cemetery. I reckoned that somebody somewhere's always gonna need to be buried. So I applied right then and there. They pretty much hired me then and there, too. Sure enough. I been diggin' holes and fillin' 'em in ever since.

EXT. CEMETERY - DUSK

Old Diggum pauses in his work, resting his chin on his hands atop the shovel handle as he watches the last of the mourners vanish through the cemetery gate. Beyond the gate, on the horizon, the sun has nearly disappeared. Diggum sets his jaw and drops the shovel to the ground by the hole. He walks toward the tool shed.

DIGGUM (V.O.)

Now you might think a man would get creeped out by takin' on a job like this. Not me, though.

INT. FARM HOUSE - FORTY YEARS EARLIER

Young Diggum is walking carefully through the remains of his house. Here and there he sees mostly burnt-up reminders of his wife and son and their life together. A ring he gifted Janie lies on the floor amid ashes, as do some of his son's Tonka-like metal farm toys.

DIGGUM (V.O.)

I seen my wife and my boy both lyin' there in the ashes of that old house, charred black and flakin' apart like the newspaper my daddy used to use to start the kindlin' burnin' in the old fireplace. I think I cried my last tears right then and there. They was both too burned up to even put 'em in a casket. Practically cremated, they was. Sure enough.

INT. CHURCH

Young Diggum sits on the front pew of the church, a young priest beside him. The priest's left arm rests on Diggum's shoulders, his hand gripping Diggum's right shoulder. Diggum's own hands are folded in his lap. He looks mournfully at the floor. People file by Diggum and the priest, paying their respects to him for his losses. Some of them speak to him. Others just touch him on the arm or on his folded hands. One much older man pauses in front of Diggum longer than the other mourners. Diggum looks up at him through wet eyes.

DIGGUM (V.O.)

You know what the old timers always said about cremation, right? If there ain't no body in the ground, it can't be raised up again come Judgment time.

The old mourner grimaces and shakes his head shamefully, as if he pities the eternal fate of Diggum's wife and son. Diggum's expression changes from sadness to anger as he transitions his gaze from the old man's face to the cross that hangs on the wall behind the pulpit.

DIGGUM (V.O.)(CONT'D)

Neither one of 'em deserved that fate. But if the old timers are right, I reckon both of 'em are lost forever. Haven't wept for a soul since them days.

(chuckles)

You think I resent what God did to me? Yeah, you damn right I do. Damn right. God's plan, the old preacher man'll tell you. God's meanness is what I think.

EXT. TOOL SHED/CEMETERY - DUSK

Old Diggum is walking out of the toolshed. In his right hand is the gas can. In his left is the ax. The shirt pocket of his coveralls contains a bulge shaped like a pack of cigarettes. In his mouth he carries a lit penlight, illuminating his path back to the grave.

DIGGUM (V.O.)

So I decided right then and there that as long as I had some strength in my hands and some will to live, I wasn't gonna let God get away with it, at least not without me gettin' away with a few things my own self.

181

Diggum drops the gas can and the ax beside the open grave. Then he leaps into it. Presently, the limp body of a stocky man launches from within the open grave and thuds onto the ground beside it. The body is dressed in a suit and tie. Its hands are huge. The body is closely followed by Diggum, who climbs out of the hole beside it. He is slightly out of breath.

DIGGUM

Evenin', Mr. Dalton.

Diggum stands, taking his ax in hand, and begins to chop up the body of John Dalton.

DIGGUM (V.O.)

Don't you go thinking I went crazy all of a sudden. Old John Dalton was just one of many that took the brunt of my revenge over the years. See, I dig up the freshly buried ones. I chop them into pieces. Then I shape them into something that'll burn easy. First, I chop off all their limbs.

Diggum stacks the pieces of John Dalton at the bottom of the grave. He forms a pyramid shape with the remains. The body's limbs form the uprights. The torso forms the base. The head of the deceased sits at the center of the structure. The body's giant hands lay on either side of the head. Diggum scans his work with the penlight. One of dead man's eyes has popped open.

DIGGUM (V.O.)(CONT'D)

I cut off their heads last, right through the meat and bone where their necks attach to it.

Never fails that their eyelids have popped loose by the time I'm ready to light 'em up, though. The light shines right in their eyes, so it looks like they're glarin' at me. That'd be spooky if I had any fear about it, I reckon. Don't make me fear nothin', though. If I happen to have my mean-streak on that night, I'll stab an open eye with the butt of my ax before I burn it.

Diggum grabs the ax from its place above his head outside the grave. He holds it with both hands, like a staff. His right hand grips the neck where the ax head meets the handle. His left hand grips the middle of the handle. He brings the ax down butt-first into the eye of the dead man. He drops the ax and relaxes again, surveying his work.

DIGGUM (V.O.)(CONT'D)

I reckon there are some folks who might do things different, but my daddy always taught me that if you wanted to build a good fire, you really need to make a pyramid.

A lot of times I can put their heads right in the middle of their torsos and burn the whole body just by lightin' the hairs of their chinny chin chins and lettin' it catch everything else. But most of the time I have to drown the whole structure in gasoline first.

Diggum, outside the grave, douses the body with gasoline and then lights a match. He pauses only a second before tossing it in. The glow from the fire in the grave illuminates his face as he watches the body burn.

DIGGUM (V.O.)(CONT'D)

I usually make sure I've got everything out of the hole before I toss in the matches.

INT. SMALL RURAL GENERAL STORE

Old Diggum is standing in the checkout line, still wearing his dirt-stained coveralls. In his grocery basket are a few necessary items, but they are quite outnumbered by bunches of boxes of wooden matches.

DIGGUM (V.O.)

Usually pick me up a bunch of little boxes of matches down at the Shop-Rite when I go for groceries. I ain't never smoked, but I always pick up a few packs of cigarettes along with those matches, just for show.

Diggum dumps the contents of the grocery basket onto the checkout conveyor. He points to a carton of Camel cigarettes that sit in a glass case behind the cashier. She glances at the contents on the conveyor, gives Diggum a bit of a disgusted look, and turns to get the carton of cigarettes for him.

DIGGUM (V.O.)(CONT'D)

Most of the time I just toss the whole pack in along with the matches. It's expensive, but if they're gonna burn down there, they might as well enjoy a final toot on the death sticks, am I right? (chuckles) Sure enough.

EXT. CEMETERY - DUSK

Diggum removes the pack of cigarettes from his shirt pocket and tosses them into the fire. He then lays on the ground beside the grave, propped on his elbows, watching the burn.

DIGGUM (V.O.)

Things went on that way for several years. Always felt it was a shame that I wasn't able to dig up the ones that was buried there already when I got the job. Let too long go by and the earth is just too hard-packed for one person to dig up by hand, so there was always gonna be a natural limit to fulfillin' my mission.

EXT. TOOL SHED/CEMETERY - MORNING

A slightly younger Diggum is leaning against the tool shed door frame, looking out at the cemetery. A beat-up old muscle car, the type a man just shy of adulthood might want to fix up and drive, turns into the cemetery and slowly approaches.

DIGGUM (V.O.)

Only way I woulda been able to dig up the older ones would be if I had a partner in crime, but there ain't no way I'd ever be able to trust anybody in knowin' what I was up to.

So you can imagine how distraught I was when the county up and hired me an assistant right around December of 1999. Sure enough.

A wild-eyed young man leaps from behind the wheel of the car. He grabs folded paperwork from the back pocket of his jeans and hands it to Diggum, who reads it silently, his eyes darkening with each pass across the page.

DIGGUM (V.O.)(CONT'D)

I didn't ask nobody for no help. To this day I can't tell you what was goin' through their damned old heads. I reckon it had somethin' to do with that old computer panic. What did they call it? The Y2K, I think.

MONTAGE

Quick clips of people reading newspapers and watching television news information about the impending changeover from 1999 to 2000. Images of bewildered, panic-stricken faces and sensationalized headlines about the potential for catastrophe as a result of the computer bug.

DIGGUM (V.O.)

Folks around here thought it was gonna be the end of the whole world on account of computers not knowin' we was headed into the year 2000 and not the year 1900. Didn't make no difference to me what year it was, but a lot of folks were thinkin' the nukes were gonna go off all by themselves, and the jet planes were gonna fall right out of the sky. I reckon there was somethin' in me that was hopin' it all would happen that way. Then my job would be done.

END OF MONTAGE

EXT. TOOL SHED/CEMETERY - MORNING

Diggum looks up from the paper in his hand and eyes the young man skeptically. He attempts a welcoming smile at the young man standing in front of him but succeeds only in appearing that he's faking a smile.

> DIGGUM (V.O.)
>
> I guess the county board figured there might be a few more bodies to bury after midnight on December 31, so they hired me this young punk who needed a supplement to his weekly allowance or wanted to save up for college or somethin'.
>
> Seein' as how he was about thirty years younger'n me, I reckon they thought he'd be stronger.

EXT. TOOL SHED/CEMETERY - DUSK

The young man is bent over a grave, pulling weeds from around the tombstone. Suddenly the head of Diggum's ax comes down on the back of the young man's neck. Blood squirts from his wounds as his body falls to the earth among the tombstones. Diggum chops at the neck a couple more times to separate the head from the body.

> DIGGUM (V.O.)
>
> He wasn't stronger. I can tell you that right now. I had to do it. I couldn't let him interfere with my mission.
>
> Truth is, I never felt threatened by the dude so much as I felt inconvenienced. He made it harder to do my job and to get away with doin' my job, so I relieved him of his. Bought

a gallon of bleach the next day to take care of the mess, and
then I had to figure out how to get rid of the damn body.

Diggum cleans the blood from the tombstone at which the young man
was working. He shoves the blood-soaked cloth into the back pocket of
his coveralls. He prepares the young man's body for cremation by chopping it up with his ax, just as he's done other bodies.

DIGGUM (V.O.)(CONT'D)

I know what you're thinkin'. You're thinkin' "Diggum, you
been gettin' rid of bodies your whole life!" And you're right.
Sure enough. But the bodies I've been gettin' rid of already
had a little slot in the earth reserved for 'em, so to speak.

Diggum glances around the cemetery, obviously trying to decide what
needs to be done with the chopped up remains. Then he drags the body to
another area of the cemetery, the area where his own plot lies. When he's
there, he prepares the young man's body to burn just as he did the man
with the large hands.

DIGGUM (V.O.)(CONT'D)

I found a spot to dig and cover up the mess, a spot where I
thought no one would ever think to look, at least until they
tried to bury me in it. By then it'd be too late. I already told
you that there's only one plot left in the place that ain't got
a marker, but you can be sure it's got remains in it.

Done with the cremation and burial, Diggum drives away from the cemetery in the young man's car, presumably to get rid of it as evidence.

EXT. TOOL SHED/CEMETERY - LATE MORNING

A sheriff's deputy arrives at the cemetery as Diggum leans against the
door frame of the tool shed. The deputy approaches Diggum and engages
him in conversation, taking notes on a notepad as he does.

DIGGUM (V.O.)

Didn't nobody really question old Diggum too much about the boy's disappearance. I just said he never showed up for work that day. Nobody else said otherwise on account of it just bein' the two of us who worked at the cemetery. That, and nobody bothers to associate with me.

The sheriff deputy nods, closes his notepad, smiles, and departs from the cemetery. As he leaves, Diggum removes the cloth with the young punk's dried blood on it from his back pocket and tosses it atop the gas can in his tool shed, intending to deal with it later. County didn't bother tryin' to replace him, either, at least not for a little while.

EXT. TOOL SHED/CEMETERY - LATE MORNING

A slightly older Diggum is weeding beside a younger, muscular, clean-cut type man. This man is not as young as the previous assistant, but obviously younger than Diggum. The younger man, Joe, is talking to Diggum. Meanwhile, Diggum is silently seething. He does not reply to the younger man. His eyes are full of hate. Occasionally, the younger man glances at Diggum. It dawns on the younger man that Diggum might be ignoring him on purpose.

DIGGUM (V.O.)

The county didn't bother again until sometime around 2004 when the local boys was comin' home from Iraq in body bags. Joe was the new guy's name. He figured out pretty quick that I didn't want nobody else around my work.

Time passes. Diggum and the new assistant continue to work together. Joe is constantly attempting to engage in conversation. Diggum is constantly ignoring him or glaring at him in response. Occasionally, the duo stands together at the tool shed while a funeral is in progress or when loved ones of the previously deceased stop by to leave remembrances. They watch in silence. Joe looks sympathetic. Diggum just looks angry.

DIGGUM (V.O.)(CONT'D)

It wasn't that I was nasty to him. I just come off cold, like I smelled somethin' on him I didn't like. I figured it was only a matter of time before I could run him off without havin' to so much as lift a finger. Sure enough.

I was all too happy to off that little punk years before, but I was afraid more than one strange disappearance by the caretaker's assistant might get me another visit from the sheriff, so I got determined to wait Joe out.

INT. TOOL SHED - DUSK

DIGGUM (V.O.)

So that's the way things stayed until that one afternoon when he was packin' up his stuff to go home, and he asked me for a damn cigarette. I'd let him into the toolshed that day on account of the rain.

Diggum is standing inside the tool shed. The door is open. Diggum is standing near it, watching a downpour. Joe enters, dripping wet and carrying some gardening tools. He shakes off the rain as he steps inside.

DIGGUM (V.O.)(CONT'D)

Don't know why I picked that day to be nice. I let him in there so he could pack up his equipment in some shelter, and what does he see sittin' there on top of my overturned bucket but a carton of cigarettes I'd bought forever ago.

Joe notices the cigarette carton and matches sitting on top of the overturned bucket beside the gas can. Diggum is obviously not paying attention to what Joe has seen.

DIGGUM (V.O.)(CONT'D)

Hell, it'd been so long since I'd burned a body that I'd forgotten the damn things were even in there. Old Joe, was all stooped over on the floor of that shed, and he eyed that carton of cigs just as he finished packin' up his tools. He sat up on his knees and looked at me all eyeballs like a little puppy beggin' for a biscuit.

JOE

Mind if I have a smoke?

DIGGUM (V.O.)

Well, damn if he didn't catch me off-guard.

DIGGUM

Aw, I don't smoke.

There's a lull as Joe looks at the cigarettes and matches, then looks at Diggum. He glances to and fro a couple of times, then shrugs his shoulders. His face betrays his confusion. He mumbles something that might or might not be "okay," then stands up to leave with his toolbox in hand. Diggum's face is flush as it dawns on him what has occurred. He sighs, suddenly resigned to what's next, and grabs the ax.

DIGGUM (V.O.)

That was when I knew I had to go ahead and kill him.

Diggum raises the ax up over his head, intending to bring the ax down into Joe's skull.

DIGGUM (V.O.)(CONT'D)

Memory is a funny thing. It has a habit of throwin' the right information at you at just the right moment, like when you suddenly realize you left the stovetop burnin' right before you back your car out of the driveway. Could be that old Joe wouldn't think about it anymore until some police detective came knockin' on his door and askin' him all the right questions. I couldn't risk it.

Joe ducks to exit the tool shed at just the right moment, and Diggum brings the ax down straight between Joe's shoulder blades. As Joe goes down, he begins screaming and howling to beat the band. He falls face-down in the mud, the ax sticking out of his back. He tries to pry it loose by himself, but to no avail. Diggum, meanwhile, appears horrified at the noise Joe is making.

DIGGUM (V.O.)(CONT'D)

I worried that old Joe's big mouth might attract some attention.

Diggum frantically searches the tool shed for something to silence Joe. He finds the five-year-old bloody shop rag that he'd used to clean the young punk's blood from the tombstone. It's still laying near the gas can, where it had been long forgotten. He grabs the shop rag and runs back outside, urgently cramming the rag into Joe's screaming mouth.

DIGGUM (V.O.)(CONT'D)

Before he was able to spit out that rag, I stomped a boot down on Joe's spinal column, grabbed that ax handle with both hands, and gave it a swift yank at an angle.

Diggum pins Joe to the ground with his boot and yanks the ax free from his back. It makes a wet ripping sound when it comes free. Joe is desperately trying to scream from behind the bloody rag. Meanwhile, Diggum strolls around him in search of the best place to strike to chop off his head. Joe's face is turning purple from lack of oxygen. His eyelids are closed, and streaming tears smear the dirt on his face.

DIGGUM (V.O.)(CONT'D)

I could see he was in right terrible pain. His face was purple, and his eyelids was all squeezed together tighter than a new jailbird's asshole. Every time he grunted, more blood poured out of that ax wound in his back. It was gettin' downright messy on the ground right outside that tool shed, and not in a way that would be an easy cleanup.

Diggum throws the ax into the open tool shed door and grabs Joe by the feet. He drags the dying man back into the tool shed. Joe attempts to stop him by clawing at the ground and at the door frame but is too weak from fear, pain, and blood loss.

DIGGUM (V.O.)(CONT'D)

Finally, I figured it might be best to wait until I got him back on the concrete pad floor inside the toolshed before I finished him off.

After that, things got easier.

Diggum kicks the carton of cigarettes and the box of matches off the top of the upended bucket. He picks up the pail and shoves it right down on top of Joe's big old melon of a head.

DIGGUM (V.O.)(CONT'D)

It was a tight fit. I imagine it was hard to breathe with the hole in his back, the rag in his mouth, and the bucket pressin' his nostrils shut like that, but so much the better for me. Sure enough.

With Joe's head snug in the bucket, Diggum grabs the ax, plants his feet beside Joe, and hefts the blade over his head. He brings it down with all his strength and strikes Joe on the neck, severing it only half way. He swings the ax two more times. Joe's head comes free. The bucket rolls out of the tool shed door with Joe's head inside. Diggum watches it roll a piece before turning to address the rest of the body.

DIGGUM (V.O.)(CONT'D)

That bucket rolled out from under my left boot and right through the tool shed door, just like some part of old Joe was still tryin' to escape. Except he didn't have to duck to get out that door no more. Sure enough. I just let his old head roll 'cause I figured it probably couldn't get very far by just gravity alone.

Thinkin' back on it, it was almost like I'd planned this whole thing all along, 'cause I already knew what I was gonna do next.

Diggum pulls two large lawn and leaf bags from a box on a shelf in the tool shed and begins the process of bagging up Joe's remains. He unrolls the first one and covers Joe's bloody neck and torso. Then he unrolls another and stretches over Joe's body feet first so that the mouths of the bags meet right about the middle of Joe's body. Once the body is covered, Diggum searches for something to secure it.

DIGGUM (V.O.)(CONT'D)

I tied the whole shebang together with some of that orange plastic weed whacker line. Not the best I probably could have done, but it was handy and easier to get at than the straps that lower the bodies into all them holes.

Diggum surveys his work, then walks outside the shed and grabs the bucket containing Joe's severed head. He examines the ground around where the head had rolled, searching for any evidence he might need to clean up later.

DIGGUM (V.O.)(CONT'D)

Lookin' around, I discovered that there wasn't much blood on the ground outside. I was lucky, I reckon. Or maybe old Joe didn't have as much blood flow to his brain as I'd thought.

EXT. CEMETERY/DIGGUM'S GRAVE - DUSK

Diggum, Joe's body, and all of Diggum's cremation and burial equipment are by Diggum's own grave. He is furiously shoveling dirt off the mound. He pauses to stretch his back. The pain of years of hard labor has taken its toll on his body. The backache is visible on his face.

DIGGUM (V.O.)

That night, for the second time in my life, I had to bury a body I'd been responsible for killin' and do it without a backhoe. If I'd done it the easy way, it might've attracted attention.

I decided the best thing to do might be to just unearth the grave I'd already dug for the young punk, toss old Joe in there, and burn him up right there in the middle of that old pile of ashes. So that's what I did.

EXT. CEMETERY/DIGGUM'S GRAVE - NIGHT

The hole is completely dug out again. Diggum is preparing Joe's body for cremation. He dumps the body in a piece at a time, then kicks the bucket containing Joe's head into the hole in the ground. He follows that with the ax and the cigarettes. Finally, he leaps into the hole himself.

After glancing around at the dark grave, Diggum lights his penlight and sticks it butt-first into the wall of mud in the side of the grave to illuminate its contents. He begins the process of propping up Joe's body parts into a pyramid shape. However, the penlight falls out of its spot in the grave's wall and rolls a bit at the bottom of the grave until it comes to rest with its beam shining on a perfectly preserved and disembodied blue eyeball.

Diggum gasps and jerks backward, surprised. He snatches up the penlight from the ground and searches around for the bucket containing Joe's head. When he finds it, he reaches into Joe's neck hole and pries the head loose from the bucket. Joe's head in one hand, Diggum places the penlight in his own mouth and pries open each of Joe's eyelids with his other hand. Joe's eyes are still there. They're also brown. Diggum is visibly distressed.

DIGGUM (V.O.)

I couldn't remember for sure what color the young punk's eyes had been, but I was pretty sure that they would've been long gone from this world by the time four years had gone past. It was right then that this old caretaker for the first time felt what you probably consider to be fear. It was kind of a cold chill that run up my back all the way to the neck, makin' me shiver. Sort of like piss shiver, I reckon, if you've ever felt that before. Could've been fear. Could've been excitement. Sure enough.

Diggum drops Joe's head, maintaining his gaze on the eyeball. He crouches down as he watches it like he's contemplating whether to reach for it.

DIGGUM (V.O.)(CONT'D)

I shored up the remainder of my courage, and I bent down and snatched up that gross old eyeball. I tossed it right onto old Joe's torso and watched as it rolled across it and came to rest up against his chin like it was givin' him a little kiss. To this day I won't swear to it, but in the split second that thing was in the palm of my hand, I thought I felt it vibratin' like it was tryin' to escape or tryin' to bite me or somethin'.

Diggum grabs the gas can and drenches the body, extra eyeball and all. He empties the container on the grave's contents before tossing it out of the hole. Occasionally, he chances a glance at the eyeball as he works and is surprised that it seems to change, to have expressions of its own even without a face. The eyeball suddenly looks angry.

DIGGUM (V.O.)(CONT'D)

I'd swear, it looked to me like I wasn't doin' nothin' but makin' it mad by pouring all the fuel on it.

Just then the eyeball rolls over, away from old Joe's chin, so that it's looking
right at Diggum again.

DIGGUM (V.O.)(CONT'D)

I'll tell you that right then and there I decided to fuck all
and get the hell out of that grave.

Diggum tosses all his equipment out of the grave and scrambles out of
there like the devil himself was after him. Panicky and rushed, he lights up
the entire book of matches and tosses it down. A roaring plume of flame
erupts from inside the grave as Diggum stands beside it, watching.

DIGGUM (V.O.)(CONT'D)

Old Joe went up like any kindlin' oughta, and it wasn't
long before that hole in the ground was glowin' hot. I figured I'd just wait for old Joe to turn to ash and then climb
down again to check on my work before I covered it all up
this time. I also figured it'd be best to wait for the sun to
come up, just in case there was somethin' still down there
in the dark besides old Joe's crispy remains. For the first
time since I started work here as caretaker, my shovel and
I walked away from an open grave, and I left it that way all
night long.

EXT. CEMETERY/DIGGUM'S GRAVE - DAWN

An exhausted Diggum stands over his open grave in the cold morning
light. An occasional drift of smoke passes over his face as if there are still
a few embers burning in the hole. Steeling his nerves, Diggum leaps into
the hole to check on his work from the night before.

DIGGUM (V.O.)

The next mornin', I rose up, grabbed my shovel and my penlight, and I headed back outside. Soon as my feet hit the ground and the beam of that penlight struck old Joe's ashes, I saw it again.

The blue eyeball is still there, where it had lain the night before when Diggum escaped the open grave and set the blaze. The sight of the eyeball takes Diggum by surprise. He jumps backward in the grave hole, nearly falling over.

DIGGUM (V.O.)(CONT'D)

That old eye was unburnt and white as the day it was buried.

Diggum scans the rest of the grave with his trusty penlight. Most of old Joe's body is nothing but ashes, just like it should've been. Then, buried just a little beneath the ashes that used to be his head, Diggum notices another little glimmer of white.

He slowly approaches this new glimmer of white amid the ashes, fearful of what it could be. He leans over it and blows lightly on the ash, attempting to clear it away from the object without touching it.

DIGGUM (V.O.)(CONT'D)

While I kept a watch on that little blue-eyed bugger that wouldn't burn (I wanted to make sure it wasn't gonna come rollin' at me), I leaned over a bit, filled my lungs full of air, and blew a gust of wind over the little white spot in the ashes. Enough of them cleared away for me to see it was sphere-shaped and pretty much all white, except for an arc of brown that disappeared into the ash that I hadn't blown away.

Diggum's mouth drops open in surprise. He can't believe he's seeing another eyeball, one of a different color.

DIGGUM (V.O.)(CONT'D)

Yeah, you guessed right. It was another goddamned eyeball.
One of old Joe's brown eyes, I suspected.

Quick as a fox, Diggum climbs out of the hole, grabs his shovel, and starts
furiously filling in the hole. He makes certain that he covers both the new
eyeball and the original blue eyeball first thing.

DIGGUM (V.O.)(CONT'D)

That was two times in the fire for the blue eyeball and one
for the brown one. Neither of 'em was burnt up, so I wasn't
gonna bother tryin' again. The logical part of my head kept
tellin' me that there was probably just somethin' about the
earth in that spot that messed up the burn. I don't know. I
ain't no scientist.

Diggum straightens up from his work. His eyes fearful, focused on the
hole he's filling in.

DIGGUM (V.O.)(CONT'D)

That's what it had to be. Somethin' about that part of the
earth that didn't want eyeballs to burn.

EXT. TOOL SHED/CEMETERY - DUSK - MONTAGE

Diggum is keeping busy, burning up the dead as they arrive. Night after
night, digging holes, burning remains, and filling the holes in again. As the
montage rolls, we see clips of Diggum's work on different days and nights.
We see him growing older and wearier as he buys his cartons of cigarettes,
buries the dead, digs them up again, and burns them.

DIGGUM (V.O.)

As the days and nights went by after that, I kept up my
bargain to myself about incineratin' the community's
loved ones as they deposited 'em with me. For the most

part, I managed to do it without re-openin' the hole that I'd dumped old Joe and the young punk into. I probably wouldn't have ever opened that old hole again if things had kept goin' the way they used to be before I offed old Joe. I told you before that I ain't superstitious, but a man still notices when two plus two used to make four and suddenly don't anymore. The night I noticed was the night I dug up and burned the corpse of that old spinster Betsy Pigg.

END OF MONTAGE

EXT. TOOL SHED/CEMETERY - DUSK

Diggum rests on his shovel as he watches the corpse of Betsy Pigg burn in her grave. His face is serene. He has his groove back, the unburnt eyeballs all but forgotten.

DIGGUM (V.O.)(CONT'D)

She must've been nearin' a hundred years at the time she died, I reckon. I took my time burnin' her corpse on account of the lack of mourners. The county buried her on the warmest New Year's Eve on record. And, if you'll pardon the pun, New Year's Day is probably the deadest day at the cemetery.

Diggum smiles at his night's work and walks away from the open grave, toward the tool shed. He's giving up for the night. He feels comfortable with the way his work is going and comfortable with leaving it on its own until after the new year rings in.

DIGGUM (V.O.)(CONT'D)

I figured I probably had a good five or six hours after sun-up before the first visitor showed up that day, so I didn't bother coverin' up her burnt remains until long after that ball in New York's Times Square had come down, and I'd had myself a good long winter's nap.

199

EXT. CEMETERY/BETSY PIGG'S GRAVE - EARLY MORNING

Diggum approaches Betsy Pigg's grave, shovel in hand, to finish his work from the night before. He glances up at an unusually warm New Year's Day sun, enjoying the feel of it on his skin. Then he looks down in the grave, and his expression changes. First, he is confused. Then horrified as memories of the unburnt eyeballs resurface.

DIGGUM (V.O.)

The next mornin', it happened again.

In the grave, on top of the burnt remains, lies an entirely unburnt woman's pelvic bone.

DIGGUM (V.O.)(CONT'D)

Hell, old spinster Pigg had broke her back sneezin' one night in her seventies when she had a particularly bad case of hay fever. I should've been able to burn hers up just by placin' her in front of my oven while I was heatin' up a pizza.

Diggum jumps into Betsy Pigg's grave to investigate further. He filters some of her ashes through his gloved fingers as if searching for signs of other unburnt remains.

DIGGUM (V.O.)(CONT'D)

All her other bones were dust now. All of 'em. There was no bones, no eyeballs, no brain, no nothin' except that pelvic bone.

Diggum thrusts the handle of his shovel through one of the holes in that pelvic bone and hefts it out of the grave hole.

The pelvic bone now lays beside the open grave. Diggum's ax wedge comes down on top of it, breaking it into two pieces at first. Diggum continues to break it up with the ax, hitting it over and over.

DIGGUM (V.O.)(CONT'D)

I broke up pretty well, but there was no way I was gonna get it down to ashes by hand. So I just put the pieces in my pail, and I filled in her grave.

EXT. CEMETERY - DUSK - MONTAGE

Diggum is shoveling dirt out of his own grave again, working hard. His face reveals a man who is both determined and a little puzzled by the recent events.

DIGGUM (V.O.)

When I had Betsy's grave filled in, I dug up part of my own grave again. I don't specifically know why I picked that one. There was just somethin' in my head, somethin' that said: "this is where the extras go." I didn't dig all the way down to where I burned old Joe and the young punk, just about half way there. Then I dropped in the shards of Betsy Pigg's pelvic bone and filled that sucker in again quick as I could.

Various shots of Diggum searching burned remains for unburnt parts. He sifts through ashes, finding pieces of bone here and there, but more often than not finding teeth because teeth are the most difficult to burn up. Each time he finds unburnt remains, he collects them and buries them along with the other unburnt remains in his own grave.

DIGGUM (V.O.)(CONT'D)

After that, I kept a closer watch on the bodies as I burnt 'em up and crushed up any remainin' bone fragments. More often than not there was teeth remainin', but that was to be expected. There'd always be a few teeth.

But more and more I was noticin' that there was parts other than teeth that didn't seem to be gettin' burnt up by the fire. I'd find a femur here or a finger there, maybe an ulna in

another place. Every time I'd chop 'em up into fragments
and dump 'em into my own grave hole.

END OF MONTAGE

EXT. CEMETERY/JOHN HANDLE'S GRAVE - DAWN

Diggum's examining the remains of another fire. He was attempting to
destroy the body of John Handle. He is shocked to find a part of an unburnt brain in the remains of the grave in which he'd burned John Handle's body. He pokes at the brain with his ax handle.

DIGGUM (V.O.)

The time I burned up old John Handle's body, I found the
right half of his brain still in the grave, not even slightly singed by the fire. I suppose that was appropriate for
old John, though. He was the guy who owned that hippie-lookin' New Age shop downtown. Figures if any part
of him was gonna survive it would be the part that's all
about creativity and flowers and daydreams and Pollyanna
shit like that.

EXT. CEMETERY/DIGGUM'S GRAVE - DUSK

Diggum is burying more remains in his own grave, particularly teeth and a
few softer unburnt remains, such as John Handle's brain. Included among
the remains are many, many unburnt teeth.

DIGGUM (V.O.)

Every single time it happened, I felt that same compulsion
to dig out the grave I'd used to burn old Joe and that young
punk. Then I'd toss that unburnt piece of body in and cover
it all back up again. Things were gettin' weird, and I didn't
want to take no chances.

INT. DIGGUM'S BEDROOM

Diggum lies on his bed, staring at the ceiling. A shadow is cast on his wall from the headlights of an approaching car. Diggum is startled and sits upright. He looks out the window. He is relieved to determine that it was just a random car driving by. Diggum rolls over on his side and tries to drift off to sleep.

DIGGUM (V.O.)

I reckon it helped me sleep at night to know that all them extra parts was in one place in the cemetery, that if I could ever figure out how to get rid of 'em for good, I'd know exactly where to go lookin' for 'em instead of havin' to dig up every grave in the cemetery.

EXT. CEMETERY/JOHN DALTON'S GRAVE - DAWN

Modern Diggum remains propped on his elbows by John Dalton's grave. The fire he'd set near the beginning of his story has died down dramatically. Smoke and ash from Mr. Dalton's cremation occasionally wisp by Diggum's face. Exhausted from his long night of work, old Diggum stands up and looks down into the open grave. At the bottom, among all the ash, are both John Dalton's huge hands, unburnt.

DIGGUM (V.O.)

Of course, if I'd figured back then what all that was leadin' to, I might've left them parts where they lay.

Angry, Diggum leaps into John Dalton's grave to retrieve the hands. He pokes at each of the hands with a finger, then reaches for them and tosses them out of the grave. He then leaps out and begins to fill in John Dalton's grave. The dead hands remain at rest by his side.

DIGGUM (V.O.)(CONT'D)

That's the other ironic, funny thing, ain't it? All I needed to do was give you a hand. And that's exactly what I was doin' out here tonight. I dug up my own old grave one more time to toss in old John Dalton's hands that wouldn't burn.

EXT. CEMETERY/DIGGUM'S GRAVE - DUSK, NEARLY FULL DARK

Diggum has just finished clearing out a deep spot in his own grave for John Dalton's hands. The hands rest beside him, as they did when he was filling in Dalton's grave. Diggum stretches his back and tosses his shovel aside. He then bends down to retrieve the hands, at which point they launch themselves from the ground and lock around his throat.

Diggum struggles with the suddenly animated hands until he finally stumbles into the open hole he's made in his own grave. The hands come loose from his throat in mid-flight and land on the ground outside the grave. Diggum lands flat on his back.

DIGGUM (V.O.)

It's funny, I reckon. I've been diggin' my own grave here for years, diggin' it out and fillin' it back in, but until tonight I was never actually bein' buried in it.

Diggum lays at the bottom of his own grave, looking up at the night sky. There's a slight gleam in his eyes and a wry grin on his face. There's no longer any fear. He begins to speak aloud to the thing standing over him.

DIGGUM

So here you are now, standin' over me with your cut up boney old arms all gleamin' in the moonlight. I reckon old God got his last laugh on me. Sure enough.

(chuckles)

I guess if God makes the rules then God can also break the rules, or at least find himself a clever way to manipulate 'em.

(laughs)

I'm bettin' that if I had my penlight with me right now, I could shine 'em on your eyes and see that you have one that's old Joe brown and another that's young punk blue. That pelvis of yours looks all cracked up and a bit womanly to me, too. I'm bettin' that's the unburnt part of the spinster Betsy Pigg that I tossed in this grave a while back.

Diggum's smile fades a little. He is perhaps wondering where his plan might have gone wrong.

DIGGUM (CONT'D)

I can almost see the whole of you in the bright of the moonlight that's shinin' off the blade of my ax now that you're standin' straddle over me and you've got it hefted way up over top of your skull like that. Sure enough.

From Diggum's point of view, a large anthropomorphic creature composed entirely of necrotic unburnt body parts stands at the edge of the grave, glaring down at him. Its exposed jaw reveals a wicked, vengeful grin. The thing has one brown eye and one blue eye. It also has a pelvis that resembles the one Diggum had earlier chopped to pieces. Its hands, the ones that attempted to strangle Diggum, are attached to it now and are wielding Diggum's own ax over its head. The tips of its toes, in addition to other parts of its body, appear to be composed primarily of human teeth.

DIGGUM (O.S.)

My God, you have a lot of teeth.

Again from Diggum's point of view, the creature arcs backward with Diggum's ax and then launches the weapon forward, toward Diggum's head.

FADE OUT.

THE END

Decision Paralysis

The scariest day of Tina's life was the day that her granny's mind broke, the day that her granny made her last decision. Her granny had driven to Tina's school that day to pick her up because both of Tina's parents worked hard at their jobs to make money so they could afford to put food on the table. There was no one else available at three o'clock in the afternoon on a weekday to drive Tina from school.

She could have ridden the bus, of course. They had tried that one time before. Her mother and father were worried about her granny's health. They said she didn't need the extra stress of having to drive into town to retrieve Tina from school during the week. Just keeping up with Tina for the few hours after school was enough of a chore for a widow in her twilight. That's what they said anyway. Tina knew her granny had argued with them about it. She had heard the whole thing that one night when her mother and father were late picking her up from her granny's house.

"I'm fine!" her granny had protested. "She doesn't need to ride the bus. I've been driving since I was a little girl on my daddy's farm. You might as well just let Tina stay with me full time during the school year anyway. She's with me more than she's at home, and I like having her around. Helps to keep me from yakking away to myself like a nut. I ain't crazy as long as there's someone else around to hear it. That was why I kept your daddy around as long as I did, Julie. Lord knows he wasn't good for much else! Except making decisions. He was always making those. You got lucky with your hubby Don there. He's got ears he uses to listen to you, and he makes real money.

"Honestly, I don't see why you don't just stay at home with the child anyway. It's not like you two need the second income when you've got Mister Mobile App Developer here wrapped around your little finger."

Despite her granny's protests, her mother and father won that argument. At least for the moment. Tina was her granny's granddaughter, not her daughter, and her mother and father wanted Tina to start riding the bus. Their feet were down. The decision was final. That's how her granny put it, anyway. She said that her mother and father had put their feet down and nailed their shoes to the floor, and that meant that they weren't going to budge.

"Just like her father," her granny had said under hot breath. "She's just like him. Has to be the one in control."

Tina had imagined her parents bent at the knees, driving long nails into the toes of their shoes with hammers like the ones that still hung on the wall in her grandfather's old tool shed. Tina played out there sometimes. She peeked in every now and then, even though she knew her granny didn't want her going in there. That was a private place, she'd explained. A place of final decisions. A place for the dead.

Tina never understood what her granny meant by that. She never saw any dead people in there, just a bunch of old tools hanging on the wall and a dead, dried up earthworm or two. Once, while playing out there, she found a dead baby bird with no feathers that had fallen from its nest, but that had been outside the shed. She thought maybe her granny was just trying to scare her into staying out of there. But it didn't work. Her granny didn't have a scary bone in her body. At least, she didn't have any scary bones that Tina knew about. Not back then.

Her granny was waiting at the end of her driveway for the bus to arrive on that day after she'd had the fight with her mother and father, but no one had told the bus driver that Tina was riding it. He just kept on driving right past her granny's house like a bat out of a gun. Tina had pressed the palms of her hands against the back window of the bus as it whizzed by the house. She had screamed her granny's name while her granny ran after her as fast as she could. The other kids might have been laughing while she screamed. Tina couldn't remember for sure. She was too terrified to notice. She was terrified that the bus would just keep on rolling forever. She might never see her granny, her mother, or her father again.

Beyond the bus window, her granny flailed her arms in the air while she gave chase on foot. Tina could see that she was shouting for the bus driver to stop and to let Tina off. For one long terrible moment, it looked like the bus driver wasn't going to heed her pleas. Perhaps Tina would be forced to continue riding the bus until it slammed right into the edge of the earth somewhere down the line; until it crashed nose-first into the place where all the roads must end, and you no longer have a choice. Where there are no decisions left to make.

Then, mercifully, she felt the massive contraption slowing beneath her. Tina could see that her granny was catching up to it on foot. Finally, she felt the gentle forward jerk and backward tug of gravity as the bus came to a complete stop. That was followed by the startled, soda can pop-top hiss of its doors swinging open. Tina was free! She broke away from the rear window and dashed down the aisle toward the open door, absently launching her backpack over one shoulder and narrowly avoiding a classmate's outstretched foot before she leaped into her granny's open arms just outside.

"Never again," her granny had said as she smothered Tina's tear-stained face against the flower patterned dress that was covering her grandmotherly bosom. She gently stroked the back of the girl's head with one pruned hand. "Never again. I'll pick you up from school from now on. We can't trust anyone else to do it. This bus incident proves that. If you want something done right, you gotta do it yourself. I've decided." Tina felt her granny lay her cheek against the top of her head.

"Never again. I've decided."

Her granny was stronger when her mother and father argued with her after that. "The bus driver will learn!" they implored. Her granny replied that she wasn't going to give that driver a chance. Tina was the only grandchild she had and, by God, she wasn't going to let anything happen to her!

"Your father wouldn't allow this, Julie," her granny shouted at Tina's mother. "So neither will I."

That's how it came to pass that her granny won her argument and became tasked with picking Tina up from school from then on. She had put her foot down—both feet, in fact. Her feet might be old, she said, but they were harder and more calloused than her mother and father's because of her many more years of walking and working on them. Her feet could stand the pain of having those nails holding them to the floor.

But her granny was never quite the same after that, either. Often Tina would catch her standing in the middle of a room, her car keys in hand, with a panicky look on her face. She looked as if she had forgotten something, somewhere she was supposed to be or something she was supposed to do.

"There are just so many decisions you have to make when you're a grown-up," her granny had explained to her one afternoon. "There are so many things that have to be done. It gets overwhelming, especially when you have reams of paper to go through and phones ringing and devices dinging at you and people harassing you about this and that.

"Makes me wish Jesse were still alive to help me take care of all this. He was always the one who paid the bills and talked to people about the dirty details of everything. I was the one who ran the errands every day and kept the house in order, but that was basically just physical labor and making decisions that didn't really have to have *correct* answers. There wasn't any paperwork or complicated questions to answer. I had to know where my purse was and how to get places. That was it. No need to think up any long-winded responses to complicated questions from tax collectors.

"Jesse was the one who talked to the man from the IRS that time we got audited. I was a nervous wreck the whole time that was going on, I tell you. It's not that we did anything wrong. We didn't. At least, I never thought we did. It was just how complicated the whole process was. I was never more glad to have Jesse there than when he was taking care of all that.

"If something like that ever happens again, I'm going to be the one who has to deal with it. But I don't know that I could. Those people are scary. They ask so many questions. Every time that man in the suit opened his mouth, I felt my blood pressure spike. It got so high that there were times when I was afraid my ears were going to launch right off my head."

She sighed.

"Sometimes I think I might have been better off without Jesse, though. I wonder if I might have been better able to handle things like that, to know what is the right thing to do. I'm too old now, though, Tina. Too old to learn how to deal with complicated stuff like that. Can't teach an old dog new tricks, you know?

"Jesse even had all our funeral arrangements all worked out way back before he died. I didn't have to lift a finger. I guess that's my only comfort now. I don't have too many more years left in this world to have to deal with it. Before too much longer, that stuff won't matter anymore."

The day of her granny's final decision had been one of the worst. She had said so as Tina climbed into the back seat of her Lincoln. The familiar aroma of sun-baked Juicy Fruit and McDonald's french fries that always permeated the car wafted to her nostrils. Her granny's news concerned Tina. Not because her granny had had a bad day. Tina knew she had a lot of those, especially when her memory wasn't working as well as it should. Tina was concerned because her granny usually asked Tina how her day at school had been before talking about her own day. It was one of the things Tina loved about her granny. She always seemed interested in the things that happened to Tina during a school day, even when those things weren't very interesting to Tina herself. Starting off the trip to her granny's house with no indication that her granny had the slightest interest in the good or bad of Tina's day made everything feel *off* somehow.

"Worst day," her granny said in answer to Tina's unasked question. "Worst day. I don't know how much more I can take. Worst day."

Tina opened her mouth to ask her granny what she meant, but her granny interrupted her, continuing unprompted.

"I saw your grandfather in my dreams last night," she said. "I saw him clear as if he were still alive. He was sitting on a little stool right there in the door of that old tool shed. Standing wide open, that door was, with all those dead man's rusty old tools hanging on hooks just inside of it. He was sitting there just like he did in life sometimes, pulling a drag on a cigarette and squinting at me through that old blue smoke when it hit him in the eye. Then he raised both his hands up and looked around like he was gesturing at all the stuff locked up in that old shed.

"And then he spoke to me, Tina. He said, 'What the hell are you doing, Janine, hanging on to all this old stuff? Who are you keeping it for? Don't you see that all you're doing is making more work and upkeep for yourself? All you have to do is let go of some of the responsibilities you've piled on top of yourself since I died, hon. Then you don't have to make so many decisions.'

"I tried to tell him that I couldn't let it go. That the tool shed was all I had left of him. I tried to tell him that if I let go of all that he'd be gone

211

forever. I wanted to explain that I can't just stop taking care of things, either. If I don't take care of them, no one will. Who'll help your mommy and daddy take care of you if I don't do it? My mouth was hanging open to say all that, but the words just wouldn't come out. It was like my tongue was paralyzed.

"And Jesse, your poor old grandfather, just sat there and looked at me for another minute. Then you know what he said? He looked at me and said, 'Tina comes in here sometimes, you know. She can take care of herself better than you think she can.' Then he waved that cigarette in the air so the smoke made a little squiggle in front of him and he recited some lines from that old folk song about the worms. The one about being dead and going to rot? How did it go?

The worms crawl in, the worms crawl out,
The worms play pinochle on your snout,
They eat your eyes, they eat your nose,
They eat the jelly between your toes.

"That's what he said to me, Tina. And I sat straight up in bed, wide awake, right then. I crawled out of bed and stood there in my nightgown, looking out the window at that old tool shed of his. The full moon was shining right on the door, bright enough to cast shadows. And there it sat, that old tool shed, just as it has been for a long time now, all closed up and silent as the grave."

"That sounds like an awful dream," Tina said, hoping that her granny wouldn't actually ask her about her adventures to the tool shed. Her granny didn't acknowledge her.

"I didn't get back to sleep all night," the old woman continued. "All I could think about was how the worms are eating at your grandfather, and I can't stop them. There's nothing I can do to stop them.

"Then, as soon as the sun was up, my phone was ringing. Your mommy. That's who it was. She was crying. She said your daddy had spent all their money—she wouldn't say on what—and they couldn't pay their bills this month. She asked me if I had any money they could borrow to pay for the water and the electric. She said they needed to know by this afternoon. She said she wouldn't ask except that they were out of options.

"I told her what I've always told your mommy," she said. "I told her that I don't believe in lending money and that the Good Lord will provide for them if they need it. But I could hear her voice quivering on the other end of the line as I was saying all that. So then she tells me that I just don't understand how things are these days, that it ain't possible to just get along without debt anymore. She said something about them not having good credit, and I was their only chance.

"So I told her that I'd think about it." Her granny chuckled without humor. "But I don't think about it, Tina. I can't think about it. It's all too much to think about. It's one more thing I have to do. One more decision I have to make. And it doesn't matter how many times I tell myself to let things go and run their own course, I know at some point I'm going to end up stepping in to take care of everything myself. I expect your mommy knows that, too."

She fell silent. Tina chose to allow it. The thought that her mother and father might be in some money trouble bothered her. How would they buy food to eat? Especially if her granny refused to help? She thought about asking her granny about this herself, but she could see that the old woman was probably in no state to make her an answer. She was staring straight ahead at the road in front of them, although perhaps not seeing it. The horns of two cars blared long in protest as her granny's Lincoln rolled full speed and without pause through a four-way stop.

Seconds later, a man pushing a lawnmower along the path where his grassy yard met the shoulder of the road looked directly at her granny and shook his fist in the air. His sweaty brow was furrowed, and his nostrils were flared dragon-like against the sides of his pinched nose. Tina wondered if her granny might be driving too fast for the neighborhood. She didn't know. She'd never been in this area of town before. The street sign at the intersection her granny had sped through indicated that they were on Wormwood Street.

The worms crawl in, the worms crawl out,
The worms play pinochle on your snout.

"Then there was the neighbor kid," her granny spat. Tina started in her seat. "He shows up at my door right as I'm about to leave for the
213

grocery. Wants to mow my lawn for a couple of twenties. At first, I tell him okay, fine, go ahead. It costs me forty, and it's something I don't have to worry about for a week or two. But then he starts asking me all these questions: do I prefer it cut high or scalped? Do I want him to avoid any specific areas where there might be flower beds or bushes he can't see? Do I want him to run the trimmer when he's done with the mowing? Where's the property line, so he doesn't get in trouble with our nasty old rear neighbor who hates anybody under fifty? I don't have the answers to these things, and I don't have time to think about them! I'd swear he asked me what to do about the worms, too. I don't know what worms he was talking about, but I heard him say something about worms. That got me thinking about your poor old Gram again, and I could feel the tears starting to well up.

"Finally, I just threw the money at him, clapped my hands over my ears, and high-tailed it to the car. Let him do whatever he thinks needs to be done. I have my own decisions to make! I can't make everybody else's decisions for them!"

Tina nodded sympathetically, although her granny hadn't bothered to check on her passenger in the rearview mirror since she'd climbed into the car. She wondered if her granny had forgotten that she was there. She'd said Tina's name a few times, so that was good. Still, she was starting to wonder how much of her granny really knew where she was and who was with her. That was when Tina heard, and felt, the loud thud on their right.

She glanced behind them to see a man in a cycling outfit and helmet laying prone on the shoulder of the road. One of his legs was twisted backward at the knee, causing the toe of his shoe to point skyward.

They eat your eyes, they eat your nose,
They eat the jelly between your toes.

A ruby pool of blood appeared to be expanding along the pavement from beneath what was left of the man's face. The bicycle he had apparently been riding lay over-ended in the ditch beside him, its front wheel spinning lazily, bouncing glints of golden autumn afternoon sunshine off its metal rim and into Tina's eyes.

Silently, Tina began to cry.

"Oh, and then there was the grocery," her granny shouted. "The grocery! There was a time when I could get what I needed, say howdy to a few folks I knew and be out of there in less than an hour. Not anymore, I tell you! Not anymore! First, you have to find a parking space that's not somewhere out in the middle of town, so you don't have a heart attack walking up to the door.

"Next, you have to fight your way past the Boy Scouts, the Girl Scouts, the Little League teams, the Salvation Army, the Pink Ribbon Crusade, or whoever is standing out front trying to pry your daily bread right out of your hands before you can even buy it. And if they don't nag you on the way into the store they nag you on the way out! Most times both!

"So, you finally make your way past all that hullabaloo only to find yourself stuck pushing your cart behind the same. Slow. Ass. Nitpicker. In. Every. Single. Aisle. They're always standing right where you need to be, too. Can't be bothered just to make their choices based on price and taste like an average person. Oh, no! They have to read the entire label and try to sound out the ingredients. Does anybody outside of someone who wears a lab coat for work know how to pronounce fucking gibberish like phenylephrine?"

Tina sobbed audibly from the back seat, although her granny did not seem to notice. She had never heard her granny use the swears before. Her father? Sure, when he was angry and not in control of himself. Her granny had never said such things in front of her. Not for the first time, the thought occurred to Tina that her granny might have hit the man on the bicycle because she, like her father sometimes, was not in control of herself.

"So you have to make another decision then," her granny said. "You have to decide whether you're going to go around them and try to remember to come back for what you need or just wait them out and hope that wherever they're headed next is the hell away from you. God! Makes me so mad!"

The left side of the car suddenly felt as if it had leaped off the ground. Tina felt a surge of terror run circles around her gut. She was sure that the Lincoln was about to flip over. To her granny's left, one of those big blue standalone United States Post Office mailboxes went flying and took her granny's side mirror along with it. The mirror bounced off the back seat window on the edge of the car opposite Tina, leaving a long black skid mark on the glass in its wake.

Tina glanced through the rear windshield and saw people watching after them, many standing at edges of yards or on the opposite sidewalk, their mouths hanging open in disbelief. One young man had apparently been struck by something as her granny drove past. He was seated on the sidewalk directly behind them, rocking back and forth on his bottom and cradling his right shoulder with his left hand. A woman who appeared to have been pushing a baby stroller was now chasing it down the hill behind them.

"Of course, once you finally have everything you need, you have to battle the lines at the checkout. Let's see, do I pick this lane or that lane? Which one's the shortest? Which one's the fastest? Oh, and no sooner do you pick a lane than someone else jumps ahead of you. That or the newest, most inexperienced cashier opens a new station and directs you there. Then you spend fifteen minutes waiting for her to figure out how to get into the system while a new line stacks up behind you, so there's no escape! Sometimes I think those kids at the grocery just want to jam everybody together like segments of some weird human worm. Like they think that it's funny."

A big green worm with rolling eyes
Crawls in your stomach and out your sides.

"Granny?" Tina tried. "Granny, I think I'm getting car sick. My tummy doesn't feel so good. Can we stop?"

No reply.

"Granny?"

They sped through another intersection, this one too fast for Tina to determine whether the light ahead of them had been red or green. Based on the loud and long *blat* of car horns fading into the distance behind them, she guessed that it had been red.

"And the worms!" her granny shouted. "There are worms all over the sidewalk when you come out of the store after a rain! Where do they come from?

"Then there's all the choices you have to make just to get out of the parking lot and find your way back home," she screeched. "Do I go up this aisle or down that one? You better believe as soon as you put your car in reverse that the asshole beside you or behind you will decide to back out at the same time. Oh, and there's a fight waiting to happen! You better believe it.

216

"And what happens when you finally get to the end of the aisle? Can you guess? All of a sudden a thousand people want to cross the parking lot to the door, so you can't get through. You have to keep watching and decide when it's safe, decide when you're least likely to run over somebody. DAMMIT! I'M TIRED OF DECIDING!

"So you know what I did?"

Tina saw her granny glance up in the rearview mirror at her for the first time that afternoon. Her eyes were full of jagged streaks of red lightning and hate.

"I just gave up trying to make decisions. I just gave up and hit the gas. I hit the gas, and I plowed right through that entire crowd of mother-fuckers! Oh, you should have heard those people scream! And I screamed back at them. You know what I screamed? I rolled down my window, and I screamed at them 'You're driving me to an early grave!' That's what I screamed. And maybe that's for the best. The earlier I get there, the earlier I can stop the worms from feasting on your grandfather.

"That's when I came to get you, Tina. I came to pick you up from school because I promised I would do that. But let me tell you something, hon. That was my last decision. Something broke inside me. I can't make any more decisions now. I'm all out of them. I mean, look at me. I can't even move! I no longer have a choice."

"Granny," Tina interrupted her. "Granny I think I'm gonna *puuu-ugh—*" That day's lunch exploded from behind her throat and out her mouth, into her lap and the Lincoln's floorboard beyond it. She could hear her granny's maniac laughter from the front seat.

Your stomach turns a slimy green,
And pus pours out like whipping cream.

"I can't make any more decisions!" her granny screamed again from behind the wheel. Tina noted that her fingers were no longer wrapped around it. "I can't do it, Jesse! I can't do it! They're driving me to an early grave just like they did to you! Just like that!"

She brayed laughter at the ceiling of the Lincoln. Tina saw a single tear creep from the corner of her granny's wrinkled old eye. "I'm coming to be with you, Jesse! I have to stop those worms! Nothing can change that now! I can't decide to stop it! Here I come!"

In the back seat, Tina sat up straight and peered through the windshield at the oncoming stone masonry of Lost Hollow's biggest cemetery. The wall was ancient, but to Tina, it looked strong enough to kill them both on impact. It might as well be the edge of the Earth, Tina thought, and the Lincoln might as well be that old school bus she'd been afraid was just going to go right off the end. Furiously, she fought against her seatbelt, pressing the release button and yanking on the strap three times in a row before the tab finally came loose from the slot.

She threw the strap aside and reached for the lever to open the Lincoln's door. She didn't know for certain whether what she was doing might save her life, but she was more than certain that hitting that cemetery wall would kill them both. She wrapped her fingers around the door lever and pulled.

Nothing happened. The door remained closed.

"Granny!" Tina screamed. "Granny please unlock the door and let me out! I don't want to go with you and Gram! I want to go home!"

From the front seat:

You'll spread it on a slice of bread,
And that's what you eat when you are dead.

Desperate, Tina snatched her school backpack off the seat beside her and dove into the floorboard behind the passenger seat. There was just enough space for her to crouch there, fetal, with her backpack and its contents filling the gap between her and the seat in front of her. She imagined the front end of her granny's Lincoln collapsing into the cemetery wall. Silently, she prayed that there was enough length on the front of the car to protect her in the back.

***

Awareness came about after some struggle.

Her knees hurt. Her shoulders and her back ached, too. She tried to open her eyes, but there was a bright light in front of her that made them sting, so she closed them tight again. She drew in a deep breath, which set her ribs on fire, and let it out in a series of short gasps and coughs. She felt the warmth of the palm of someone's hand on her brow.

"There there," a familiar voice whispered. It sounded a little like her granny, but without much of the hoarseness that comes with old age. "There there. Everything's alright. Everything's going to be all right."

Tina opened her mouth to speak, but her lips were met instead by the mouth of a plastic straw. "Sip," said the voice. Her tongue felt thick, and her throat was scratchy. Swallowing was painful, but the cool water felt good as it rolled down her esophagus.

"Granny," she managed.

"No, sweetie," the voice whispered. "It's Mommy. Mommy's here."

"Mommy?" Tina replied. "Mommy the light's too bright."

There was a metallic squeak, and suddenly the blinding haze in front of her eyelids was gone. She opened her eyes and, when her vision cleared, was able to make out the forms of both her mother and her father standing over her. She knew that she must be laying down because behind them was a white ceiling with a lot of little holes in it, like the one in her classroom at school.

"Where?"

"You're in the hospital, pumpkin," her father said. "You were in a nasty accident, but the doctors think you're going to heal up just fine."

"Accident? Granny?"

"Now now," her mother said. "Don't you worry about that right now. You just lay back and get some rest. Let your body heal. Everything else in the world can wait, okay?"

"Okay," Tina replied. Her eyelids suddenly felt heavy again.

"Mommy and Daddy are going to go talk to the doctor for a minute, sweetie," her mother said. "You'll be okay here. Just relax. We'll be right back."

There was the sound of multiple footsteps on linoleum, then what was most likely a closing door, and the room was quiet. Tina was overcome by the need to sleep.

"Granny?" she whispered into the darkness. "Where are you, Granny? What did you do?"

"I made one more decision after all," she thought she heard a voice say from a distance. "I'm with your Gram now, Tina. I decided to be with him."

"But you didn't let me have a choice," Tina whispered in reply. "I didn't get a choice." There was a long pause. Tina was nearly unconscious when the voice spoke again.

"It's strange here," it said. "Just like the old song says. The worms crawl in, the worms crawl out. You can't stop them. No matter what you decide to do, what choices you make, you can't stop the worms."

Tina drifted into a deep sleep, glad of the fact that she did not need to make any more decisions that day.

Legit

Hello? Is this thing on? Ha! Here, buddy-boo. I don't feel like holding the phone the whole time I'm recording this. You take it again. I want to send a new message to all my new fans now that you and I all over the news. Oh, I guess you can't do this anymore, huh? Seeing as how you're dead now. Well, let me just prop it up in your hand here, like so. Maybe we can use Officer Simpleton's head laying against your neck here to make a nice little stand. There we go. All set!

Hi, world! It's me again. Tiffany. Let's recap. After the good old Clarington PD showed up and started shouting at us, I thought it might be fun to see what Officer Asshat had in the trunk of this patrol car that might give me a little bit of a chance in this fight. Turns out the trunk was empty except for a spare tire. Pretty much like buddy-boo's body stuck behind the camera here. Ha!

So I don't know why the cops haven't rushed me yet. I'm sure that between my live streams and the sounds of gunshots they probably already know that both their own little Officer Interfere and buddy-boo are dead now. So I'm all by my little bitty lonesome in this empty garage, just waiting out the inevitable end of it all.

I guess you might be wondering what happened to buddy-boo, huh? His fat naked ass was alive and recording my first little live stream just about half an hour ago after I heard the cops outside and figured out I didn't have any guns in here to fight them with. I guess I was hoping that them knowing I'm defenseless in here would make them go ahead and rush me and get this done. They wouldn't kill me. They'd just take me into custody. I'm a pretty girl, for God's sake. They're just another means to end, really. Who knows what I would do once I got out of this dead end and back into a populated area like a county jail, right? Ha!

Anyway, we were talking about buddy-boo here. I thought about keeping him alive. Really, I did. I mean, he had managed to fool me twice in the same night. That's not easy to do. I figured if I could keep him alive long enough I'd be able to break him. Make him kind of my pretend hubby or a sidekick. Clyde to my Bonnie. Kid to my Butch. Robin to my Batman. Someone to do the dirty work of cleaning up after me. I've been there too many times tonight already, believe me. If I were going to keep fulfilling my destiny, I'd need some help with the more disgusting parts. Did you know a body will leak shit and piss after it dies? I sure didn't. That's not how it happens in the movies. I hadn't really noticed it anyway, not until I took out old buddy-boo. The backseat of this car and part of Officer Stupid's leg are coated in piss and liquid shit now. Smells awful in here. I've even gagged a few times. Guess that was the hazard of killing buddy-boo while he was still naked, fat with food, and half hung over from our time in the bar, huh? Ha! You would've thought that his bare-assed run through the nighttime desert after I ran out of gas would've scared all the shit out of him already, or at least frozen his asshole closed.

I guess it all just comes down to the fact that buddy-boo was a fuck-up no matter how you slice him. So that's what I ended up doing after he dropped my phone during my last attempt to live stream this ordeal. I sliced him. Well, I sliced his brain in two with one of Officer Shitface's bullets. Ha! You'd think having his wrists strapped together would help him get a grip on something expensive like a smartphone. Guess not. He dropped it right onto the patrol car's floorboard. It pissed me off—as in final straw pissed off—so I killed him for it.

Yeppers peppers, after waiting all night long, I finally got to watch old bare-assed buddy-boo's journey into the Great Beyond. I don't know what I was expecting. Fireworks? A parade of some kind across his glazed over eyeballs? No idea. It was a real letdown, though.

Don't get me wrong. I was happy to finally get to kill him. I felt real good about that. I just hated the look in his eyes when he went. Maybe there wasn't enough light behind those eyes to bother going dark, I don't know. But it just wasn't the same as the others. It was just kind of a blankness into more blankness, and then the smell of piss and shit. Motherfucker didn't even put up a struggle this time. Didn't even try. He saw me pick up the gun. Saw me aim it at his temple. I guess I figured he'd dropped the phone on purpose or something like he'd thought of some other way to escape me and dropping the phone was part of his plan.

So I shot him again. Two more times, actually. Once for not having a more spectacular departure from this world and then again for making me think he had more brains than he really did. I thought I had underestimated him before. Guess not. I think there might have been a part of me that was hoping he was planning something else. I guess I kind of wanted the foil. The Batman has his Joker, you know? Why shouldn't I have a fat naked one?

Okay, before I go any further: yes, I can see all those little emoji popping up on the screen as I'm talking. I'm not blind. I'm ignoring you. I'm not really sure how many ways I can say it, though. You don't matter. I'm not doing this for you. I'm doing this because I figure it's a means of getting what I want. So, you know, get over yourselves. You need to be paying attention to me, not those stupid cutesy little social buttons. Fucking egomaniacs on your little phones there, thinking you're so legit because you're *sharing* your lives. You're not sharing, you're blathering into the void. You're not legit. I am. I'm legit. You wanna know why? Here it is. And it's real.

Yeah. Take a good long look at buddy-boo here and his friend and lover Officer Corpsey. Wait, let me turn on the flashlight on this phone here. There. See? This was all me. All real. I did this. See buddy-boo's brains dripping out of that hole in the side of his head? See the drop of piss still dangling from the end of his dick? I wish I could text you the smell in here. Why hasn't anyone invented that yet? Ha! Yeah, while you sit back in your comfy little coffee shops with your lattes and your laptops, I've been out here doing things, making something of myself. See? *See?* I. Am. The. Real. Deal.

Well, I'm not a little girl anymore anyway. That's for damn sure. I'll tell you all a little secret, though. There's a part of me that wishes I was, at least for a little while. If I could just go back, I might do some better planning. It's been a long night, and I've been through a hell of a lot of shit. I wonder if I made a mistake not killing buddy-boo at the get-go. I do make my mistakes sometimes. Looking back, I could've just offed him in the parking lot in back of that bar. Nobody was out there at the time. I can't imagine anyone in that place would have been sober enough to stop me anyway. Maybe if I hadn't had to deal with his hairy ass, I would've thought to stop for gas somewhere. Maybe I would have put a little more effort into doing my job and a little less in trying to hunt down and eliminate a problem. Coulda, woulda, shoulda, I guess. No point in dwelling on it. In fact, I think I'm going to stop calling any mistakes I made tonight "mistakes." From now on, I'm going to call them "happy accidents." Without those happy accidents, I would have just spent this night like any other boring night before it: wishing I was doing something else.

Besides, I'm not sure that I'm really done with all this yet. Sure, there are a few cops outside who want to put a stop to me. But there are a whole lot of people left alive in this world, and I'm guessing that if I'm meant to keep killing, I'll get out of this somehow and keep on killing. I mean, maybe prison is where I'm supposed to be after all, right? Maybe I'm supposed to spend the rest of my life killing people in prison. Though I'm not really sure I believe in that, either. Is there *actually* some higher power guiding me? Maybe. But probably not. No, looking back on all this, I think I just did it because I wanted to. I was bored, and I hate being bored. There was no purpose other than that.

Hey, you. Whoever you were. I saw that comment pop up there on my screen. What did I tell you about trying to make this about you? It ain't. So don't. But to answer your question (because I feel like it): no, I don't regret one fucking bit of anything I've done tonight. I've decided. It's all good. There's just nothing worth regretting. Whatever happens next happens. That's all. I look back on it all, and I'm satisfied. I did it, and I did it my way. So, you know, fuck you.

Anyway, what was I saying? Oh, right. I was bored. I don't think I actually knew I was bored until I saw my mom die in the bathroom. All of a sudden then it hit me that I had been missing out on something. And, well, you know everything that happened after that from the last live stream I did before I offed old buddy-boo here. I'm not bored anymore. At least not yet.

Jesus, what is taking those cops so long to get in here and deal with me? The wait is killing me. I starting to feel like a fucking elderly invalid, just laying in a hospital bed and waiting to die and hoping the kids come see me before I go. I've dealt with more in the past ten minutes than they have all night. Bust down the door already! Are you worried because I have Officer Douchebag's gun? I think I've already emptied it. Let's find out.

Ha! Did you see that? There were two shots left! Good thing I pointed it out the window of the car and not at myself, huh? I wonder if I hit anything on the other side of that garage door there, though. Looks like I busted out some of the glass that buddy-boo here hadn't already shattered when I made him break in. The ringing in my ears is pretty bad right now, so I can't tell if there's any shuffling or shouting or anything going on outside. Maybe I just got lucky and hit one of them. That oughta bring them running in at me, don't you think? Well, maybe not. You'd think I'd be hearing *something* by now.

I wonder if the cops know that I don't have any other weapons in here? Maybe that's the problem. Hey, all you people out there watching this, can you let those guys outside know I'm unarmed now? That'd be awesome. Come on in, guys! Join the fun! Ha! Or, maybe they're afraid because I still have Officer Butthead's patrol car in here. Hmm. I guess I have been able to make use of a few non-traditional weapons over the course of this evening, haven't I? Ha! Maybe they're afraid I'm going to turn this car into another one? You know what? That's actually not a bad idea. Don't they build houses like this pretty much paper thin these days? I'll bet if I started her up and revved the engine real good before I kicked it into gear, I could bust right through that garage door and mow down a few officers before they could even get off a shot.

What do you think, followers? Should I try it? Hmmm? I'll be right back.

***

Hello again, live stream followers! If you can't tell from the view, I'm now sitting in the driver's seat of Officer Dumbass' patrol car. Pretty sure you can hear it, too. The engine's running. I know, I know. You're not supposed to run a car in an enclosed environment. Carbon monoxide and all that. I can assure you that I won't be in here long enough for that to matter.

Your hero Tiffany isn't trying to off herself. I might be the elderly invalid in this situation, but I think I've still got a little fight left in me. I've just got to be a little creative about the way things go from here on out.

Since it looks like the good old PD are all wrapped up in their own little worlds and not paying attention to this live stream, I've decided to give them a little show. After all, I don't want them to get bored waiting for little old me. I hate being bored. They probably do too. Hell, doesn't everybody? So, I pried my little smarty phone out of buddy-boo's cold dead hands back there and clipped it as best as I could do what I think is this patrol car's dash cam. I don't know that for sure, but I do know that from this angle it looks like I can watch you watching me. I guess that means all's well.

Here's what's going to happen. I think I already mentioned that I make mistakes sometimes. Well, I made a mistake when buddy-boo and I drove this patrol car into the garage. I should have thrown it into reverse and backed the piece of shit in here. Instead, I did the easy thing and drove it straight on in, nose first. Almost bumped the back wall, which would've left a nice big crunchy stained hole in this brand spanking new house! Ha! I hate to mess up all that pretty drywall and contractor white paint on the back of the garage, so I've decided to kick this patrol car into the backward way and crash through that shiny new garage door instead.

Of course, I can't see what's on the other side of the door. Why? Because doors are opaque, silly! I might make mistakes sometimes, but I'm not stupid. I have to make sure I have all the power this patrol car can muster in reverse before I throw it into gear. I want to bust all the way through that door. And if any poor little soul happens to be standing behind it with a weapon drawn—well, I guess we'll just see what happens. It's all going to be on video, of course. And you lucky people get to watch it all unfold live! Hey, maybe it'll turn into a car chase and get aired on live TV. But only you live stream followers will get the real inside story, huh? Ha!

Oh, but that just opens up all sorts of new possibilities, doesn't it? I'm getting tingles just thinking about it. Not only do I want to survive this now, I need to. Think about it. If they catch me, they'll put me in prison. They might even try to give me the death sentence. If they did, I would still have years to wait and live before they shot me up. I'd be world famous by then. Before you know it, reporters would be clamoring to do interviews with me for television, magazines, radio, podcasts, websites—you name it! I'd be totally legit then: the badass girl unrepentant of her killing spree. I already know how I'd answer the two questions that all those reporters are guaranteed to ask me.

"Why did you do it, Tiffany?" they'll ask.

"I was bored," I'll say.

"Do you regret what you did, Tiffany?" they'll ask.

"Not one bit," I'll say. "Beats being bored any day."

And I wouldn't be lying. What I did tonight does beat being bored any day. Looking back on all of it, I'd say I've grown up over the course of it all. I mean, first I was just bored. Then I had to deal with everything buddy-boo and Officer Shit-for-Brains here tried to throw in my way. And now? Now all I can think is that I am now everything I wanted to be. I made it. Did it my way. And I'm going to keep doing it my way for as long as I can. Head's up live stream followers! My new destiny, whether it's freedom or confinement, lies beyond that garage door. I'm sure you've always heard, as I have, that life is about the journey, not the destination. My poor dead little daddy used to lay that one on me from time to time. I don't know for sure what's going to happen next, but I can tell you that for me it's been one hell of a ride.

The carbon monoxide is probably thick in here now. I'm starting to feel a little sleepy. I guess I'd better get moving while I still have the energy to do it. I dumped buddy-boo and Officer Butthead out of the patrol car before I went live again. They're laying on the concrete just beside the hood of the car. I put buddy-boo on top of the cop and pointed his bare ass toward the ceiling, just because the two of them pressed together looks funnier that way. I don't need them bouncing around the backseat while I'm making my getaway, especially now that buddy-boo is dead. I sure do miss him.

Ha! No, I know what you're thinking. That's not a regret. I was never really going to allow him to live. He would just drag me down with him. I miss him kind of like I miss my crowbar. I had plans for it, too. But Tiffany is meant for greater things than a fat naked redneck for a companion. Greater things are coming just beyond that garage door. I really do wonder what those cops outside have been doing all this time. I hope I'm about to give them the surprise of their lives.

Here I go then, my live stream followers. Get ready. On the road again like Willie Nelson. That's where I'm going. No turning back now.

Pedal to the metal.

Right hand on the shifter.

Left hand on the wheel.

My way.

Totally legit.

About These Stories

I sat down to write each of these stories over a span of my life that began sometime in 2012. This collection was not even a glimmer in my eye at that point. I simply knew I had an idea for a short story that I wanted to write and then release as an ebook. Frankly, I never dreamed I would even follow up that effort with a second story, much less the ten stories and single screenplay that comprise this volume.

When the idea did finally occur to me to collect these stories and place them into a single volume, I knew that I wanted to have a theme. When I looked back at the content of the stories I had written up to that point, most of them involved incidents in cars or were at least connected to a trip or the road somehow. That's why this volume is titled *Road Kills*. Now that I've wrapped it up, I wonder if my next short tale of dark comic horror will involve the road at all. Part of me hopes it does not. There are always other dark corners to explore, after all.

That said, what follows is a little background on each of the works you've read herein.

Nobody Was Here

This was the first story I wrote and the first story I released. It developed out of a real-life incident that occurred when I was on my way back home from a trip to New Orleans. I stopped at a Burger King for lunch and encountered a young man in the men's room who was very obviously on something and who attempted to proposition me. Unlike Reese in the tale, I managed to get out and get away from him without further incident.

Hoppers

There's not much to say about this one other than the fact that I find the idea of killer bunnies to be quite hilarious. This was also written at a time when I was sick of being in near head-on collisions with other drivers because of their fixation on their smartphones. Strike those two ideas together, and you get the spark that fanned the flames of this tale.

Dislike

I'm not a particularly social fellow. Never have been. Although I have managed to branch out quite a bit on social media since way back in 2012 when I first started releasing stories. Each of us has at some point seen the damage that drunk driving or drunk dialing can do. This story spawned from me wondering what horrible things could ever come of being drunk on social media.

The Murder of Crows

This story actually pre-dates The two that were released before it. I was hesitant to put it out into the world. At the time this was written, gossip shows calling themselves "news" were following celebrities like Charlie Sheen around, trying to dig up whatever dirt they could find or provoke a new reaction to get on camera. Apparently, their audiences simply enjoy watching public breakdowns. I started to wonder what might happen if such places ever ran out of people to harass into meltdowns. Out of that, came this story.

Because Reasons, Deal With It, and Legit

As you might have noticed, all three of these stories focus on the same murderous young woman named Tiffany. She was born primarily out of a desire to take common horror tropes and turn them on their heads a bit. Instead of a young woman in her underwear being chased around by a deranged killer, I wondered what it might be like to follow a young woman who *is* the deranged killer. It naturally followed then that the primary victim in the story would be a young naked man.

After Liane Moonraven performed the role of Tiffany for her audio theater group in *Because Reasons*, several people asked me What was going to happen next. In truth, I hadn't planned to write any more to the story. The young man runs away into the desert and Tiffany follows him, confident in her role as the hunter. Ultimately, I chose to continue her story because it occurred to me that I had only allowed her character to grow into the first stage of adulthood: that phase where you're young and idealistic and trying to make your way in the world. There were still two whole stages left to go.

The second story explores the second stage of her development, which is the phase of adulthood in which one has tasted success and starts to settle down into an everyday life, perhaps even finding a partner with whom to continue the journey. The third and last story explores the end of the adult phase of life when you're reflecting on your achievements and wondering whether it was all actually worth it.

Bedside Manner

You can't pull together a collection of horror shorts and not have a ghost story. Well, I suppose you can, but why would you want to? Ghosts are horror tradition, and this one just might be the most traditional story in the book. It has all the elements, after all: the ghostly figure beside the bed at 3:15 in the morning who wants some sort of revenge or closure for a slight in her life.

Diggum

If I were forced to pick a favorite of my stories, this would be my current one. Diggum has a special place in my heart. He grew up in an area similar to the one I grew up in and, as such, surrounded by people with religious beliefs similar to his. I had much fun writing Diggum, and then *being* Diggum in the audio book form of this story and in the book trailer I made for it (those are my boots and my gloved hands if you've seen it). An abridged version of the audio book was also aired by Liane Moonraven's Carmen Audio Theater Group.

The screenplay came about because I felt like I wasn't quite done with Diggum. Of all my stories, it was the one to which I felt most *visually* connected. Although I'd written much of the audio adaptation of *Because Reasons*, I'd never written a film script before. I wanted to try my hand at it. So the screenplay was born. On somewhat of a lark, I submitted it to various film festivals and have been overjoyed by the attention it has received from them. As I write this, *Diggum* the screenplay has already been lauded three times and awarded the 2017 Best Violence award in the 2017 Chemical Film Festival.

Decision Paralysis

I don't remember who told me that human anxiety has reached an all-time high largely because of the number of decisions we are required to make in a day. When you think about it, every button we tap on a smartphone and every effort we make to get where we're going involves another decision on our part. We spend much of our lives deciding how to get from point A to point B, whether those are physical destinations or emotional ones with other people. So I began to wonder where the breaking strain is. How many decisions in one day is too many for one person? And what happens when that limit is reached? Is there a fail-safe shutdown somewhere? What if there isn't?

Safety First

Years ago, a scene popped into my head that featured two space explorers on a deserted planet: one standing on an outcropping at the end of a long drop, and the other pointing a weapon at him. I wrote about 800words of that story, but I didn't know where I wanted to go with it, so I put it away and forgot about it.

One day, while looking for something to do, I happened upon the start of that idea in my files. I reread what I had already written, and the rest of the story just fell into place from there. The result is the only off-world story I've ever written. It's probably as close to science fiction as I'll ever get,

***

If you've read this far, thank you. If you skipped this whole section, that's fine, too. The only people who like to talk about a writer's process are other writers, and mostly they only want to talk about their own. I provide the above as only a brief glimpse into the twisted thought processes that led to these stories. I hope you enjoyed your journey reading them as much as I enjoyed laying the asphalt.